Clara Poole

and the

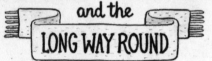

LONG WAY ROUND

Clara Poole

and the

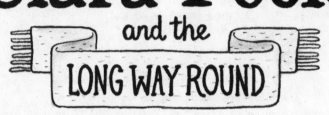

LONG WAY ROUND

TAYLOR TYNG

PIXEL✛INK

PIXEL✚INK

Pixel+Ink is an imprint of TGM Development Corp.
www.pixelandinkbooks.com
Printed and bound in May 2023 at Lake Book Manufacturing,
Melrose Park, IL, U.S.A.
Book design by Jay Colvin

Library of Congress Cataloging-in-Publication Data

Names: Tyng, Taylor, author.
Title: Clara Poole and the long way round / Taylor Tyng.
Description: First edition. | New York : Pixel+Ink, [2023] | Audience: Ages
8-12. | Audience: Grades 4-6. | Summary: When an unintended balloon
flight over Michigan brings twelve-year-old Clara Poole instant
celebrity, she is invited to be the spokesperson for a round-the-world
adventure race, but it soon becomes clear that someone is trying to
sabotage the competition.
Identifiers: LCCN 2023000013 (print) | LCCN 2023000014 (ebook) |
ISBN 9781645951599 (hardcover) | ISBN 9781645951605 (ebook)
Subjects: CYAC: Balloon racing—Fiction. | Contests—Fiction. | Adventure
and adventurers—Fiction. | LCGFT: Adventure fiction. | Novels.
Classification: LCC PZ7.1.T966 Cl 2023 (print) | LCC PZ7.1.T966 (ebook) |
DDC [Fic]—dc23
LC record available at https://lccn.loc.gov/2023000013
LC ebook record available at https://lccn.loc.gov/2023000014

Hardcover ISBN: 978-1-64595-159-9
E-book ISBN: 978-1-64595-160-5

First Edition

1 3 5 7 9 10 8 6 4 2

For my daughters, who asked for a dream at bedtime
and gave me back a bigger one than I could've ever imagined
—T.T.

CONTENTS

One: The Accident That Started Everything 1

Two: Touch Down 7

Three: Harold Habberdish's Very Bad Day 12

Four: The Windmill 19

Five: An Unlikely Proposal 27

Six: Departures 41

Seven: A Poor Start 52

Eight: Orientation 64

Nine: Unintended Results 77

Ten: A Worse Alternative 89

Eleven: The Reliability of the Mail 99

Twelve: Go! 117

Thirteen: The First Test 136

Fourteen: A Sea of Sand 149

Fifteen: The Blue People 161

Sixteen: The Five Perils..176

Seventeen: A Place with No People 191

Eighteen: Pieces of the Past 207

Nineteen: A Coo-rious Situation.............................217

Twenty: The Making of Enemies 232

Twenty-One: Paper Birds.......................................245

Twenty-Two: A Dodge-Size Wrinkle........................252

Twenty-Three: Roman Candle 258

Twenty-Four: The Cheater Revealed........................272

Twenty-Five: Mountains of Truth 279

Twenty-Six: Fur, Feathers, and Scales 298

Twenty-Seven: Striking Twice.................................312

Twenty-Eight: Monkey Luck....................................322

Twenty-Nine: A Sudden Change of Heart 329

Thirty: Mayhem 337

Thirty-One: The Dovie Cup....................................353

Sometimes in life, forgiving yourself is the hardest part.

—Greta Gildersleeve

CHAPTER ONE

THE ACCIDENT THAT
STARTED EVERYTHING

CLARA WATCHED FROM HER PLASTIC lawn chair as the news vans sped below. There were more now—fifteen by her count—jockeying for position among the flashing lights and blaring sirens of an endless string of police cars. She had been in the air for over six hours, long enough for every news outlet within a hundred miles to scramble a team of reporters, locate her, and join the hunt. Finding her hadn't been difficult. After all, how many twelve-year-old girls were hurtling through the skies of Michigan in a plastic lawn chair tied to hundreds of colorful balloons?

Clara closed her eyes as the wind whipped her face. She felt more herself. At least more than she had in the year since the accident, before she became the girl her father had always wanted her to be—the *safe* version of Clara Poole.

Still, as freeing as the heights were, she knew it was only a matter of time until she'd have to land. Soon the pinks and purples of the evening sky would be replaced with the black of night. She would reach the coast, and then once over Lake Michigan, things would turn very serious, very quickly.

A symphony of honks blared from the convoy below as another van swerved to the head of the pack. But this vehicle was not a news van. It was a minivan—*Clara's* family's mini-van. She knew this not because of its powder-blue exterior or the cargo carrier on top, but from the panic-stricken face of her Grandma Sue screaming through the moonroof. Yet, as much as it pained Clara to cause her grandmother such fright, it was the person driving whose emotional state concerned her the most. For underneath his red baseball cap, Clara knew her father's face must be an equally vivid shade of anger.

Not that this was new. His face was always like that these days—fed up with and fuming over one of her countless poor choices. *Eyes down . . . feet on the ground . . . safety first . . . think before you act.* Those had been her life directives ever since the accident, reminders given freely each day by one Mr. Oliver Poole, risk-averse father extraordinaire. She could only imagine the lecture awaiting her when she finally touched down. The idea chilled her to the bone. Or was it the temperature dropping?

Clara gave a sheepish wave, hoping it might calm her grandmother, then retreated back in her chair as a *pop-pop* sounded above, and she dropped altitude. In no time, she'd be on the ground, and no doubt *grounded*.

Just tell him you didn't mean it—that it was an accident.

It wasn't exactly untrue.

Flying over Western Michigan in a homemade balloon had never been Clara's intention. It wasn't even her creation—at least not solely hers. The whole thing had begun as a science experiment in Mrs. Chelsea's sixth-grade classroom, which was to be unveiled at the end-of-the-year fair. After their unit on gravity, the students had decided to investigate how many balloons it would take to send a person airborne. After three days inflating hundreds of balloons and tying them to a white plastic lawn chair, which had been tethered to the ground, the kids took turns testing who could be lifted into the air.

Many of her classmates had been too heavy, but a small group including Clara floated with ease. These lucky students were assigned to sit in the chair in shifts during the fair to demonstrate the experiment.

Clara's had been the last slot of the day. At two p.m.,

she climbed in, buckled the crude safety harness, and let out the rope one crank at a time until she reached a piece of tape labeled STOP! 10 FEET.

Then, she sat.

Most people, of course, had already seen the experiment and turned their attention to getting in one more bounce in the bounce house or devouring one more funnel cake before the fair's close. Even Mrs. Chelsea had wandered off to chat with a few other teachers. That was fine with Clara, who frankly preferred being alone. Still, after a while, even she grew bored of the quiet.

Guess I'll just crank myself back down and be done with it, she thought.

But then a new idea called to her from an old forgotten voice.

Or . . . it said. *You could go higher.*

And so she did. With each revolution of the crank, she floated up until she was twenty feet off the ground. The wind jerked at the balloons, and still, no one was watching. Clara let out even more rope.

The tether sang, a high-pitched hum, as the wind tugged at the chair. But there was something else tugging, some-thing inside—something that demanded attention.

Clara considered the pin securing the rope to the chair, and before knowing why, pulled it free. The balloons caught the wind, and in an instant, she launched into the sky.

Jump! she thought.

But before she could, the chair soared even higher.

A chorus of bloodcurdling screams cut through the air as Mrs. Chelsea and the other teachers raced across the fairgrounds waving their hands furiously as if doing so might stop Clara from flying away. It did not. A split second later, their panicked faces were gone, the school grounds of Gerald Ford Elementary had disappeared, and Clara was rocketing west.

Thwack! Pop! Poppity-pop! The chair lurched left, jogging Clara back to earth—or rather, *back to air.* She grasped the white plastic arms, clenching them with even whiter knuckles, and looked up.

Of the hundreds of balloons originally tied to the lawn chair, she couldn't count how many remained, but she knew there weren't enough to keep her airborne much longer. These were not the type of balloons meant for long-distance flight—or short distance, for that matter. Clara doubted they'd be strong enough to last a toddler's birthday party.

Landing was either good or bad, depending on how she

looked at it. On the one hand, it meant she'd live to see another day, on the other, she'd have to face her father. *Accident* or not, she was positive her punishment for this escapade would be legendary.

However, that inevitability would have to wait for the more serious matter in front of her. After a day of sailing over farmland and foothills, the vast silver mirror of Lake Michigan emerged, and once she left land behind, there would be nothing but water until she reached Wisconsin—if she even made it that far. Quickly, she decided not to try.

Clara pulled a bobby pin from her hair, then started hauling down balloons string by string. She stabbed at them feverishly, popping one after another, until she started to descend—far too quickly.

Closing her eyes, she braced for impact.

CHAPTER TWO

TOUCH DOWN

CLARA SMASHED INTO THE GROUND and ricocheted back into the air like a human skipping stone. Pieces of lawn chair flew in all directions as she tumbled, the earth biting into her arms and legs, tearing her sweatshirt and jeans. And then suddenly, she hit something with a shuddering thud.

Her eyes watered, stars flickering in her vision, before slowly, a picture formed: black, hairy, and awful-smelling. Clara groaned as she stared into the glazed eyes of an enormous wet-nosed cow.

"Stop breathing on me," she grumbled.

The animal mooed its apology as Clara sat and tried to blink away her blindness. This time, however, the flashing stars were not all in her head, but coming from a crowd of reporters snapping pictures of her among the wreckage.

"Why did you do it?" one blurted.

"Yeah, what gave you the idea? Was it the influence of video games?"

"Were you running away?"

"Do your parents know anything about your flight?"

"What's your name?"

"My name?" she repeated, shielding her eyes. "My name's—"

"CLARA ABIGAIL POOLE!"

The horde swiveled their heads as one at the new voice, though Clara knew it instantly.

Slowly, the crowd parted, revealing the flannel-shirted shape of her father. He was not nearly as red-faced as Clara thought he'd be. In fact, he looked tired. She wiped the muck from her cheek and pulled twigs from her hair, trying to resemble anything other than the muddy mess she knew she was.

Her father stopped, looming over her, and spoke two words: "You're grounded."

THE DRIVE HOME was long and silent. Clara's father kept his full attention on the road, while Grandma Sue, drained from the day's excitement, snored in the passenger seat. Clara stared out the back window at nothing in particular, trying to pass the discomfort of each minute by playing a one-person game of License-Plate ABC. She was on her second round at Q when a news report came on the radio:

"That's right, Kirk. A twelve-year-old girl stole a hot-air balloon and took law enforcement on an all-day chase across the—"

Her father switched the station.

"Here's an unusual story, Joan. A young Michigander built a hot-air balloon and launched herself from her family's farm. After flying across the state, she splashed down in Lake Michigan, resulting in what is being called a daring Coast Guard rescue. When asked why she did it, she explained it was to encourage other young girls to be passionate about STEM education. After she—"

Clara's father grumbled and clicked off the radio.

"That's not true," she said with a huff. "I wasn't encouraging anyone to do anything with—"

Her father's hand went up and the car returned to silence.

A few miles later, they turned right at a stone gate, its

familiar painted sign announcing BITTER BEND FARM. As they pulled up to the house, Clara noticed the front door was wide open, no doubt left that way after her father received a call that his daughter was rocketing over Michigan in a lawn chair.

"Oh, we're home," said Grandma Sue, stirring in the front seat. "I don't know about you, but that was quite enough excitement for one day. I'm just glad you're safe and sound, dear."

Clara gave a faint smile as her father cut the ignition, and they sat in silence, watching Grandma Sue make her way from the car down the gravel path to the guest cottage. "That could've happened, you know," he said eventually.

"What could've?"

"Those things they said on the radio. You could've been blown out over the lake . . . drowned . . . who knows what else."

"But I wasn't. I was—"

Her father raised his hand again.

"Dad, seriously, I was—"

"The only thing you were doing was thinking about yourself," he snapped. "Because you sure weren't thinking about your grandmother or me. And you certainly weren't thinking about—" He closed his eyes and inhaled deeply.

"Go ahead," Clara said, after a moment. "Say it."

Her father's eyes stayed shut.

"Say it," she pressed. "I know it's how you feel. . . . That I certainly wasn't thinking about Mom."

"No, Clara, that's not what I meant."

"Yes, it is. You think everything's my fault. That Mom would still be here if it weren't for me."

"No, that's not—"

Clara kicked the car door open.

"Clara—"

"Forget it," she snapped, and stormed into the house. She didn't even pause to switch on the light. She marched through the darkened kitchen, stomped each stair, and slammed her bedroom door with such force, the whole house shook.

Or maybe, it was just Clara who did.

CHAPTER THREE

HAROLD HABBERDISH'S
VERY BAD DAY

"BUT . . . YOU CAN'T BACK OUT NOW! But . . . it will ruin everything. But . . . we have a contract!"

Those words had come from the mouth of Harold Habberdish less than an hour before. He'd heard himself say them, the drastic pleas, futile appeals, and hopeless supplications, knowing full well they meant only one thing: disaster.

Harold's day had started well enough. He'd put on his coat, pulled his blue bowler hat down over his gray curls, and stepped out the door of his Paris apartment. Rain spat, but not enough for an umbrella, nor enough to keep Harold, a Brit by birth, from walking the city streets he loved.

Turning into the Tuileries Garden, he proceeded along the manicured pathways in the direction of the Louvre, the former palace of French kings turned world-renowned art museum. Surrounded by the richness of history, Harold reflected. *I'm about to make history, too.*

In little more than a week, pilots from around the globe would descend on Paris for the World Organization of Balloon Aeronauts' one-hundredth air race. And as the newly appointed president of WOOBA (as it was commonly known), Harold had spared no expense in creating what was guaranteed to be the greatest adventure competition ever conceived.

From the colossal stadium, where the opening ceremonies would take place, to the thrilling aerial venues, to the star-studded parties in the clouds, nothing could hold a candle to what Harold was planning. Surely, his father and former WOOBA president, Harrison Habberdish, would be proud, as would his father's father, Hugo, WOOBA president before him. Legacy was everything to Harold, and as the fifth generation of Habberdishes, from Harold to Harrison, Hugo to Henry, all the way to WOOBA's founder, Hubert Horatio Habberdish, the thought of continuing such lofty family tradition filled him with pride like . . . well, like a hot-air balloon.

The rain began to fall harder as Harold crossed Rue de Rivoli near the sloping glass of the Louvre's pyramid. He paused to take in the neatly lettered sign of Sutton & Crumwell, considered to be as fine as the bespoke clothiers of London's Savile Row. As Harold crossed the threshold, the smells of mahogany, wool, and leather made him feel like he'd been transported back to his childhood England. A bell chimed in back and, as if on cue, a small man dressed impeccably in gray tweed emerged from behind a green velvet curtain.

"Good day, Mr. Crumwell," Habberdish said, removing his coat and hat. "Going to be a wet one after all, eh?"

The shrewlike man squinted out the window over half-moon glasses. "Mmm, yes, Mr. Habberdish, so it would appear. Please, sir, this way. Your suit is ready."

Harold stepped past the curtain and up onto a dressing platform, his excitement reflected in the surrounding mirrors.

He had commissioned a one-of-a-kind suit made of brilliant royal blue linen and patterned with WOOBA's insignia, the white dove. "It must be a suit that will stand out above the rest," he'd proclaimed. He'd even gone so far as to provide a sketch to illustrate precisely how the doves should be sized and positioned on the fabric.

"Your jacket, sir," said the tailor, helping Harold slip his arms through the sleeves. "The fit should be perfection."

And it was. In fact, it was the best-fitted piece of clothing Harold had ever worn. The shoulders were precisely cut, the taper at the waist just so, and the drape of the cloth was nothing short of exquisite. Yet, Harold's attention was focused not on the fine craftsmanship of the tailoring, but rather the unusual pattern adorning it.

"*What* is this?" he asked, holding out the sleeve.

"The dove pattern you requested."

"I'm sorry, Mr. Crumwell, but I assure you it is not."

The tailor fiddled with his glasses, raising his chin as he squinted. "Yes, yes . . . this is it—your doves—all up and down, precisely as you wished."

Harold stared into the mirror. "But they don't look like doves. They look like . . . like *chickens*!"

"Sir, this fabric was made using the exact specifications you yourself supplied."

"What do you mean, my specifications? I most certainly did not order a *chicken suit*!"

The tailor readjusted his glasses and disappeared behind his curtain once more. When he returned, he held out a piece of paper—Harold's sketch. On it, perfectly sized and precisely spaced, was a pattern of what Harold now realized looked remarkably like chickens, or at best, chicken-like doves. He conceded that the jacket's pattern was an exact match. "Surely, though, it can be fixed?"

"I'm afraid, sir, there is nothing to fix. We would need about six weeks to have new fabric made."

"Six weeks?"

A short while later, a much-deflated Harold Habberdish left Sutton's, chicken suit in hand, just as the rain began to fall in sheets. By the time he hurled himself through the doors of the Société Credit Bank, a block away, he was soaked to the bone.

As he approached the teller one squishy footstep at a time, the bank's manager, Victor Arnaut, hurried to greet him.

"Monsieur Habberdish, sir. You have gone swimming in your clothes!"

"Bonjour, Monsieur Arnaut. Yes, I, uh, forgot my umbrella at home."

"Do you require a towel, monsieur?"

"No, no," said Habberdish, pulling an envelope from his coat pocket. "But you can deposit this check for me. It's the big one from our premier sponsor, Groem and Stratmire. Without this check, nothing's getting off the ground." Harold chuckled at his own joke, beginning to feel a touch better after the incident at the tailor's. That was until he noticed the confusion on Victor Arnaut's face.

"I'm sorry, monsieur, but haven't you heard?"

"Heard?" Harold's chest tightened. "Heard *what*?"

"Groem and Stratmire . . . they filed for bankruptcy this morning. The reports say it was something to do with executives secretly spending millions on big yachts and fancy houses. I can try to deposit the check for you, monsieur, but I doubt it will clear. They have no money."

Harold blinked, replaying the words in his mind. Certainly, Arnaut was wrong. But as the senior executive manager of France's largest bank, Victor Arnaut's job very much entailed always being right. Then Harold locked eyes on the newscast playing on the lobby's television. A reporter was speaking in front of a large stone building as people exited carrying boxes and desk lamps. Though the television had been muted, Harold could still read the chyron scrolling across the bottom of the screen: GROEM & STRATMIRE DECLARES BANKRUPTCY AFTER 125 YEARS OF BUSINESS. CLOSURE EFFECTIVE IMMEDIATELY.

Harold floated through the remainder of the day, numb: watching news stories; verifying that his check was, indeed, worthless; trudging back to his office in the pouring rain; taking in the dumbstruck faces of his employees when he announced what had happened. A phone call with the head of Groem & Stratmire confirmed that there would be no sponsorship money. He was indeed sorry, but that if there were still tickets to the opening ceremony, he'd enjoy bringing his family.

Harold looked out his window into the courtyard where brazen pigeons crept like spies among café tables, stealing pastries from the plates of unwitting tourists. After a hundred years, was this really it? No more race? No more balloons? No more WOOBA? How would he be able to tell his family that in his first year as president, he'd botched everything?

After a deep breath, he picked up the phone, steeling himself to call his father, when his assistant, Marie Lemot, stormed through his office doors.

"Turn on the TV!" she ordered.

Harold returned the phone to the cradle. "Ms. Lemot, please, the last thing I want to see is more bad news."

"But, sir, you don't understand. It's not over! I think I've figured out a way to save the race!"

Harold stared blankly as his assistant seized the remote from his desk and switched on the television. On the screen, a young girl covered in mud was standing next to a broken lawn chair and what appeared to be bundles of children's balloons. 12-YEAR-OLD GIRL FLIES HOMEMADE BALLOON ACROSS MICHIGAN . . . BECOMES INSTANT CELEBRITY.

"Ms. Lemot? What is this?"

"Trust me, sir. I'll explain on the way. I'll get your coat."

She marched to the coat stand, pausing to take in the royal-blue lump forming a puddle on the floor below.

"Mr. Habberdish? Are those chickens?"

CHAPTER FOUR

THE WINDMILL

CLARA SAT ON THE GABLE outside her window trying to clear her mind. The roof was her favorite place to think. Often, she'd sit there after dark, watching the stars shimmer overhead while lightning bugs flickered their response in the fields below. Like most farms, life was busy, and privacy limited. But the roof was all hers.

Clara's parents had bought Bitter Bend Farm when she was four, hoping to escape the rat race of the city for literally greener pastures. Even after, her father had continued traveling to the city for work, leaving Clara and her mother alone to manage the farm. The two of them were happy— they were a team. And though Clara always hoped for a little sister, her parents never had more children. She'd grown to assume they were too nervous they might have another child like her.

Whether daredevils are born daredevils no one knows, but Clara should've been born with a warning label: *Danger Sure to Follow*. And though daredeviling can take many forms, Clara's particular sort manifested in an obsessive need to climb—anything and everything—the higher the better.

As a toddler, she'd break out of her crib only to appear hanging like a monkey from the canopy of her parents' bed. At mealtimes, she'd escape her high chair the instant her mother turned away, determined to scale the cupboard. Ladders of any type—step, folding, telescoping—were kept under lock and key, as the exploration of such things was sure to end in a trip to the emergency room.

As she grew, Clara climbed every tree in the orchard, the high beam of the hay barn, the rickety metal ladder of the old grain silo; anything she could get a grip on. She was no stranger to scrapes or bruises—so much so that her mother kept Clara's pockets full of Band-Aids. She wore each one as badge of honor, there to show off her many daring risks and accomplishments. That is, until the day her world crashed down.

HARVEST WAS OVER, and life at Bitter Bend had slowed for winter. It was a welcome break from sore muscles and dirty fingernails, and long days of grunt work on the farm. For Clara, it meant free time and maybe even a new climbing challenge.

The problem was there weren't any left at Bitter Bend—not the trees in the orchard, not the side of the barn where her mother had hung rock-climbing holds, nothing. Clara figured she'd climbed everything there was to climb on the farm. Everything except the windmill by the frog pond.

The windmill was magnificent: a fan of galvanized steel blades connected to a red tail that read BITTER BEND in fancy white script, all of which sat atop a wooden tower fifty feet high. It was her father's gift for her mother, one he had bought from a rancher in Texas and spent months secretly restoring to its original glory.

It was assembled the day of their anniversary, and that evening the family had spent the night watching frogs dart under lily pads as they hid from the bright lights strung across the pond.

Returning to the house under that star-filled sky, her father had paused. "Promise me, Clara. No climbing."

But that was then.

Her father wasn't home, her boredom had reached Code Red, and the windmill stood there taunting her. She checked quickly that her mother was inside the house, and without another thought—except *Game on*—she began to climb.

The lower sections were easy going, the posts angled at a gentle slope. In no time, Clara had ascended the first two levels and was atop the tower's third belt. When she glanced back at the house to make sure her mother hadn't seen, she found herself well above its roofline, higher than she'd ever been.

Or higher than I've ever been—yet, she thought, eyeing the next level.

This portion, however, proved more challenging, as the tower's angle tapered more severely. To compensate, Clara adjusted her technique, bear-hugging one of the center braces with her arms and legs. Up and up, knot by knot, she shimmied, squeezing the timber tightly to keep from sliding back down. It was tougher than it looked. Yet, she was so close. There was no stopping now.

"*Ouch!*" she yelped, scattering the birds in nearby trees.

Pain bit into her thigh, and with it a rush of adrenaline, willing Clara up onto the last belt. Immediately, the discomfort in her leg took a back seat to the view.

Whoa . . . I can see downtown . . . the church steeple . . . the roofs of Main Street.

Somewhere, a great horned owl hooted long and low. Clara searched the treetops until she found him perched atop a neighboring elm before he spread his wings and dropped into the air.

"I'd give anything to fly," she whispered, stretching her own arms wide.

She watched in a kind of daze until the bird was a speck in the sky before the sting in her leg brought her firmly back to the top of the windmill.

The splinter had cut deep, far more than any Band-Aid would help, but nevertheless, she took one from her pocket. She hadn't even peeled back the wrapper when she felt the first drop.

And then another . . .

And then another . . .

And then the storm.

Rain fell in torrents, almost washing Clara from her perch. Thunder boomed, shaking the ground like a monster waking. It juddered up the tower with an angry roar as she

23

scrambled to clutch the nearest post. But it was the lightning, ripping across the sky in jagged arcs of electricity, that brought the most wicked part of all: panic.

Clara screamed, but found no voice. She suddenly felt trapped, terrified, and very, very small.

An eternity passed in that moment high up in the windmill, and then another before she heard her mother's voice. Not daring to move, Clara craned her head back and mustered enough voice to call out, "In the windmill!"

Head aching, arms numb from clinging to the post, she strained to hear a reply over the whipping wind. What came instead was a clang of metal, and then the top of a ladder appeared against the beam behind her.

"Hold on!" shouted her mother. "I'm coming."

Clara closed her eyes, tears blending with the rain, and then curled her toes inside her shoes as if imagining them digging into solid ground. *It's over*, she thought. *I'm safe.*

Finally, her mother's face appeared, peeking over the edge of the beam.

"Can you reach me?" she called.

"I . . . don't know." Clara tried to focus, but the noise was deafening.

"I need you to turn around and take my hand."

Clara heard the words perfectly, but her body refused to budge.

"Clara, you need to try."

She shook her head. No, the storm was too angry.

"Listen to me," her mother insisted.

Clara's heart was in her throat. The world around her roared. "I can't," she heard herself say.

"There's no time."

"I can't. I can't move!"

"Do . . . it . . . now!"

Never once in her entire life had Clara heard her mother's voice so clear, so urgent. She loosened her grip on the post and turned.

And then the world flashed white.

LATER, CLARA WOULD read that when a person is struck by lightning, time stops, and they feel like they're trapped in a bubble of light. To date, it's the best description she's ever heard. Bystander reports she'd seen suggested singed clothing and burns were the only ways to piece the event together. Clara had none of those. There were no bystanders. Her clothes weren't singed, and she hadn't suffered so much as the tiniest of burns. All she remembered was waking up in a hospital bed to the unshaven face of an exhausted man who resembled her father. When he looked at her, Clara knew instantly she'd been the only one to survive the accident.

The months that followed were blurry at best. Her grandmother moved in to help, and her father came and went like a ghost. Clara spent her days alone, huddled in her room staring at nothing.

When her mother's funeral came, she didn't go. She couldn't face her father. She couldn't face the truth. She couldn't even face herself in the mirror.

And even if she had, she wouldn't have recognized the girl staring back.

The lightning had turned her brown hair a shocking white.

CHAPTER FIVE

AN UNLIKELY PROPOSAL

THE TWO DAYS AFTER HER flight over Michigan felt like a year. Being grounded has that effect, she supposed; time slows to the cruelest of crawls.

Clara had said nothing to her father since that moment in the car, keeping to the sanctuary of her room. She sat by her window wrapped in her mother's scarf as the sun set over the mob of reporters camped at the edge of their property, each eager to interview the now infamous Balloon Girl.

She drew the scarf tighter as a cold breeze blew through the open sash. She had found the scarf after the funeral, casually forgotten on the coatrack in the hall. It had still smelled like her mother—hints of lily and fig—as though she was still somewhere in the house or had just left on an errand but would return soon. The scent began to fade with time, like all the other signs of her mother's presence. Desperate not to forget, Clara had placed the scarf inside a plastic bag and hidden it in her bedside table. She only opened it on the worst days when nothing else could help—days like today.

A series of short honks sounded as a long black sedan wove through the news vans and down the driveway. It stopped in front of the house, and two unusual-looking people emerged. The first was a woman, a little younger than Clara's mother would've been, wearing a navy pantsuit accented by a red neck scarf and cat-eye glasses, her chestnut hair pulled back in a bun. Her companion, a shorter and much odder-looking man, wore a royal-blue bowler hat, from which a frizz of gray hair puffed out, and a matching blue suit with a strange pattern. He patted his chest before removing a note from his inside jacket pocket, which he studied for a moment as if ensuring he was in the right place. Then, the pair headed for the door.

"This is private property," Clara heard her father say from the porch below. "I told you people, no press allowed. Go back to the road or I'm calling the police."

"Oh, goodness. Indeed, Mr. Poole," said the man with a quick bow. "But we are not from the press. No, no. We are from WOOBA. If I may introduce myself, my name is

Harold Habberdish, and this is my assistant, Marie Lemot. We've just arrived from Paris, and we were hoping to have a word with you."

"Woo-huh?" replied Clara's father. "Paris?"

"It's pronounced *Woo-bah*, and yes, Paris, France," said Habberdish. "Mr. Poole, if you would permit us inside, I can explain further. I think you'll be very interested to learn why we're here . . . as will your daughter."

CLARA STRAINED TO HEAR through the air grate by her bedroom door. She had only made out a few muffled words since the strangers had entered the house, mainly her father's: *balloon, too young,* and *too dangerous.* Beyond that, the man from Paris was doing most of the talking, and sounded very excited.

Where did he say he was from? she wondered. *Wubah? Who-bah?* Whatever it was, it sounded official, like the FBI.

Clara slumped back onto her bed, waiting for the inevitable, imagining what kind of trouble she was in and how bad the punishment might be. She concocted scenario after scenario, each worse than the last, before she decided enough was enough. After all, if all this fuss was about her, then surely she had a right to be part of the conversation.

"Not my daughter!" her father exclaimed as she rounded the door to the kitchen.

"Mr. Poole, I assure you, it's completely safe," insisted the man in the blue bowler hat.

The trio sat at the kitchen table, her father with his arms crossed, scowling.

"What's completely safe?" Clara asked.

"Oh, darling, we didn't hear you come down," said Grandma Sue, drying dishes at the sink. Her eyes softened as they moved to Clara's neck. "Is that scarf—"

"Yes," Clara replied, instinctively clutching at her neck. "It's Mom's. But what's completely safe?"

"Oh, nothing, dear. These nice people were presenting a proposal to your father."

"A proposal? You mean they're not the FBI?"

"The FB . . . what are you talking about?" said her father. "No, these people are from an organization called Wahba."

"WOOBA," corrected the man in the blue bowler hat. "W-O-O-B-A. It stands for the World Organization of Balloon Aeronauts. Perhaps you've heard of us?"

"Uh, no," said Clara, still trying to figure out exactly what was happening.

"Well, Miss Poole, I can certainly remedy that. But

first, introductions! My name is Harold Habberdish. I am WOOBA's president. And this brilliant woman to my right is my assistant, Marie Lemot. We've come all the way from—"

"Paris," Clara finished. "I heard. But what I don't know is *why* you Organization of Balloon People are here?"

"Balloon *Aeronauts*," corrected Habberdish. "The World Organization of Balloon *Aeronauts*. Aeronauts are pilots who fly hot-air balloons."

Clara furrowed her brow. "Then why not just call them pilots?"

Habberdish inclined his head. "Interesting. I honestly can't say I've ever thought of it that way. Though I suppose *WOOBP* isn't as easy to pronounce as WOOBA, now is it? In any case, we're here because we have a proposal for you. An invitation, really."

"To which I've already said no," her father cut in.

"Yes, well, some of us are still warming up to the idea." Clara's father shot Habberdish a thunderous glare, which the odd man ignored. "You see, Clara, every year WOOBA puts on a race—a hot-air balloon race. The only of its kind in the entire world. And this year's event is to be an exceptional one, as we are celebrating our hundredth anniversary. As such, we have spared no expense to create the most ambitious and breathtaking adventure race ever conceived.

And, as part of that planning, we are inviting celebrities like you to participate."

"*Celebrities?*" repeated Clara. "I'm not a celebrity."

As if on cue, Ms. Lemot removed a stack of newspapers and magazines from her attaché case and fanned them out across the table. Each featured a picture of Clara under a bold headline:

CLARA POOLE: YOUNGEST PERSON TO BREAK
THE AERONAUT DISTANCE RECORD

ACADEMY AWARD—WINNING DIRECTOR
ALREADY TAPPED FOR BALLOON GIRL MOVIE

YOUNG AERONAUT CLARA POOLE:
A ROLE MODEL FOR GIRLS EVERYWHERE

"As you can see, you are much more than you think," Ms. Lemot said warmly. "Your recent adventure has ignited the imaginations of young and old alike. Why, look outside your window at all those reporters waiting—hoping—to interview the brave young Clara Poole. If you're not a celebrity, I don't know who is."

"Imagine this!" said Habberdish, arcing his hands above

his head like a director delivering a pitch. "'Media darling and amateur pilot, Clara Poole, to be the youngest person to fly around the world in the hundredth annual WOOBA Hot-Air Balloon Race.'"

Clara wasn't sure she'd heard correctly. "You want me . . ."

"Yes," said Habberdish.

". . . to fly around the world . . ."

"Indeed."

". . . in a hot-air balloon?"

"Yes, that's right, you've got it!"

Clara fell into her seat. Suddenly, the ordinary world did not feel so ordinary. Days ago, she'd almost crashed in the waters of Lake Michigan, and today a pair of strangers from France was in her kitchen asking her to join some wacko race she'd never heard of. "This is a joke, right?"

Habberdish frowned. "Joke? My dear Miss Poole, we are entirely serious. You are being invited to participate in the Hundredth Annual WOOBA Air Race."

For a moment, the room was silent apart from the ticking second hand of the wall clock. Clara replayed the conversation in her head, trying to put two and two together. It didn't add up. "I don't get it," she finally said.

"Sorry?" responded Habberdish. "Get what?"

"You said I'm a celebrity, right? But there's tons of

people more famous than me. And I'm not ... whatever you called it ... an *aeronaut*? And you flew all the way from Paris when you could've just called or emailed. It doesn't make sense. Why me?"

Habberdish glanced at Ms. Lemot, who shrugged and nodded. "Well," he said with a small chuckle. "Not only are you correct, Clara, but quite perceptive. That's good! That kind of quick thinking will serve you well in the race, especially during your television appearances."

Clara decided not to interrupt, though she made a mental note to ask what he meant by television appearances.

"Indeed, there is a tad bit more to the story," Habberdish continued. "Recently, some, er, issues have come to light, which have delivered us to your doorstep. Our largest sponsor, the famed watchmaker Groem and Stratmire, has unexpectedly dropped out, leaving us in a bit of a pickle, financially speaking. In fact, it's a rather large pickle. A huge pickle. The pickle of all pickles—"

"Too many pickles, sir," said Ms. Lemot, politely waving him on.

"Right. I will save you the boring details, Miss Poole. The simple truth is without Groem and Stratmire's sponsorship, I'm afraid there won't be a race. In other words, we're grounded."

"I know how that feels," Clara grumbled, prompting a scowl from her father.

"However, Ms. Lemot has worked wonders in an incredibly short time to secure an entirely new group of sponsors, ones who have generously agreed to fund our race. There is just one catch—a stipulation, really."

"Stipulation?"

"A requirement . . . that we have a particular individual participate. And, that individual . . . is you."

"Clara, they want you to be something called the Face of the Race," her father explained. "It's because you've received all this media attention. These sponsors think your participation will help sell their products. That's the only reason they want you in their race. Isn't that right, Mr. Habberdish?"

Habberdish cleared his throat to respond, but Clara wasn't listening. Nor were her thoughts occupied with sponsors or products or whatever the Face of the Race was. She was thinking of bluebird skies and the wind on her face and the freedom she'd felt in her plastic lawn chair.

"Is it dangerous?" she asked.

"Oh, very!" Habberdish replied eagerly. "The race is actually a series of stages held all over the world, each with its own unique challenges and special features, all of which have been designed to thrill. This year, there's even a stage where pilots will navigate blindly through an alpine pass shrouded in clouds. It's going to be spectacular."

Clara had to admit it did sound exciting, but from her father's expression, he had a decidedly different take. Habberdish seemed to sense this, too.

"Really, though, it's not *that* dangerous. . . . *Action-packed* is a better description. Plus, we have a world-class support crew to ensure complete safety at all times. I should add, Mr. Poole, that we want you there, as well."

Clara's father laughed awkwardly. "Me? Yeah, fat chance I set foot in a balloon."

"Oh, I see," said Habberdish, raising his eyebrows. "Is it because of the heights?"

Clara's father pushed his chin into his neck and pursed his lips. "What? Puh, no."

"Because there are therapies to help overcome a fear of—"

"I don't need therapy for anything, thanks."

"In any case, I'm speaking about a much different kind of balloon. *You* would be riding aboard the *Zephyrus*, our official airship. It's quite a marvel of engineering. More like a floating cruise ship with every creature comfort imaginable. You might call it our home base. After each stage, pilots moor their balloons at air docks for refueling, maintenance, and safety checks, so you'd be with your daughter before and after each race."

Clara looked at her father, hoping to catch some glimmer of interest.

"You're not listening," he said. "I'm not sending my daughter into danger. She's a child."

Clara bristled. "I'm in sixth grade."

"In that case, Mr. Poole, you'll be thrilled to know many of the pilots have children who participate in our race. It's considered something of a rite of passage. Why, one of our young pilots is only nine. Can you imagine? Wait until you meet her, Clara. She really is quite brilliant."

"I thought you said I'd be the youngest?"

"Did I?" Habberdish bit his finger. "Merely a little spin, I suppose . . . to make things more exciting for the spectators. A touch of embellishment never hurts, right?"

"And what do I get if I win?" she asked.

"Well, if you ask me, the thrill of the experience should be reward enough. However, the winner does receive a—"

"It doesn't matter." Her father waved a dismissive hand. "My daughter is not a balloon pilot."

"You mean, she's not a balloon pilot . . . *yet?*" mused Habberdish.

"I mean *never*."

"I can speak for myself, thank you," said Clara.

"Technically, Mr. Poole, Clara would only be a *copilot*. In fact, we've already selected the perfect pilot to escort her. He's an Oxford graduate, former Olympian, and most notably, was our champion a few years back. All she would need to do is ride along and enjoy the sights."

Clara's father rose from his chair. "She's not going, and that's final. We're flattered you've come all this way, but my daughter is far too young to fly in a hot-air balloon, let alone go round the world in some cockamamie race. She's lucky she didn't kill herself the other day."

"But—"

"No."

Habberdish rapped his fingers on the table, and opened his mouth a few times to object, but ultimately gave a sharp nod. "It's late. Perhaps it would be best to discuss this matter another time. But the offer stands. Please sleep on it at the very least. We're staying at the inn downtown, and return to Paris tomorrow." With that, Harold Habberdish and Marie Lemot picked up their belongings and left.

As the screen door shut with its customary *thwack*, Clara's father shook his head. "Of all the crazy things . . . WOOBA!"

"I didn't want to interrupt," said Grandma Sue, chirping up for the first time, "but I thought they were lovely people. And Paris? Why, I went to Paris once when I was young— such a magical place for a girl. Sometimes, I still dream of the pastries."

A moment later, the screen door opened again, and Harold Habberdish reappeared. "I almost forgot," he said, removing a small silver box from his jacket pocket. "You may want these." He pressed the side of the box—a small balloon inflated from its top—then grinned as he sent it sailing. It glinted in the light, bobbing softly until it found Clara. When she caught it and looked back, the man from WOOBA was gone.

Clara turned the box, finding a thin drawer on one end, which she slid open. Inside, folded in metallic tissue paper, were two silver tickets.

"Dad, these are plane tickets to Paris!"

"I don't care if they're tickets to Mars. You're not going to a foreign country, jumping into some balloon, and racing to who knows where with who knows who. Seriously, Clara, use your head. I wouldn't do this."

"But . . . I'm not you," she mumbled.

"That's right. What you are is a twelve-year-old girl who's

demonstrated that she knows very little about what's best for her. Now, we're done talking about it. Besides, there's something much more important we need to discuss."

"Well, whatever it is, I didn't do it," she said, crossing her arms. "I've been grounded, remember."

"It's not anything you did, honey."

Clara frowned at her father.

"*Honey?*" she repeated. "You only call me that when you have bad news."

He rubbed the back on his neck, then opened his mouth to speak.

CHAPTER SIX

DEPARTURES

"WE'RE MOVING."

The words didn't compute.

"What do you mean, *moving*?" said Clara.

Her father fidgeted in his chair, then sat up with authority. "I've decided to sell the farm and move us back to the city."

"To *Chicago*?" she yelled.

"Yes, with my job there and all the travel time in between, it would be easier if we were there together. Plus, I wouldn't have to leave you with your grandmother and worry about you so much."

"Then don't," she snapped, drawing out breaths to stay calm. "Quit your dumb job and find one here."

"It's not a dumb job, Clara. It's actually quite a good one.

But that's not the only reason." He paused. "I think it's time we had a fresh start."

"A fresh start? I don't need a fresh start."

"Honestly, honey, it would be good for you. . . . The best thing for you, really."

"That's a lie." She clenched her jaw, fighting back tears.

"Clara, listen—"

"No. You're doing this because of the accident . . . Because you can't be here anymore . . . Because . . ."

"Clara, that's not tr—"

"No," she spat, backing away. "I won't . . . I won't do it."

She dashed from the kitchen, stopping first in the front hall, then the living room, wanting to scoop up each room in her arms and run. She screamed in frustration and bounded the stairs two at a time, each step cracking underfoot. *Cracks!* Her whole world was cracking. Rushing into the safety of her bedroom, she slammed the door and collapsed on her bed.

Moments later, footsteps sounded down the hall.

"Go away!" she hollered before her father could say anything.

"Can I come in?"

"I said, GO AWAY!"

Silence followed, though she could still hear him

breathing on the other side of the door. She stared at the knob, waiting for it to turn.

It never did.

"I'm sorry," he finally said. "If you don't want to talk now, I get it. But I'm leaving for the city first thing in the morning. I have an appointment about renting an apartment while we look for something permanent. I'll be back in the evening, and maybe we can talk more then." He went silent again, as though waiting for a response. She didn't give him the satisfaction. "Okay, then. Your grandmother is downstairs if you need her."

His footsteps receded, and her room fell quiet.

Move? He can't. I won't. I'll run away before I ever go to Chicago.

A glint of light reflected off the floor near the foot of her bed, and Clara's gaze fell on the pair of silver tickets. Had she carried them upstairs without realizing it?

She rose, stepping silently across her room, picked one up, then flipped it from front to back, studying the words.

The grandfather clock in the hall chimed the hour.

Aeronauts.

By the tenth bong, Clara had made up her mind. In nine hours, her father would be on his way to the city and her grandmother would be waving Clara off to school before heading to her garden club. But Clara wouldn't be going to school, and she definitely wasn't going to Chicago.

No. Clara was going to Paris.

CLARA WAS RELIEVED to find her father already gone when she woke the next morning. Though anger had fueled her dreams, she wasn't sure if she could've faced him and still gone through with her plan. Deceiving her grandmother, who smiled lovingly as Clara left for the school bus, was painful enough.

So, it turned out, was the wait. In fact, it wasn't until after lunch, before Grandma Sue left the house, that Clara could finally emerge from her cramped hiding spot in the chicken coop, bent like a hook and spitting feathers. As her grandmother's old Volvo rumbled off down the gravel drive, Clara noticed the last news van leaving. Perhaps its crew had come to grips with the fact that they wouldn't be getting their big headline, all the while not realizing there was a new one in the making.

CELEBRITY BALLOON GIRL RUNS AWAY TO FRANCE

Clara returned to the house and packed quickly, taking only the clothes and toiletries that would fit in her backpack. She tied her mother's scarf around her neck, zipped her hoodie, and glanced at herself in the hall mirror. Her hair, too short for a proper ponytail, fell in her face. She brushed it away like a fly. What she needed was a hat, but the only one on the coatrack was her father's—his *favorite* red hat. She couldn't take it. He loved that hat. And then it hit her. *You're running away. Who's gonna care about a stupid hat. Besides, you'll be suspicious enough traveling alone, even without white hair.*

Dilemma solved. The hat went on her head.

She placed a hand on the doorknob, on her way to the barn to get her bike, then stopped.

My passport!

Luckily, she had one. Her family had planned a trip to Europe before her mother's death, and her passport had sat unstamped, collecting dust on her bookshelf since—yet another symbol of life postponed.

She rushed to her room to retrieve it, and was almost out the door when yet another thought occurred to her:

A note! I should leave a note.

But what should she write? Clara knew her father would be beyond furious. That didn't mean she wanted him to worry. Still, she couldn't say where she was going or he'd be on the next flight to Paris to stop her.

This running away business is hard.

Quickly, Clara grabbed a Post-it note and pencil from the kitchen junk drawer.

Dear Dad,

I can't go to Chicago. I know you always worry about me. Please, don't be mad. I promise, I'll be safe.
—Clara

P.S. Whatever you do, don't sell the farm!

She placed the note on the kitchen table, pinning it underneath the saltshaker, and then pulled her ticket from her pocket. The airport was maybe twenty miles away. If she rode fast, she might get there before lunch. She was surprised to see that the ticket listed no specific time or date, only the name of the airline and the destination:

SILVER ALLEGIANT
Passenger: One
Destination: Paris, France

She was checking the back again to make sure she wasn't missing something when she heard the metallic brakes of a car squeal to a stop outside the kitchen door. Clara froze. *Grandma can't be home already.*

She moved like a ghost to the window and nudged back the curtain.

It wasn't her grandmother. Instead, she saw the same black sedan Harold Habberdish and his assistant had arrived in the day before. A driver dressed in a dark suit and sunglasses opened the back door and then stood to the side, waiting. Clara waited, too. No one emerged. After a moment, the driver consulted his watch, then walked toward the kitchen door and knocked.

"Yes . . . hello?" Clara mumbled.

"Good morning, Miss Poole, my name is Pembley. WOOBA has sent me to drive you to the airport."

"They . . . did?" she said, marveling at both the strangeness of the moment and her sheer stroke of luck. A chauffeured ride would be much easier than biking. "Uh . . . okay."

Clara exited the house, her hand lingering on the doorjamb, and followed Pembley to the car.

"Is Mr. Poole joining us?" asked the driver, handing her his business card.

"Er . . . no," she replied as she climbed into the back.

"Very good," he said, satisfied.

Pembley shut the door without another word, and seconds later they pulled away. Clara watched through the rear window until the farm disappeared, wondering if it would be the last time.

In no time, they arrived at the airport, but to Clara's surprise, they drove right past the main terminal.

"Don't we stop here?" she called to the front.

"No, miss. Your plane is departing from the private jetway."

She was about to ask what he meant when the car pulled through a gate labeled SILVER ALLEGIANT and onto the runway, stopping near a gleaming metal jet, its gangplank extended in welcome.

Marie Lemot appeared at the plane's door, holding a phone to her ear as Clara stepped onto the tarmac. She flashed a warm smile, cupped the receiver, and whispered, "Bonjour," waving Clara aboard before promptly disappearing back into the plane, chatting frantically with the person on the other end.

Clara blinked. All this was really, truly, very much happening. Fear swelled in her stomach, but nothing like the kind that had paralyzed her in the windmill. It was a feeling that her life was about to change forever.

"Miss Poole," said an airline attendant, appearing in the doorway. "If you please, we need you to board. There's bad weather moving into the area, and we need to depart now to avoid it."

Clara saw dark clouds swirling to the west—the same direction as Bitter Bend—and for a brief moment, she saw her father's face in the brewing storm.

"Please, this way, Miss Poole."

With each step across the tarmac, another objection popped into Clara's mind. What would her father do when he found her note? Did she have any clue what she was getting herself into? Would she really be able to fly around the world in a hot-air balloon with a complete stranger? Had she packed enough underwear?

One step, two steps, three steps, and she was on board.

Plush leather chairs lined the cabin on either side. She chose the nearest one and buckled her seat belt. As the door swooshed closed, a bolt of panic raced down her spine.

"Welcome aboard. This is Captain Gregory," crackled a voice over the intercom. "We have a small patch of weather to clear after takeoff, which might slow us down a bit, but then it's smooth sailing all the way to Paris. So please sit back and make yourself comfortable."

The plane taxied down the runway as the edge of the storm arrived. Rain pelted the sleek fuselage—a sensation not unlike being inside a tin can—before the jet engines roared to life, forcing Clara into her seat back. They lifted effortlessly into the sky, and Clara watched the geometric patterns of farms below fade to cloud.

"That man can be quite the talker," said Ms. Lemot, waving her phone as she collapsed into the seat across from Clara.

"Who?"

"Mr. Habberdish, of course."

"Where is he?"

"He had to depart last night. The poor man has so much to do. But he requested I stay to take care of you and your father. Speaking of your father, where is he?"

"Oh. Ah . . ."

"He's not on board?"

"Uh . . . no. He, er, needed to stay to finish something for work. Like you said . . . the poor man has so much to do. But he knew that I would be with you, so he let me come ahead. He's taking the other plane tomorrow."

"We only have one plane."

"I meant, you know . . . a regular plane."

"I see," murmured Ms. Lemot. She frowned slightly, biting on her bottom lip.

Smile, thought Clara. *Smile like everything's okay.*

Finally, Marie Lemot beamed back. "Well, I'm happy to be your chaperone until then, and I look forward to greeting your father when he arrives in Paris."

Clara smiled awkwardly and pulled on her ear. "Yeah . . . Me, too."

CHAPTER SEVEN

A POOR START

THE PLANE'S INTERCOM CRACKLED TO LIFE. "Good morning and bonjour. This is Captain Gregory. We are making our descent into Paris and will be on the ground shortly. Please ensure your seat belt is fastened and bienvenue en France."

Clara rubbed the sleep from her eyes, gave a tug on her lap belt, and glanced out the window at the approaching dawn. She'd never been abroad before, and the only things she knew about France were that the Eiffel Tower, initially considered an eyesore, was now its cultural icon, and that the food was supposedly the best on Earth. Her stomach gurgled at the thought of baguettes, chocolate croissants, and omelets.

The plane tilted, and Paris unfolded below her. A river

snaked through the city's center, its banks flanked by long rectangular barges. Wide boulevards fanned out like spokes, connecting at rotundas, around which cars raced madly like ants at a picnic basket.

In minutes, the plane was on the tarmac, and Clara found herself riding with Ms. Lemot in the back of a long sedan along boulevards filled with quaint shops and patisseries. Slowly, the city thinned and became more wooded until they turned down a long drive and stopped in front of a massive cigar-shaped building of glass and steel. It reflected the morning sun, rising a dozen or so stories, with tall cylindrical structures at each end, and a series of wide balconies that jutted out like wings.

Ms. Lemot led Clara up a wide metal gangplank toward what resembled an enormous glass porthole. Air hissed like a soda can opening before a door rolled effortlessly into the wall, and then they descended into a tubular hallway illuminated by rings of lights.

"Ms. Lemot, what kind of building is this?"

"An extraordinary one," she replied, hurrying along. "You'll learn more about it soon enough. But right now, we need to find Mr. Habberdish. He's making the final touches to his speech, and I'm sure he'll want to review parts of it with you before calling you to the stage."

Clara's stomach lurched, but this time not from hunger. "Stage?"

"Yes. We don't have time to get you properly dressed, but you shouldn't be up there for long. You won't need to say much, unless that is, you've prepared a speech."

"A speech?"

Ms. Lemot paused. "Clara, did you read the folder of materials I gave you on the plane?"

"What folder?"

"The one that said 'Read Me' on the cover."

Clara gave something between a shrug and a cringe.

Ms. Lemot sighed. "In that case, we have quite a bit to review—and rather quickly. Today is orientation."

Clara shrugged again, desperately wishing she was better prepared.

"WOOBA orientation is a presentation for pilots, during which we review the details of the racecourse, rules and regulations, and make any important announcements. It is also the first day of WOOBATech, where pilots purchase supplies and equipment, and experience the latest in aeronautical technology. Come. You can explore the exhibits while I find Mr. Habberdish."

Ms. Lemot gestured Clara toward a set of smoked glass doors. They slid open, and Clara's eyes went wide. It was as if she'd been transported to one of those wild bazaars in Morocco; people bustled about yelling and haggling. She turned to ask Ms. Lemot a question, but the woman was gone.

A banner spanned the exhibit gateway: WOOBATECH 3000: THE FUTURE IS NOW. Yet it was the hastily written sentence below that drew her attention: SPONSORED BY BIG DOG JERKY—DON'T BE A BIG JERK. GIVE YOUR DOG BIG DOG JERKY! Clara wasn't sure what dog treats had to do with a round-the-world air race, but she was quickly distracted by a man in a balloon costume who shoved a map of the exhibit floor into her hand.

The show was divided into three main pavilions, though taking in the chaos around her, it was impossible to be sure. One thing, however, was certain: everyone had something to sell.

The first booths were dedicated to raw materials, which Clara assumed were used for making balloon baskets. She examined barrels of different types of wicker: ash, oak, hickory, rattan, bulrush, and bamboo.

"You don't want any those, miss," whispered a raspy voice in her ear. She spun on her heels and gazed into the deep-set eyes of a weaselly looking shopkeeper. "That kind of wicker is outdated. What you need is Aerostat

Performance Wicker—3D-printed carbon fiber. It's ten times stronger than steel and half as light as aluminum. Here. Let me show you."

"Er, no thanks," Clara replied, stepping back out of his reach and right onto the toes of a stout, aristocratic-looking man.

"Ow!" he howled through his thick mustache. "Where are your parents? Children shouldn't be walking the floor alone. I say, the riffraff they let into the race these days!"

Clara apologized and darted into an area marked CABLING AND FASTENERS. Ropes of every color hung from rows of wooden pegs, though Clara had no clue what part of ballooning they were used for.

"Look, Mum, racing baskets!" said a boy to her right. His head was buried inside a sleek black basket that looked more like a bobsled than something attached to a hot-air balloon.

"Alfie Woodrow! Get out of there," snapped a red-haired woman in a leather coat and green leggings.

"Seriously, Mum, why can't we fly one of these?" The boy emerged from the basket, his disheveled mop of red curls falling around a freckled, rosy face. "We could go so fast."

"Alfie, the race is not only about speed. Strategy is equally important. Trust me, you'll understand once you've had some experience."

As she wrapped her son in a tight hug, Clara's thoughts wandered to her father. What had he done after reading her note? Where was he now?

"Is everything okay, dear?" the red-haired woman asked.

"Huh?"

"You're staring at us."

"Oh! Erm . . . sorry."

Clara ducked her head and continued on past a rowdy group of pilots shooting fireballs from something advertised as an IGNITUS BURNER: LET THE DRAGON OUT WITH 6-COIL TECHNOLOGY, until she found herself immersed in a world of blinking screens and electronic gadgetry.

There was a hum and whoosh as something beelike zipped past her ear. Clara whirled to find two zombie-faced boys with controllers, piloting a pair of miniature drones.

"Hey, watch it!" she snapped.

"Dude, you almost hit her," said the first boy in a perfect monotone.

"Yeah . . . almost," deadpanned his friend.

Clara shot them her best mean-girl look, then continued

toward an area promoting the latest and greatest innovations in balloon navigation. She picked up a device at random—something called the WOOBAnometer All-in-One Aerostatic Assistant—and tapped the screen.

The machine jumped to life, screeching out an alarm.

Clara pressed button after button, though somehow that only made the dumb thing louder. "Will you stop!" she hissed.

A group of nearby pilots cast disapproving glances in her direction as Clara fought madly to silence the demon device. Finally, with no inkling of what to do, she threw it—much, much harder than intended.

The WOOBAnometer sailed across the exhibit floor, cartwheeling end over end into the skull of a large woman wearing a virtual headset. She stumbled, shocked and sightless, tripping on the hem of her polka-dot dress, and went careening across the aisle, tumbling into the two zombie-faced boys.

"Berta!" cried a tiny man, no larger than a jockey. He rushed to the woman's aid, pulling at her in vain as she struggled to get upright.

The miniature drones, now pilotless, zipped in all directions. Some exhibitgoers dove for cover, while other used cardboard standees to shield themselves from the buzzing rotors. One drone even buried itself in the updo of a fleeing woman, chewing through her thick curls before dismantling the handheld electronics shelf, sending devices clattering to the floor. Clara ducked as the second drone buzzed by, heading for the burner exhibit, where after being engulfed by an Ignitus fireball, it landed in the wicker booth, igniting a barrel of reeds. The blaze was quickly extinguished by a terrified exhibitor.

All eyes turned to Clara.

"Oh boy . . . ," she mumbled, before picking one of the few surviving devices off the floor and placing it gingerly back on the shelf.

"Don't . . . touch . . . anything!" pleaded a man in a WOOBA event staff shirt, approaching her cautiously. "This is all very complicated and very expensive equipment. Please, perhaps you'd like to move on to another exhibit? Or the food court, maybe? Or even the exit?"

Red-faced, Clara nodded apologetically, then sulked away from the Electronics Pavilion, seeking refuge in the bits and bobs of an old junk booth.

"Can I help you, miss?" A deeply wrinkled face popped up from behind a dusty stack of flight manuals. "Barnaby Bixley, of Barnaby Bixley's Balloon Bazaar and Other Big Baubles," he said proudly. "Over seventy years offering only the best service to only the best aeronauts."

"Barnaby Bixley's Balloon Bazaar?" she repeated, twisting her tongue around the words.

"And Other Big Baubles," he added with a grin.

He resembled someone from a bygone era in his white shirt and tan suspenders, which held up a scratchy-looking pair of wool pants far higher than where an average person's waist should be. Bixley was bald aside from a thin band of hair that ran from one ear to the other, but his eyes, a stunning electric blue, teemed with life.

"Looking for something? Maybe a slide rule for celestial navigation?"

"Oh, sorry. I'm not here to buy anything," Clara said.

"Then you've come to the right place," he replied with a chuckle. "No one buys anything from me anymore."

Clara could see why. Bixley's goods spanned from battered to broken-down. Strange telescopes, sextants, and other ancient contraptions, none of which had seen a polishing cloth in decades, spilled carelessly from old wooden crates.

"People don't need these old things anymore," Bixley explained, disappearing behind a shelf of weathered almanacs. "Nowadays, piloting is all done with computerized gadgets and gizmos."

"Then why sell these . . . antiques? Why don't you just retire?"

"What's to say I haven't? Mind you, at ninety-five, I can't fly anymore, but I still love being around pilots." Bixley puffed out his chest. "As I'm sure you know, it takes a certain breed to be one."

"Actually, I don't."

"No? Why's that? I've seen quite a few pilots in my time. You look like one to me."

"Sorry, Mr. Bixley, but I'm not."

"Then I suppose we'll have to do something about that, won't we?" Bixley had a bit of giddyup in his step as he hurried off, rummaging through drawers, cabinets, and cluttered bins.

"Not that . . . no . . . too big . . . aha!" he said. "Here, Miss . . . ?"

"Poole. Clara Poole."

"Well, Miss Clara Poole, try this on. It looks about your size."

Clara slipped her arms through the well-worn sleeves of a jacket, and then Bixley escorted her to a standing mirror with splotched edges. The jacket was made from well-weathered brown leather, with large pockets on each side and a tall collar that buttoned to her chin. She tucked her mother's scarf into the neckline and examined her reflection. She did look like a pilot.

"Mr. Bixley, thank you, but I'm afraid I don't have any money."

"Nonsense! I already told you no one buys anything from me anymore. How about this: you borrow it and then give it back after you win the race."

"There you are!" called Ms. Lemot from across the aisle. "Did something happen at the Electronics Pavilion?" Before Clara could explain, Ms. Lemot cut her off. "No matter. I'm just glad I found you."

"Mr. Bixley lent me a coat," she said with a small twirl.

"And what a nice coat it is, too. Now, Clara, we need to hustle. Orientation begins in less than thirty minutes, and Mr. Habberdish must speak with you beforehand."

"Thank you, Mr. Bixley," said Clara.

"Wait," he said. "I have one more thing. Something I never flew without." He scurried to his desk and removed a small object from the drawer—a silver compass with a white dial. Neatly written beneath the *N* were the words *Always Follow True North*. Clara couldn't help but notice the compass's needle spinning at random, and something rattling inside the case.

"Mr. Bixley, I think this might be broken."

"No, no, it works," he assured her. "You'll figure it out."

Clara was quite sure she didn't know how to use a broken compass, but she smiled politely and slipped it into her pocket.

"Clara, we really must go," Ms. Lemot urged. "You don't want to be late to your big Face of the Race introduction."

"Are you this year's Face of the Race?" Bixley asked, sounding impressed. "Well, Miss Poole, you're in for quite a wild ride!"

Clara gulped. "Am I?"

She turned to Ms. Lemot, but the woman was already marching away. Clara smiled once more at Barnaby Bixley, then hurried to catch up. "Ms. Lemot, what did he mean by 'wild ride'? Ms. Lemot . . . ?"

CHAPTER EIGHT

ORIENTATION

BELLS CHIMED OVER THE LOUDSPEAKER, signaling the race participants to make their way to the auditorium level for the start of orientation. Vendors shouted last-minute bargains as pilots peeled away from the booths and queued by the elevators. It was there that Clara and Ms. Lemot found Harold Habberdish.

"There she is, our Face of the Race!" he exclaimed. "Welcome, welcome, Clara. I knew you'd convince your father to come!"

Clara forced out a smile. "Yeah, my dad . . . it was, uh . . . easy."

The elevator doors opened, and Habberdish ushered Clara and Ms. Lemot inside along with a stiff-looking man in a dark suit. With his slender face and the rimless glasses that rested on the tip of a hooked nose, he reminded Clara of an undertaker.

"This is Mr. Lester Longing, WOOBA's legal counsel," Habberdish explained. "He and I were just discussing a new rule that's caused a bit of an uproar with some of the participants—the qualifications that must be met to be officially recognized as a copilot."

Mr. Longing did not speak or smile or move. He didn't even blink.

"He's dreadfully dull," whispered Habberdish, leaning close to Clara. "Aside from legal work, I don't think he does anything else."

The carriage jumped to life, and Clara's knees buckled. "Careful, dear," said Ms. Lemot, grabbing her arm. "These elevators take some getting used to. Tell them where you want to go, hold on, and hope they take you there."

Clara ran her finger against the brushed metal walls, bare apart from a small window that glowed in alternating colors. "There're no buttons or labels? How do you even know what to say?"

Ms. Lemot frowned. "Trial and error, I'm afraid. It took me a while to learn that the dining hall was actually called the *canteen*. I had to bring a packed lunch for months."

Eee-orrr!

"What on earth was that?" said Habberdish, his gaze darting around the compartment.

"Me," Clara confessed. "I haven't eaten since yesterday, and Ms. Lemot said *lunch*." She pressed her face against the little window, hoping a hamburger or pizza might magically appear, but only saw the light fade from blue to green.

Habberdish patted his suit jacket, patterned in strange white birds. "They're doves," he explained flatly, noticing Clara's confusion. Finally, he fished out a package of candy from an inside pocket. "Here. One of the new sponsors gave this to me. I haven't tried it myself, but you're welcome to it."

"Thank you," Clara said. "I could eat my sock right now." She unwrapped a piece and popped it in her mouth.

To say the candy tasted bad would have been an understatement. Bad was moldy bread. Bad was spoiled milk. This was infinitely worse than bad. Part nutty, part spicy, and part cheesy, the candy was the most revolting thing Clara had ever tasted. Her brain did acrobatics trying to put together a complete and horrifying picture of the ingredients. Was it slug sprinkled in chili powder? Maybe stale cheddar gummy bear? Or worse, cheesy rotten banana rolled in pepper?

"Wha . . . ith dis?"

"I'm not sure," replied Habberdish. "Gum, I think. There are so many sponsors now that I can't keep up with all their products. Why? Is it unpleasant?"

Clara spat the vile substance from her mouth and then eyed the words on the package: WIBBLE BIBBLE BUBBLE GUM—NEW SPICY NACHO RAISIN!

"Anyhow, here's more if you want," he continued, stuffing another package into her jacket pocket. "Now, we don't have much time, so I'll do my best to run through all the details. As you know, we have a new group of sponsors replacing our long-standing one, Groem and Stratmire. That's made your job as our Face of the Race a touch more complicated. Some of our sponsors are, how shall I say it, a bit less sophisticated. But don't worry! We've enlisted a hotshot creative team to write your product placements, a top fashion team to design your grand reveal at the opening ceremonies, a veteran race announcer to help mold your public image, and an A-list production team responsible for pulling it all together. Sound good?"

What it sounded like was scary, but Clara nodded anyway.

"Splendid. The final matter is your contract."

"Thorry, wha con-thrack?" Clara asked, picking the last of the sticky candy from her molars.

"Per agreement with our sponsors, we must have a signed contract before we can announce you as the Face of the Race."

"Okay . . . I think?"

Clara had never seen a contract before, let alone signed one. But after blowing up the exhibit floor at WOOBATech, she thought it wise not to cause more trouble.

Mr. Longing handed Clara a pen, then removed a stack of papers from his briefcase, which Habberdish began flipping through madly. "Sign here," he said, pointing. "And here . . . and there . . . and initial this twice."

"Should I be reading this?" Clara asked. "What exactly am I signing?"

"I'll summarize. This clause says you agree to participate in the race as a pilot. You've signed that one, so we'll move on. This next section says you agree to be the Face of the Race for the competition's duration and that you'll market our sponsors' products through various means of promotion."

"What are *various means*?"

"It means that they are, well, *various*. In any case, you agree to promote them—mostly on television. Okay, next."

"I'm not sure I want to be on television."

"Don't be silly. All children want to be on television. Now, this next section gives us the right to use your likeness however we see fit. Sign here . . . and there, thank you. And this last part says that you are who you say you are, that you are sound of mind, and that we may take legal recourse if you've lied. But really, why would you do that?"

Clara thought of her father and his soon-to-be-totally-make-believe arrival in Paris.

She signed and initialed, initialed, and signed. Once she'd finished, Mr. Longing placed the papers back in his briefcase and gave the WOOBA president a solemn nod.

Swoosh. The elevator door opened, and Habberdish escorted Clara into a busy hallway. Pilots—some dressed in tuxedos and evening gowns, and others in sun-beaten jackets—milled about the space. Camera flashes bounced off the walls as people wearing press badges spoke loudly into television cameras. There must've been a hundred, many times the number of reporters who'd been camped outside Bitter Bend.

"Now . . . ," continued Habberdish, yelling to be heard over the racket as they hurried toward a sign marked backstage, "pilots are an odd breed. Quite superstitious, which is sometimes warranted, as bad things do happen in balloon racing. But they do love their stories. So . . . once

I've introduced you, tell a little tale, something funny to warm up the room. No doubt, they'll adore you."

As they passed through the stage door, the din of the crowd vanished. Two stagehands appeared from the shadows. The first attached a microphone to Clara's ear while the other clipped a receiver unit to her belt. She spun, lost in the commotion, only to walk face-first into a stylist's makeup pouf.

"But I don't have any stories," Clara said, coughing.

"Nonsense. Everyone has stories. This is it, Clara. The moment—your moment! Are you ready? Any last questions?"

"Mr. Habberdish, I don't think I can—"

"Fantastic! Let's do this!"

The lights dimmed, the audience roared, and Habberdish took the stage.

"Welcome to orientation for the hundredth annual WOOBA Air Race. This year is historic. We have constructed a tournament to outshadow every other event known to mankind. Our race will bring more people together than the World Cup, have more heart-pounding action than the Super Bowl, be more dramatic than the Tour de France, and be more high-spirited than the Olympics. Thus, it is only fitting that we begin our hundredth year by looking back at our storied history through a montage that exemplifies our courage, exalts our heroes, and inspires our very humanity."

The screen lit up with black-and-white footage chronicling the earliest days of the race. Men (and only men, it seemed) dressed in tweed suits and ivy caps laughed as they boarded small balloons fixed with odd propellers above their baskets. The grainy clips cut between takeoffs, landing in hayfields, and pilots sharing a toast with local farmers.

As the film moved through time, the balloons became more recognizable and modern-looking. The scenery changed, too, gradually and then more dramatically. Farmers' fields were replaced with mountains and deserts, and the smiling airmen were substituted with hard-faced, sun-blistered adventurers. The balloons changed once again, this time to sleek airships and zeppelins equipped with sails and rotors, and with them, the harshness of the terrain evolved, as well. Pilots parachuted from burning baskets after crashing into rugged peaks, while others fought frozen waves, downed and adrift on iron-gray seas.

Clara's stomach lurched again, this time not from hunger but from fear. Nothing she saw in the film reminded her of any part of her flight over Michigan.

THE RACE IS ON! appeared onscreen and then faded

to black. The lights went up, and Habberdish reemerged onstage to a cheering crowd, arms outstretched like a circus ringleader. "Now, what say we talk about this year's race?" he exclaimed. The houselights dimmed slightly, and a map of the world illuminated onscreen with a blue line corkscrewing across it. "This year's course is divided into ten stages, each with its own unique challenges. Some will be straightforward sprints, others untimed and technical, and others still designed to test a pilot's endurance. Unlike previous years, all stages will conclude at floating finish lines. Winners of each stage will be named at medal ceremonies along the way, and will be given the honor of flying the Dovie, or leader's flag, during the next race."

A royal-blue pennant with a white dove in the center faded in onscreen.

"As always, our racecourse is subject to change given global weather patterns, including but not limited to: hurricanes and cyclones, government missile testing, and the alteration of commercial flight paths. Fortunately, with the aid of the *Zephyrus*, which can travel large distances quickly, we can reposition if needed to ensure the action never stops."

Hurricanes? Missiles? Suddenly, moving to Chicago sounded like a much better idea to Clara.

"Excuse me, Ms. Lemot," she whispered.

The woman bent low. "Yes? Exciting, isn't it? You're on in a moment."

"I don't think I can do this."

"Don't be nervous. You won't be onstage for long."

"No, I mean the race."

A spotlight hit Clara, and Habberdish smiled at her from center stage, his hand outstretched.

"That's your cue, kid," said a stagehand, nudging her in the back.

"Here she is," trumpeted Habberdish. "This year's spokesperson, our very own Face of the Race, Clara Poole!"

The stagehand pushed her onto the stage to loud applause. The houselights were bright enough that Clara could still see the crowd's faces clearly. Alfie, the boy from the basket exhibit, sat in the front row with his mother. Behind them was the mustached aristocrat whose toes she'd stepped on, looking extremely bored. Seated beside him was a primly dressed girl with long auburn hair. However, unlike her father (Clara assumed), the girl didn't appear bored in the least. In fact, she stared at Clara with a look that could only be described as loathing. Clara wondered what other horrible offense she'd unknowingly committed during her WOOBATech fiasco.

"As many of you know," continued Habberdish, "Miss

Poole rocketed to fame after her record-breaking flight in a homemade balloon. We are beyond privileged to have her represent us in the running of our centennial competition. Clara, say hello to the audience and the countless fans watching at home."

Thousands of eyes fixed on her as cameras flashed from the mezzanine.

"Uh . . ." She scanned the watchful faces waiting for her to say something exciting, something magical, something important. "Um . . . I think I need to go home."

A few people laughed. Others screwed up their mouths, confused.

"Home! Indeed! Isn't she great, folks? Just brilliant!" Habberdish nudged her to the stairs at the edge of the stage. "Well done. Why don't you sit down?" he whispered before turning back to the crowd. "Clara Poole, everyone!"

A smattering of applause filled the otherwise dead air. Clara slumped into a seat in the front row and pulled her collar up to hide her face as the crowd began to stir, anticipating the presentation's end.

"Not yet, folks," said Habberdish, raising his hands. "There's one last important announcement before we conclude. Over the years, we've seen a wave of innovation in aeronautics. And as exciting as these advances are, they have come at a great price: we have lost the true art of piloting. Therefore, to honor our sport's humble beginnings, we'll be returning to our roots. All modern technology is banned from this year's race."

The crowd grumbled and gasped, expressions of excitement turning into confused frowns.

"Is this a joke?" yelled a pilot behind Clara.

"How do you define *modern technology*?" called out another.

"But I just bought all this new stuff at WOOBATech!" cried a third.

"I understand this might come as a shock," Habberdish continued, his face grave, "but this rule is effective immediately. Pilots are not to use any new technology that aids their navigation, communication, or propulsion. Naturally, you will be given ample time to retrofit your balloons before Stage One. And with that, I bid you goodbye for now, and look forward to seeing you at the opening ceremonies."

The house lights went up, and the crowd dispersed, still grumbling. Clara rushed to the edge of the stage where the WOOBA president had been joined by Ms. Lemot. "Mr. Habberdish, may I speak with you?"

"Yes, yes, of course. You know, that was a funny thing you said to the audience. For a second, I thought you were serious. It made for fantastic television!"

"But I wasn't joking," Clara insisted. "I want to go home."

"Ha! Yes, very convincing." He eyed her for a moment, and his expression changed. "Good grief, you're serious! Well, I'm sorry, Miss Poole, but that's impossible."

"Why?"

"Because we just announced you as the race's spokesperson on international television. And because you signed a contract."

"But—"

"Clara, come now. You're about to have the adventure of a lifetime."

"But I don't want an adventure. I want to go home."

"And that's precisely where you're going!" said someone behind her. Clara spun and met the eyes of a man with brown hair and glasses—a man missing his signature red baseball cap.

"Mr. Poole, you're here!" Ms. Lemot chirped cheerfully.

"Dad," squeaked Clara. "You're . . . uh . . . here."

CHAPTER NINE

UNINTENDED RESULTS

CLARA WAS SITTING IN THE morning light of her hotel room window watching children sail toy boats in the fountain outside when the door slammed shut.

"It's hopeless," her father said, collapsing into the wing-back chair beside her. "I've spent all morning talking with attorneys, combing over that ridiculous contract you signed, trying to find a way out. I even wasted three hours with that mind-numbing lawyer, Mr. Longing, who droned on and on about the binding nature of the agreement and what he claimed would be 'WOOBA's unfortunate recourse, should you withdraw.'"

"What does that mean?"

"It means he'll sue our pants off if you don't participate."

"Dad, I—"

"Please. I don't want to hear it. Last night was enough, and I need all my energy to figure a way out of this mess."

It had been a long night. Her father had shifted from anger to relief, relief to worry, and worry to exhaustion. Clara had stayed silent through all of it. What could she say? In forty-eight hours, she'd single-handedly managed to ruin their lives.

"So there's really no way out?" she finally asked.

"Not unless you're dead or injured." He rose and headed for the bathroom. Clara could hear the faucet running. "I'm still searching for a loophole, some clause to disqualify you, but right now the only choice I really have is . . ." His voice quavered. "The only choice I have . . . is to join you."

"Join me?"

"I'm certainly not letting my twelve-year-old daughter fly around the world on her own." He reappeared, rubbing at his face with a towel. "Habberdish agreed. We have an appointment this morning to meet your—*our*—pilot, and tour the balloon docks. Habberdish also suggested I watch the documentary from last night's orientation to get a better understanding of the race."

"Oh, I think you can skip that. . . ." Clara winced as she recalled the scenes of flaming balloons. "Really, Dad, it was super boring."

"Fine, then I guess we should go to meet Habberdish." He turned to head out the door, but stopped short. "Is that my red hat?"

"Yeah," she replied sheepishly. "About that . . ."

THE HÔTEL LAURENCE was the epitome of French elegance. Considered a national treasure since the seventeenth century, the hotel catered to the most refined and private clientele: royalty, movie stars, artists, prima ballerinas, world diplomats, and other eminent guests. At least, so said the magazine in Clara's room. However, no one would've known it stepping off the elevator.

Staff scrambled to slip drink coasters under the sweating glasses of a group of rowdy pilots resting their stockinged feet on a three-hundred-year-old table, while the concierge spoke urgently to a crowd of women in climbing harnesses about removing their ropes from the Tiffany chandelier. Even the maître d' was arguing politely with a thickly-bearded pilot the size of a bear, explaining that the dining room's rococo serving trays could not be used for takeout. Amid the mayhem sat Harold Habberdish taking tea as he read the morning paper.

"Ah, here they are—father and daughter," he said, setting aside his newspaper. "I trust you two had a good night to rest and reconnect? Well, we have lots to see today, and I'm sure you're excited. Shall we begin?"

"Harold Habberdish, don't you move an inch!"

A woman stormed across the lobby toward them. Clara could see she was old, but *how* old was tough to tell given her abundance of energy. She wore a worn, waist-length flight jacket with a fur collar that appeared to have been devoured by mice, and her hair, hastily pinned back, was a nest of white snarls. Her gaze, however, was as resolute as an army general's.

"Ah, Greta. We were just on our way to—"

"Did you tell that bore of a man, Longing, to give this to me?" she snarled, shaking a piece of paper in the WOOBA president's face. "*This* was pinned to my basket this morning. Perhaps I should read it to you."

Dear Ms. Gildersleeve,

We regret to inform you that your request for a waiver of Rule 10.4 of the WOOBA Race Guidelines ("Rules for Copilots") has been denied. This rule states that for safety reasons, all balloons must have a full complement of crew members, comprising at least one pilot and one copilot. Furthermore, the recent addendum to this rule, Subset Rule 10.4.1, now stipulates all pilots and copilots must be human.

Your participation in the race is determinant on all criteria being met.

Sincerely,
Lester Longing, Esq.
Law Offices of Longing, Ernst & Burnsly
London

Habberdish sighed and motioned in the direction of Clara and her father.

"Greta Gildersleeve, please meet the Pooles, Clara and Oliver. Greta, this young girl is our new Face of the Race. Perhaps you saw her at yesterday's orientation?"

The woman shot Clara a sideways glare. "I don't attend those dumb events. All that puffery and people who call themselves aeronauts . . . which brings me back to my question: I thought we'd solved our copilot dispute, Habberdish. This letter suggests otherwise."

"I'm sorry, Greta. As you already know, this new rule

was put in place for safety. However, your problem is easily solved. Find a copilot."

"I *have* a copilot. *Copilots*, to be precise."

"Yes, well, go find some that are *people*."

Clara tried to imagine what kind of copilot *wasn't* a person.

"Now, if you'll excuse us, I'm taking the Pooles to tour the balloon docks. If necessary, I can come to your mooring afterward and continue this conversation."

"You know as well as I do that my copilots could fly circles around any pilot here!" Gildersleeve threw up her hands and stormed off muttering something about belief in Darwinism.

"Well," said Habberdish. "You've now met Greta."

AFTER A SHORT DRIVE, they stood staring into the mouth of an enormous hangar with the number three painted thirty feet high on its door. The sounds of welders and rivet guns competed with the high-pitched beeping of forklifts. Plumes of smoke filled the air, and hot embers rained down as if someone inside was breaking up a ship for scrap.

"The balloons are moored in three main hangars," explained Habberdish, "and a fourth is used by event production and rescue-and-recovery. Shall we go inside and take a look before meeting your pilot, Pascal Berg?"

Inside was an odd choice of words. Hangar Three was so vast that it still felt like they were wandering outside.

"Each hangar has its own personality," Habberdish continued. "This one, nicknamed the Hive, was inspired by the ceilings of Paris's train stations." The roof, made of massive hexagonal glass tiles, cast shafts of amber light across the walls and floor. Clara wouldn't have been surprised to see gigantic worker bees buzzing overhead.

Habberdish led them down a wide central causeway where balloons were moored on each side to tall girder towers. They rested like slumbering monsters; their stillness broken only by the fiery blasts of pilots testing burners.

"You may notice the shapes of some balloons are not those you'd typically associate with hot-air ballooning. The design of each envelope is different, based on its pilot's experience and distinct style of flying."

"What do you mean by *envelope*?" asked Clara's father.

"Ah, yes, good question. You see, the top part of the balloon where the hot air is forced inside is called the *envelope*, or *bag*, which connect to the *basket* or *gondola*. Our racing balloons are unique from ordinary hot-air balloons in that they have semirigid forms inside, which give them added structure for enduring extreme winds and collisions. As such, they remain partially inflated throughout the race."

"What about that one?" said Clara, pointing to an odd-shaped green balloon. "It looks like two zucchinis."

"That's *Rumor*, piloted by the Woodrows. It's what we call a bi-envelope—two pontoon-shaped bags with a center-hung gondola. Excellent in strong winds. And the blimp-shaped ship on your right belongs to Sir Wallace Chins-Ratton. It's called *Brigadier Albert*, though most pilots call it *Big Al*. However, don't say that in front of Chins-Ratton. He's a rather formal fellow."

"Indeed, formality is what holds the civilized world together. That, and impeccable taste." The mustached aristocrat appeared suddenly on the causeway behind them. He was a stark contrast to the other rough-and-tumble-looking pilots in Hangar Three, dressed impeccably like a naval admiral. Behind him scowled the sullen-faced girl with auburn hair. She wore a crisp, gray knee-length skirt and a navy sweater with a white collar, monogrammed with the initials *OCR*. The girl stared at Clara so intensely, she thought a hole might burn into her forehead.

"Ah, good morning, Wallace. We were just admiring

head. The ambulance just left. I assumed you saw it when you came in?"

"*Ambulance? Sandbag?*" repeated Habberdish, frowning.

"To the head," Berta confirmed. "The good news: He was semiconscious when they left. The bad: He didn't seem to have a clue who he was."

Harold Habberdish opened his mouth, but only managed a feeble *uh*. He turned, pointing at the hangar's entrance, then back at Berta, and finally to Clara.

"So," she said with an awkward smile, "does that mean I can go home now?"

your balloon. And a good morning to you, too, Ophelia."

"What's your name?" Ophelia said flatly, ignoring Habberdish's greeting. "Carrie, is it? This year's Face of the Race? Too bad. After Groem and Stratmire dropped out, word is WOOBA had to scramble to replace them. The new sponsors I've heard mentioned sound utterly . . . common. I'm rather glad I'm not you." With that, the girl marched off toward the hangar door.

Clara scowled. "My name isn't Carrie. It's Clara."

"Whatever," Ophelia called back, flicking away the comment with her hand.

"Habberdish, a word, please," said Sir Wallace. "I'm afraid there's been a colossal mistake—one I expect you will remedy promptly. *Brigadier Albert* was given mooring here in Hanger Three rather than in Regency."

"My apologies, Wallace, but is there really a difference between here and there?"

"A *difference*? My good man, there is an enormous difference! I am *always* moored in Regency. Surely, you don't expect *Brigadier Albert* to be docked in a place this pedestrian. As I said before, good taste is important."

Habberdish forced a smile. "Of course. I will speak with our dock manager about having you relocated as soon as possible."

"Today, Harold. Soot is getting all over my basket." Chins-Ratton turned and wobbled after his daughter.

"He's special," said Clara's father.

"Quite," Habberdish replied before continuing down the causeway. "The Chins-Rattons have a long history with WOOBA. They've participated in the race for decades. This will be Ophelia's fourth competition. She was the youngest to participate until the Hoshi child this year. Needless to say, the Chins-Rattons are very—"

"Rude." It was the large woman Clara had accidentally struck in the head with the WOOBAnometer. She sat in a rocking chair at the base of a mooring surrounded by pots of chrysanthemums and forget-me-nots, knitting what looked like the world's largest sweater. "Those two have been acting like royalty all morning, stomping about and hollering, telling the rest of us how awful it is in here."

"May I introduce Roberta Bortles, the pride of Scotland and pilot of *Primrose*." Habberdish turned to smile at the rose-faced woman. "Roberta, these are the Pooles, Oliver and his daughter, Clara."

"Aye, I saw you onstage at orientation," she said. "It's lovely to meet you and your father. Everyone calls me Berta, or Berta the Bug, on account of my polka-dot dresses. And up there is Signore Furio. Say hello, Alberto!"

Clara gazed up to see Berta's tiny companion suspen[ded] from a wooden scaffold strung together by a tangle of ro[pe]. He tiptoed nimbly from board to board, depositing fl[ow]ers into brightly colored window boxes. Clara tho[ught] *Primrose* more closely resembled a cozy cottage than a[n] air balloon.

"Ciao!" said Furio with an exuberant wave.

"The darling man doesn't speak a lick of English, b[ut] trying to learn some Italian of my own. Alberto come[s] a long line of brave men. His father was a Formul[a] racer and his grandfather was a tank commander [in] World War II. At least, I believe that's the case. Either [one] one was a shepherd and the other a plumber. I conf[ess] having a wee bit of trouble with translation."

"Ms. Berta, I think I may have hit you in the he[ad] terday at WOOBATech," said Clara, blushing. "I pr[omise I] didn't mean it."

"That's all right, dearie. Mind you, I was a bi[t] wally after, but I'm right as rain now. Speaking of a[ll] Harold, it's such a shame about Pascal."

"Sorry . . . Pascal? What about him?"

"Oh my, don't you know? Harold, the poor [man] knocked out cold not an hour ago. Terrible acc[ident] was retrofitting his balloon when a sandbag fell ri[ght]

CHAPTER TEN

A WORSE ALTERNATIVE

HAROLD HABBERDISH HADN'T STOPPED pacing since he got off the phone, anxiously rubbing his temples and muttering to himself. "This can't be happening again. Without a pilot, Clara can't fly. Without Clara, I don't have sponsors. And without sponsors, there is no race. Good grief, what if the sponsors catch wind of this? Think, Habberdish. Think. There must be a solution."

"Mr. Habberdish?" Clara said cautiously. "What did the doctors say about Pascal?"

"What? Who? The *doctors*? The doctors said the man has suffered a traumatic brain injury and has no idea who he is. He should be fine, eventually, but there's no way he'll be able to race. At any rate, none of that matters right now. No, no, there are far more urgent things to focus on."

Clara's father frowned. "Like what?"

"The sponsors, Mr. Poole! The sponsors! We must find a new pilot for Clara—someone who can take Berg's place."

"His place? Honestly, do you ever think about anything other than this stupid race? There are people involved—real people."

"Yes, of course. Real people," Habberdish muttered. "The question is which people? People who can pilot . . . People who need copilots . . . Copilots who are people . . . Wait, *copilots must be people!* Mr. Poole, you're a genius!"

Habberdish sprinted off down the causeway. Clara and her father chased after him, but somehow the little man ran like the wind, turning back every now and again to wave them on. They passed balloons of every shape and size, even one that resembled the head of a giant bear. When they finally stopped, Clara's father doubled over, sucking in air, while Habberdish gaped at the last mooring tower.

It was empty.

"That can't be," he said. "They should be here."

A hot blast roasted Clara's backside. She whirled around to see a tall, ratty-looking basket sitting among a mishmash of grimy boxes and crates, which, by comparison, made Barnaby Bixley's Balloon Bazaar look downright modern.

A figure in a hooded cloak huddled nearby over an ancient-looking burner, which lay on its side, coughing flames into the belly of a half-inflated balloon.

"Thank heavens," said Habberdish. The burner blazed again, its snarl deafening. "Sorry to bother you, but I must have a word. Excuse me? Hello?"

The person lifted his head, looked in both directions, then went back to work.

"Could you stop, please? I have a solution to your problem!"

This time, the person cut the burner, then turned to face them. He wore welding goggles with black lenses, which made him look menacing beneath his hood. But it was the three blue faces in matching goggles that appeared behind him that surprised Clara most. The faces weren't human.

The person removed his hood and goggles, and Clara realized it wasn't a man at all, but the gruff old woman from the hotel lobby.

"Greta," said Habberdish. "I need to speak with you."

"I'm busy," she said, turning back to her work.

The strange faces disappeared back into the shadows.

"Greta, please. It's urgent. And, I have an official decision regarding your copilots."

"Do you?" she said. "Well, don't tell *me*. Tell them."

The three creatures reappeared behind her. Two were the size of toddlers, while the third was twice as big and extremely plump. All had reddish-gold hair, which stuck out in all directions.

Clara's father stumbled back. "What are those things?"

"They are not *things*," Gildersleeve replied tersely. "They are monkeys. Golden snub-nosed monkeys."

Hairy arms rose to remove the goggles from their blue faces, revealing eyes as black as the lenses that had covered them. The monkeys curled their lips back in awkward gummy smiles, emphasizing large canine teeth, then moved toward Clara and her father, sniffing the air. The big monkey, who was nearly as tall as Clara, wrinkled his nose and huffed loudly.

"Are they dangerous?" asked her father nervously.

"Only if you're rude," Gildersleeve replied.

"So that's why Mr. Habberdish told you to find a copilot who's a person," Clara blurted out. "Your copilots are monkeys! But can they really fly a balloon?"

"Better than any pilot in this race. Habberdish knows it, too. He just refuses to admit it."

The monkeys circled Clara, lifting her arms and peeking inside her leather jacket. The smallest one tugged her mother's scarf from her neck and draped it around his own.

"That's not yours," said Gildersleeve sternly. "Give it to the child."

The monkey hesitantly handed it back.

"What are their names?" Clara asked.

"Dunno. I've never asked them. I call the skinny one who took your scarf Houdini because he can escape from anything. Sneaky, that one, and a bit of a thief, too, if you don't watch your belongings. The medium-sized one with the hair sticking up, I call Mayhem. He's by far the best pilot of the three, albeit a bit of daredevil."

"And what about the smelly one here?" asked Clara's father. The big monkey barked and pounded his hands on the ground. "Easy now. Just joking." Even so, he took another healthy step back.

"I call that one Bob."

"Why Bob?" asked Clara.

"Because he doesn't look like a Frank. He's quite sensitive, though, so don't get on his bad side. He tends to hold a grudge."

Bob glared intensely at Clara's father and pushed out his chest, trying to look intimidating. Still, Clara caught him sniffing at his armpits a moment later when he thought no one was paying attention.

"Greta, we've decided to bend the rules and allow you to fly with your monkeys," said Habberdish.

"So then you do have a brain?"

"Yes, well, the monkeys can join you, but only if Clara and her father fly with you as well."

"Wait," said her father. "We're flying with *her* now?"

"Fat chance!" Gildersleeve scoffed. "I have a full crew already. Besides, you know I don't fly with other people. Nor am I WOOBA's babysitter."

"I don't need a babysitter," Clara shot back.

"Greta, I'm afraid you don't have much choice," said Habberdish. "I've brought the rule book, and you are welcome to read it yourself. The monkeys can join you—they can even pilot—but you still must have one human copilot aboard. Mr. Berg's accident means he can no longer accompany Clara, yet it is a condition of our sponsorship agreements that she participate in the race. As I see it, I need a replacement for Berg, and you need a human copilot. It's that simple."

He held out the rule book to Gildersleeve, who snatched it and threw it over her shoulder. "I've read it," she said, stepping closer until she was face-to-face with Clara. "Have you ever been in a balloon, child?"

"Yes, I flew in one my class made as a science project."

"A science project?"

"It was a lawn chair, actually."

"That so? And what can you tell me about piloting?"

"I'm not sure I understand."

"Have you ever worked a burner?"

"No."

"Do you know what the Venturi effect is? Or what a pressure scoop does?"

"A what?"

"Can you fix a faulty fuel line? Or deflate a parachute?"

"Um . . ."

"What's your experience with maps and navigation? Can you read the stars?"

"Read them how?"

"What about wind? Know anything about wind patterns?"

"I learned about the different kinds of clouds once."

Clara's father placed a protective hand on her shoulder. "Ms. Gildersleeve, this isn't an inquisition."

"Don't tell me my business, Mr. Poole. I've flown this race more times than any living pilot. These questions are vital, if not lifesaving."

"Greta, you of all people can teach her what she needs to know," Habberdish interjected. "Plus, she'll learn quite a bit when she attends pilot training."

"And if I say no?"

"Clara joins you, or you don't race."

Gildersleeve walked back to her basket and ran her hand along its side, then turned and squinted at Habberdish. "The child can come."

"Thank you, Greta," he said, relieved.

"But only the child."

Clara's father raised a hand. "Wait . . . what?"

"I will take the child with me, provided she stays out of my way at all times."

"That's unacceptable. There's no way Clara is going without me."

"Greta, surely you can see your way to accommodating one more?" Habberdish pleaded.

"You said it yourself: the requirement is that the child goes. That's all the space I have for passengers."

"Then tell one of those fleabags not to go!" snapped Clara's father.

Bob barked loudly, followed by Houdini and Mayhem.

"Those *fleabags* happen to be expert pilots. Are you, Mr. Poole?"

"No, I'm her father. And if Clara is going to fly in that rickety basket over mountains and oceans and deserts . . . thousands and thousands of feet in the air . . . then so . . . am . . ." His face went pale, and he started wheezing.

"I understand your concern, Mr. Poole, but she'll be in expert hands," said Habberdish encouragingly. "You really have nothing to worry about. And you'll be aboard the *Zephyrus*, of course, so you'll be with Clara every moment she's not racing in the comfort and safety of your luxurious cabin."

"Dad, it's okay," Clara added. "I have to be in this race one way or another. Besides, it might be easier if you . . . weren't there."

Her father's glare softened and his heavy breathing slowed. Clara could see the parental gears turning in his head. Finally, he turned to Habberdish. "If anything happens to my daughter, I swear I'll—"

"Nothing bad will happen, Mr. Poole. You have my word."

"Nothing bad will happen," repeated Gildersleeve, "so long as she does what I say without question. And one more thing, Habberdish. No television cameras in my basket. I won't be subjected to any of her celebrity nonsense."

"I'm not a celebrity," said Clara.

"Apparently, child, the world thinks differently."

"And I'm not a child, either."

Gildersleeve and the monkeys turned back to their work, and soon the burner was firing into the mouth of the balloon. Clara followed her father and Habberdish from the hangar as the men discussed the details of her involvement like she wasn't there.

How she wished she weren't.

That night, she lay in bed staring at the distant orange glow of the hangars' roofs. Inside them, a thunder of dragons rested silently, waiting for their fiery ascent into the skies. Clara tossed and turned, wondering if she could really fly around the world with that surly old woman and three monkeys. She'd find out soon.

The race began in two days.

CHAPTER ELEVEN

THE RELIABILITY OF
THE MAIL

THE KNOCK CAME AFTER JUST SUNRISE. Clara wrapped herself in her comforter and shuffled to the door, one eye still closed, to find a man from WOOBA. He apologized for the earliness of the hour, said something about a mailroom mix-up and not receiving these materials the night before, then shoved an envelope in her hand and disappeared.

Her father groaned. "Who was it?"

"Someone from WOOBA."

"Did they bring coffee?"

Clara fell back on her bed, yawned, and pulled out the card inside the envelope.

Dear Miss Poole,

Your presence is required at tomorrow's Pilot Training and Safety Demonstration. Class will begin at eight in the morning outside the balloon docks. Please wear something that you don't mind getting ripped, singed, or vomited upon.

Sincerely,
Dodge Barlow
Safety Instructor

With a jolt, Clara realized that eight in the morning meant eight *this* morning. She bolted from bed and rushed to get ready, throwing on the same sweatshirt and jeans she'd worn the day before. "Dad, I'm going to the dining room to get something quick to eat. I have to get to the balloon docks for training."

"Sure, honey. You can wear my maroon socks if it's raining," he said through a snore.

She left him sleeping and slipped into the hall to call the elevator. It chimed, and the doors opened to reveal Ophelia Chins-Ratton inside. She was dressed like an equestrian in white breeches and leather boots, a crisp white shirt, and a cropped velvet jacket with *OCR* monogrammed on the lapel. Her hair, pulled tight in a single perfect braid, rested on one shoulder.

"Oh, it's you," Ophelia said dryly. "Hurry up then or wait for the next one."

Clara stepped into the car and pressed herself against the opposite wall. "I just got my invitation to pilot training," she said, trying to make polite conversation. "I was supposed to get it yesterday, but I guess there was a mix-up."

"It's a requirement, not an invitation. Any person under the age of eighteen must attend until they pass a flight test."

"Oh, so you've done this before?"

"Of course I have. I've done it multiple times."

"But you haven't passed your test yet?"

Ophelia shot Clara a nasty look as the elevator dinged, and the doors slid open.

A slender boy stepped onto the carriage, his eyes twinkling under a mop of dark hair. "Hey, OCR. Did you hear about the new instructor for pilot training? Guess last year's went hang gliding into a tornado and hasn't been seen since. I swear, the people WOOBA finds are completely mental."

"*OCR?*" Clara asked.

"Oh, hello." The boy smiled, revealing a mouthful of braces. "Didn't see you there. Harbinder Jolly, though everyone calls me Binder."

"Hi, I'm Clara."

"Pleasure's mine. And, yeah, OCR is what everyone calls Ophelia here. It's because of those monograms she has plastered all over her clothes. Ya know, OCR . . . Ophelia Chins-Ratton." Binder leaned close to Clara's ear. "Or you can call her *Rat Chin* like I do."

"I heard that, Harbinder Jolly," snapped Ophelia. "At least I know how to dress myself."

"Are you mad?" he answered, pulling on the hem of his shirt. "This is my brand-new India National Cricket Team jersey. It's absolutely brilliant."

"It's also on backward," Ophelia huffed.

Binder eyed his jersey. "Blimey, you're right." He pulled his arms inside, spinning the shirt around his neck, momentarily catching it on the thick iron bangle he wore on his wrist. "There we go. As I said, brilliant."

"You do know you're an idiot?" The elevator dinged once again, the doors slid open, and Ophelia marched out.

"Love you, too!" Binder called after her.

"Is she always like that?" asked Clara.

"Like what? Rude? Superior? Grumpy?" He paused. "Hey, do you have PTSD today?"

"Excuse me?"

Binder laughed. "It stands for *Pilot Training and Safety Demonstration.*"

"Oh, I thought you meant——"

"*Post-traumatic stress disorder?* Yeah, truth is, it could be called that, too."

"I got my letter this morning, but I don't really know much about it."

"Oh, right, first-timer. Then the less you know, the better." Binder clapped Clara on the shoulder. "One word of advice: don't eat a lot. The first day can be a bit rough on a full stomach. I ate an entire cheese pizza before my first class. It did *not* go well." He winked and sauntered off toward a group of kids.

Clara went to find the breakfast buffet. She was ravenous, but decided to heed Binder's warning, choosing a slice of buttered toast and orange juice before settling at a table in the corner, far away from Ophelia and anyone else. She pulled her hood over her head and did her best to become invisible.

"Miss Poole, I presume?" said a smooth, calm voice.

Clara peeked out from her hood to see its owner, a tall,

slim man dressed in black leathers and an overcoat. His silver hair was slicked back, and he had a narrow face scarred from years of exposure to sun and weather. His eyes, set closely over his raven-beak nose, were so dark, it was hard to distinguish where iris ended and pupil began. However, it was the small tattoos under each eye that drew her attention: an infinity symbol on the left and a ship's anchor on the right.

"Godfrey Sway," he said, pronouncing each syllable with significance, "and this is my grandson, Landon."

Clara hadn't noticed the boy standing next to him. Other than the long black bangs that swept across his face (and no tattoos), he looked every bit like a younger version of his grandfather, and about her age. But when she made eye contact, Landon quickly focused on his feet.

"You are Miss Poole, are you not?" Sway asked again. "The one flying with Pascal Berg?"

"Yes, sorry. I *was* flying with Mr. Berg, but there was an accident, and he can't race now."

"Then it is true? I heard chatter among the pilots, but didn't know for sure. Sandbag to the head, was it?" Sway smiled thinly. "Too bad. Berg's a fine fellow and quite an accomplished pilot. As much as I don't mind fewer rivals, I will miss the competition. He is all that's *good* about pilots."

"To be honest, I wish I was still flying with him," Clara said.

"Funny you should mention that. It's precisely why I wanted to speak with you." Sway pulled out the chair across from her and sat. Landon remained still as a statue. "Is it also true that Habberdish paired you with another pilot?"

"Yes, Greta Gildersleeve. She's the one that flies with monkeys."

"Yes, I know Greta . . . and her monkeys—dangerous and unpredictable things if you ask me. Miss Poole, from one concerned pilot to another, I feel I should warn you about Gildersleeve."

"Warn me?"

"As I'm sure you are aware, Greta is quite old—well over eighty. Why WOOBA still allows her to participate is beyond me. She may be a former champion, which is surely good for business, but that was many lifetimes ago, back when racing was simpler. It's remarkable the old woman hasn't killed herself yet. I only bring this up because I'd hate to see you become another one of her unfortunate copilots."

"What do you mean by *unfortunate*?"

"I guess I mean . . . *dead*."

Clara studied the man's face to see if he was joking, but it remained expressionless.

"Well, Miss Poole, it was nice to meet you, but we should be going. Like you, we still have much to do to prepare for before opening ceremonies. Perhaps you still have time to find another team to join. I would."

Sway left the dining room, but Landon lingered by Clara's table.

"What?" she finally said after an awkward silence. "Do you talk?"

Landon gave a small grimace, then hurried after his grandfather. Clara watched him go, wondering how this whole ordeal could get any stranger.

"Can you pass the syrup?"

Clara jumped, nearly toppling her chair. Next to her was a little girl in a bear hat kneeling on the seat behind an enormous stack of pancakes.

"How long have you been there?"

"Long enough," the girl said. "Syrup, please?" Clara passed the pitcher and watched the girl dump the entire container over her pancakes. "People say you're a celebrity. You don't look like one, but then, I've never met one before." She pointed to another syrup pitcher across the table. "Can you pass that, too?"

Clara slid the container to the girl, who emptied it on top of her plate.

"I'm not a celebrity," Clara said, sighing. "I wish people would stop calling me that."

But it seemed that was enough conversation. The girl took a moment to fix her hat so the ears pointed in the right direction, and then tucked into the tower of pancakes like a truck driver.

"Who's this?" Clara's father asked, approaching the table.

"I have no idea," she replied. "She just appeared."

"I don't think I've ever seen anyone eat that much."

"Dad, there was a man here a minute ago. He warned me about Gildersleeve. He said she was dangerous and not to fly with her."

"Oh no. That's not good." Quickly, Clara realized her father's attention was not on her, but on the little girl, who was lying facedown in her pancakes. "She was eating one moment, and then the next, she went *plop*."

"Hatsu!" A woman rushed across the dining room. Her black hair was pulled back into a low ponytail and she wore a sleek brown single-piece leather suit with a Japanese flag embroidered on the sleeve. "I'm so sorry," she said. "I thought Hatsu was still in our room. She has a mind of her own sometimes, and a bit of a problem when it comes to sweets. They tend to give her sugar crashes."

"We noticed," said Clara.

"She knows better, but we're still working on willpower. I'm Satomi, by the way. Satomi Hoshi." She pulled the comatose girl from the plate, her hat and hair dripping with syrup. Clara sensed from Satomi's reaction that this had happened before. "Are you both flying in the race?"

"I'm not. I was, well, kinda, but not now. I'm Oliver Poole."

"And I know you already from orientation," replied Satomi, grinning at Clara. "Nice to meet you both. If you'll excuse us, I should get Hatsu cleaned up before training. I'm sure she'll see you there, Clara. I know she was excited to meet you." Satomi Hoshi lifted her daughter over her shoulder like a sack of sugar.

"Is it breakfast time?" asked the semiconscious girl.

"No, dear. Breakfast is over."

"Bummer."

As the Hoshis made their way out of the dining room, Clara's father scratched his head. "Did that really just happen?"

"I think so."

"Can this place get any more bizarre?"

Clara didn't answer. Because, so far, every time she'd turned around . . . it had.

A SHORT TIME LATER, that feeling was once again confirmed as Clara stood in a field outside the balloon docks staring at a strange-looking platform hovering above the ground. Even stranger was the man atop it. He was well over six feet tall with sun-bleached hair that stuck out in all directions like a fright wig, bushy eyebrows, and a deeply tanned, stubbled face. Clara thought his faded orange flight suit, which he'd rolled up at the elbows and knees, gave him the distinct look of an escaped prisoner on a surfing holiday.

"Good morning, dudes and dudettes," he bellowed. "My name is Dodge Barlow, and I have been given the immense honor of filling in for Mr. Haskell, WOOBA's longtime safety instructor. I'm sure Mr. Haskell regrets not being here himself, but he was . . . er . . . taken away from his duties unexpectedly."

"Yeah, by a twister," whispered Binder, snickering behind Clara.

"So," continued Dodge, clasping his hands excitedly, "if

you will each grab a flusterboard over there, we'll get this party started. Because today, we're going to jump right in."

Clara took a sleek silver board with black foot straps from a rack of dozens, then followed the other kids onto the hovering platform.

"Excuse me, Mr. Barlow," said a mouse-faced girl with glasses. Her stick-on name tag announced her as Raylee Price, and she stared at the strange board in her arms with a look of dread. "When you said, 'jump right in,' you meant that figuratively, right?"

Dodge flashed a wild grin. "No way, chica. As soon as we get high enough, you're going to jump into the air on that board you're holding. Intense, huh?"

Raylee gulped, as did a few other kids. The bear-hatted Hatsu, for some reason, however, was licking her lips.

"How does this have anything to do with pilot training?" asked a stork-like boy with the name tag *Felix*.

"Or safety?" added Raylee.

"Don't worry about it," Dodge said with a dismissive wave. "You're going to love it."

He jabbed a red button on the post beside him. Children's knees buckled as the platform blistered upward until Paris looked like a toy model, then stopped abruptly.

"Okey-dokey, who's first?" said Dodge excitedly, holding up a parachute pack. "How about you with the white hair. What's your name?"

"Clara," she mumbled.

"Well, all right, Clara. Strap on that pack and step to the edge. You're going to flusterboard from here down to that training platform, the one with the red flag on top."

"You mean, you're not going to demonstrate how to do it first?" asked Raylee.

Dodge waved his hand again. "What, and ruin all the fun?"

Clara inched forward, buckling the parachute around her shoulders, waist, and legs. Her knees knocked and her hands trembled so much, it was a wonder she was able to secure the harness at all. All around her, she met expressions of shock, except from Binder and Alfie, who seemed genuinely envious.

"Hey, give that back," yelled Felix. "The bear kid stole my Wibble Bibble pop out of my pocket!"

Clara turned to see Hatsu scrambling toward the side of the platform, clutching a lollipop in her hand.

"Seriously," whined Felix. "It's my last one."

Possibly it was the thought of the lollipop being the last, or maybe it was the overwhelming power that sugar had on her, but Hatsu clutched her flusterboard, wild-eyed, and leaped off the platform.

The class rushed to the edge just in time to catch a glimpse of a small form with bear ears rocket into the clouds.

"That must be really good candy," said Binder.

"I'd say," Dodge replied. "She didn't even take a parachute."

He stood unmoving, watching the sky with a curious expression.

"Aren't you going after her?" cried Raylee.

"I would," he said, pulling his ear, "but I only brought kid-sized parachutes."

Raylee's eyes went wider than they already were. "But you're the safety instructor!"

A few desperate seconds ticked inside Clara's head before she heard a voice. It grew, louder and louder, fighting for attention as she rocked back and forth, until it was crystal clear.

You're wearing a parachute, it said.

In a breath, Clara willed herself forward and jumped into the air.

She spiraled downward, the flusterboard chattering in the wind, but only for a moment, before her adrenaline kicked in. Working against the wind, she placed one foot into the foot strap, and then the other. A second later, she was standing.

Clara swerved right and left as she barreled forward, trying to control the board. If she was scared, the emotion was a distant second to the one thought that consumed her—*catch Hatsu.*

A blur vanished into a cloud below, and Clara followed it, leaning forward to increase her descent. Cold burned her cheeks, and the corners of her eyes watered from the whipping wind. When she broke from the cloud, she caught sight of the little girl and the red flag of the training platform beyond. Immediately, Clara knew Hatsu was too far off. She'd miss the platform for sure, which meant a race to the ground—a race Clara didn't think she could win. Already, the rooftops of Paris were far closer than she liked.

She grabbed the edge of her board, tucking into as small a ball as she could, rocketing forward in a sweeping arc until she was below Hatsu, then pulled up hard on the nose. The flusterboard shot up, ramming Clara right into Hatsu, forcing them both higher into the air and then dropping them into the soft webbing of the training platform.

"Are you okay?" she asked, lying breathless on top of the little girl.

"Clara Poole," Hatsu said casually, as if they'd bumped into each other on the street.

"What were you thinking? You could've been killed!"

"Even worse. I could've dropped my lollipop."

Cheering came from above, and then the training platform broke through the clouds. Dodge was clapping, Binder and Alfie were going bonkers, and the rest of the class was a chorus of hurrahs. All except Ophelia, who stood with her arms crossed and her mouth pursed.

"Now that's how you do it," declared Dodge.

"But they almost died," Raylee protested.

"Yes," replied Dodge with a nod. "But they almost died *safely*."

AN HOUR LATER, the class had returned to solid ground, boarded the awaiting WOOBus, and were pulling back into the hotel. Hatsu hadn't stopped talking to Clara the whole way, mostly about bears being her favorite—and the undisputed best—animal in the world. (It also explained her choice of headwear.) Meanwhile, Clara tried to figure out how she could avoid telling her father that she'd spent the morning plummeting through the sky on something called a flusterboard.

The bus stopped.

"See you soon, *celebrity*," chirped Hatsu, and bounced out the door.

"That was brave," said Ophelia, passing by Clara's seat before she could follow. "And stupid. But you're flying with that old loon, Gildersleeve, so I suppose stupid is right up your alley. On the bright side, at least you don't smell as bad as her monkeys . . . yet." The girl flipped her ponytail with a smirk and exited the bus.

"Why does she hate me?" Clara mumbled aloud, and then jumped when someone actually answered.

"She was the Face of the Race before you," explained Landon Sway from a few seats back.

"Sorry?"

"OCR. She was the Face of the Race, but this year, you are. That's why she hates you. Because you're the one everyone's watching now, not her."

Landon rose and made his way to the front.

"So, you do speak," she blurted out.

He stopped, but did not look back. "When I have something to say." And then he was gone.

"Hey, wait . . ."

But before she could exit, a woman in a blue blazer blocked the door. "Excuse me, Miss Poole. Mr. Gerard needs to see you immediately."

"Mr. Gerard?"

"WOOBA's official race announcer. He sent me to bring you to the stadium to get ready for the opening ceremony."

"But that's not until tomorrow."

The woman raised an eyebrow. "Miss Poole, the opening ceremony—and the beginning of the race—is later today."

"Today?"

"Yes, in two hours. Haven't you been receiving your daily schedule?"

"What daily schedule?"

"Oh my, there must've been a mix-up in the mailroom."

"Really?" huffed Clara. "You think?"

CHAPTER TWELVE

GO!

PLANNING FOR SOMETHING that's meant to occur the next day, only to find it happening *that* day, does funny things to one's mind. Mainly bad things.

As the afternoon sun waned, Clara was whisked from the hotel back to the balloon fields and into the belly of the stadium where the opening ceremonies were about to begin. A team of stylists descended on her, curling her hair and throwing her into a sparkly white bubble-shaped dress, which made her feel like a Christmas ornament. All the while, Clara wondered if her father had any idea what was happening. Moreover, Clara wondered if *she* knew what was happening. After applying *a touch of makeup* (which, Clara thought bordered on clown-like), the stylists released her into a dark tunnel looking and feeling anything but herself. It was there she met the plastic-haired Mr. Gerard—or *Guy* as he introduced himself—and his too-bleached, big-toothed smile.

"Listen up, Sara," he said.

"My name is Clara."

"Whatever. In a few moments, the ceremony will begin. This is how it works: I run out, welcome the fans, announce you, and then you tell me how excited you are, what a dream this is, blah blah blah. Then comes an entertainment segment, during which we chitchat and say corny things like, 'Boy, don't you just love all the colors,' and 'Gee, isn't this all so amazing.' Every now and then, on my cue, you'll read one of the promotional lines from that sponsor page."

Clara eyed the paper in her hands, given to her seconds before, which had a dozen short paragraphs about companies and products she'd never heard of.

"Okay . . . ready, Sara?"

"Clara."

"Whatever."

Suddenly, she was a deep well of thoughts and emotions. Chicago popped into her head, and with it, the life she could've had, followed by flashes of Bitter Bend, her father, and her mother.

The stadium went dark, and an explosion of lasers blanketed the stands. The beams morphed into a series of balloons, and then merged together over the stage in the shape of the WOOBA dove. The crowd erupted, and Guy Gerard came alive as if someone had pushed a button, his eyes bright and a smile plastered across his face. He ran out the tunnel toward the stage as a spotlight hit him.

"Hello, fans of WOOOOBAAAA! Welcome to the hundredth annual running of the most dangerous, most exciting, most thrilling by-the-seat-of-your-pants, round-the-world adventure race on Earth! You all know me, Guy Gerard. I will be your host for every action-packed stage, every heartrending crash, every sparkling party in the clouds, until we crown our hundredth WOOBA Grand Champion!"

All at once, the giant screen filled with the image of a flock of birds rising from the Dovie Cup trophy.

"Before we begin, let's say hello to last year's winner, Callum MacDougal, who spent all year training to defend his title. Unfortunately, poor Callum had a teensy crash last month and couldn't be here in person, but we have him live via satellite from his beloved Scotland."

The screen cut to a man in a hospital bed, who gave a thumbs-up with his right hand, the only thing other than his eyes and mouth not covered in a full-body cast.

"Hello, Callum old chap! Looks like you're on the mend. I'm sure we'll see you back in the skies again soon!"

A hush fell over the crowd as the mummified man's image disappeared. Guy Gerard, however, didn't miss a beat.

"There's no glory without danger, folks, and no danger without glory. And speaking of glory or *glorious*, are you ready to meet a special young lady? No doubt you've read about her in the papers and seen her on TV. Why, I can't go anywhere without seeing her face plastered on the side of a bus or a billboard. Please give a rousing WOOBA welcome to this year's Face of the Race, Clara Poole!"

The crowd cheered as stadium lights cut to black and a spotlight materialized inches from Clara's feet. She stepped away from it, into the shadowy safety of the tunnel.

"I guess that's not enough applause to get our young celebrity out here. C'mon, folks, we can do better! Let's say hello to our very own Clara Poole!"

The crowd exploded, louder than before. This time someone shoved her into the spotlight. She turned to run back and saw the same stout stagehand from orientation standing in the shadows with his arms crossed.

"Don't even think about it," he said.

"There she is," boomed Guy. "Come say hello, Clara!"

Timidly, she made her way toward Guy, guided only by the red-blinking recording lights of the television cameras. The entire stadium was pin-drop silent.

And then, in an instant, the stadium came alive. Troupes of dancers rushed from the wings holding gray cutouts shaped like waves. They rose and fell, imitating an angry sea, while a single dancer in a white balloon costume thrashed about wildly. It seemed Harold Habberdish had adapted his orientation movie into a full-fledged Broadway production.

"What did you think of that number, Clara?" Guy asked, yanking her to center stage.

She trembled beside him, her mind completely blank, fixed on the mass of strange faces. "Errrr . . ." She racked her brain, trying to think of anything to say. "Don't you just love all the colors?"

Guy frowned. "Yes, I suppose there are quite a few shades of gray," he said, searching for a segue. "Hey, speaking of colors, don't you have a message for our audience?"

Clara gave him a confused look, and he motioned to her paper with his eyes, his smile never wavering.

"Oh, right," she whispered, scanning the first paragraph. "Say, Guy, have you ever been coloring a picture and run out of crayons? It's a daily problem for millions of people. But now, there's a solution. They're called Cray-Longs, and they're just like regular crayons, only ten percent longer."

"Did you hear that, folks?" shouted Guy. "A whole ten percent! Wow, what amazing innovations will people think up next?"

He nodded again toward the paper. Clara scoured the other paragraphs, searching for her cue. The silence was deafening, and she felt the weight of thousands of eyes. "Uh . . ."

"Say something, kid," he hissed through smiling teeth. *"Anything."*

"Gee . . . isn't this all so amazing?" she squeaked out.

Guy Gerard dropped his head, disgusted. Clara, having no idea what to do next, read one paragraph after another. First was a promotion for LumiSheets, the glow-in-the-dark toilet paper, and then one for metal-detecting shoes called Sneakatectors, followed by KornerFrames, the only solution for hanging your pictures around corners, before wrapping up with a plug for Shoebrellas, *guaranteed to let you wear suede in the rain*. She smiled awkwardly at Guy, who could only gape back at her.

Finally, he gave his head a little shake. "Wow, I think that says it all, don't you folks?" Then, out of the side of his mouth, he muttered, "I do." He gently nudged Clara out of the spotlight and turned his dazzling smile back to the audience. "In that case, why don't we meet this year's aeronauts!"

A stagehand waved Clara offstage and thrust her regular clothes into her arms. Clara hoped he'd tell her what happened next, but she only got a thumbs-up and a meek "Good luck."

The next thing she knew, pilots were flooding the stage, forming a long line by the ramp leading to the balloon field. The Chins-Rattons took their place beside Guy, Ophelia dressed in a crimson flight suit with England's Cross of St. George embroidered on each shoulder, and an extra-large *OCR* stitched onto the lapel. On the far side of the stage, Alfie Woodrow and Binder Jolly stood with their mothers like wild-eyed racehorses champing at the bit. Bear-hatted Hatsu grinned as Clara slid beside her, before resuming her expression of steely determination. Nowhere, however, did Clara see Gildersleeve.

"Our first pilots are a pair you all know well," said Guy. "Flying Her Majesty's Airship, *Brigadier Albert*, say hello to Sir Wallace Chins-Ratton and his daughter, Ophelia. Now, here's an amazing aeronautical accomplishment: not only did Sir Wallace win our eighty-ninth and ninety-fourth races, but a member of the Chins-Ratton family has participated in every race since WOOBA's thirty-seventh year. Who knows? Maybe this will be Ophelia's first win!"

Ophelia snatched the microphone from the announcer's hand. "Thank you, Guy, and so good to see you again. As you might know, I've moved on from my time as Face of the Race. While it was an honor to represent the prestigious Groem and Stratmire, I find the Face of the Race to be a little juvenile now. And with this being my fourth race, I'm making a prediction here and now: the Chins-Rattons aren't *maybe* winning. We're definitely winning!"

Ophelia threw the microphone back at Guy, spun on her heels, and flicked her ponytail in the air.

"How about that, folks? Sounds like those Chins-Rattons mean business."

The Jollys representing India in *Samsara* were next, followed by a host of other teams, including the Prices in *Jubilee*, the Woodrows in *Rumor*, and the Hoshis in *Ussuri*. Hatsu was positively electric (or maybe just sugar-charged, if the chocolate ring around her mouth indicated anything). Next came Charles "Five Fingers" Patten of *Endurance*, a rugged-looking man from South Africa with a chiseled face and a noticeable hobble. Evidently, he'd lost the fingers on one hand and his all toes to frostbite the prior year.

On and on the introductions continued. Clara stifled a yawn, feeling her eyes drifting closed, but perked up again as the Newlins stepped forward.

"From Australia, flying *Albatross*, welcome Norman 'Nine Lives' Newlin and his son, Niles. Those familiar with the Newlins know they've had a few crashes over the years. Well . . . every year."

"Yes, but not this one," Norman assured the audience. "This year is the year of the Newlins!"

"Love that confidence! Just don't add another life to that nickname of yours. Next, from Wales, flying *Providence*, a single-chamber dirigible, is a man you know all too well. Put your hands together for Godfrey Sway and his grandson, Landon."

Sway suddenly appeared on the stage, waving to the crowd, while Landon lingered in the shadows.

"So, Godfrey, how many years have you been racing?"

"Far more than I have fingers and toes," replied Sway with a thin smile.

"Ha . . . I would think so. Still, you've won quite a few championships, both as a pilot and a copilot."

"I don't really count my copilot days, but yes, I've won seven times as the captain of *Providence*."

"Well, here's hoping for one more!" exclaimed Guy as he turned back to the crowd. "All right, friends, it appears we've reached our last team. Though they need no introduction—in fact, you've met one member already— the pilot of this team is a living legend. Now some might say, 'Guy, how can a woman that old still be racing?' Fiddlesticks! Why, she's won the Dovie Cup so many times we've stopped counting! In fact, there's not a pilot dead or alive with more wins. So, without further ado, from England, flying *Amelia*, a traditional single-envelope balloon, let's hear it for Greta Gildersleeve and her copilot, Clara Poole!" The line of faces turned to Clara. "Where is she?" Guy hissed, cupping a hand over his microphone.

All Clara could do was shrug.

"Well, folks, a champion of Greta's caliber is probably already halfway to the Stage One finish line. That must mean it's time to get this race going!"

Guy raised a starting pistol into the air, and the aeronauts crouched like athletes at a track meet.

Clara turned to Hatsu. "What's happening?"

"PILOTS, GET READY!"

"Hatsu, I'm serious. What happens next?"

"You're funny," she said with a giggle. "I should call you Bakagari."

"Huh?"

"Bakagari—it's my father's version of silly goose in Japanese. He has a thing for American sayings. Although, the actual translation is probably closer to *stupid goose*."

"PILOTS, GET SET!"

"Hatsu, please!"

BANG!

"Run!" Hatsu squealed over the thunder of feet. Pilots sprinted from the stage to the balloon field. Clara was swept up in the horde, churning her legs as fast as the hem of her bubble dress would allow, all the while clutching her regular clothes.

Long tongues of fire licked the air, and burners erupted, turning night into day as pilots scrambled into their baskets and took flight.

Clara found *Amelia* in the middle of the pack. Gildersleeve stood inside the basket, frowning at a map, while the monkeys scampered up and down the envelope, checking the rigging.

"Oh, I was hoping we lost you," she grumbled, not looking up from her chart.

"Well, I'm ready," exclaimed Clara.

"We'll see about that."

Clara struggled up the ladder in her bubble dress,

still holding her normal clothes, and fell onto the deck.

"Release the mooring lines," ordered Gildersleeve.

The next thing Clara knew, the monkeys had darted over the side. Suddenly, she felt very unprepared. It was all happening too quickly. She patted the jacket in her arms, feeling Bixley's broken compass, the extra Wibble Bibble Habberdish had given her, and a soft bulge in her chest pocket. Reaching inside, she pulled out her mother's scarf, tied it around her neck, and clutched it tightly, Slowly, her heartbeat settled.

"Wait!" she heard her father cry as he scaled the outside of the basket. "Swear you'll stay safe."

"Dad, let go. We're taking off!"

"Just swear it!"

"Yeah, yeah, of course. I swear."

"Okay . . . good," he said, rubbing his forehead. "Here, I made this for you. It has every crumb of information I could find about each stage." He thrust a three-ring notebook as thick as an encyclopedia into her arms. On the front were the words: EVERYTHING YOUR FATHER WOULD DO THAT YOU SHOULD, TOO. "Promise me you'll read it."

"I promise," she replied, tucking it under her arm.

Houdini released the last line, the balloon shot upward, and her father tumbled to the ground.

"See you in Morocco!" He waved, running across the field.

"Morocco?"

"It's where Stage One ends. It's in the book!"

Gildersleeve gave a long pull on the burner, and *Amelia* surged into the air with a snarl of heat. Clara stumbled as her father's face dropped out of view.

"Try not to fall off in the first five minutes," the old woman chided.

Suddenly, the night was a sea of orange as the sky filled with paper lanterns. They rose and fell like waves of light, rolling in the breeze. Clara peered over the edge of the basket and watched as people below launched more lanterns into the air.

"It's a tradition," Gildersleeve explained. "Look closely. You'll see each one has a wish written on it."

As a lantern passed, Clara read *Bonne chance, mes amis* and another, *May the winds be kind*. There was even one with her name on it.

"'Vole haut, petite Clara.' What does that mean?"

"It means 'Fly high, young Clara.' Just don't let those lanterns hit the balloon," said Gildersleeve. "Last year, Norman Newlin's *Albatross* went up in flames before it even left the field."

Houdini scurried above in the hammocks, pushing away lanterns that drifted too close with a long pole. With each poke, they erupted in flames and extinguished themselves in puffs of ash. It was mesmerizing to watch, and Houdini gibbered with delight each time one ignited.

Amelia shook as a great crack, like an earthquake, reverberated through the air. Clara looked to the ground to see the top half of WOOBA headquarters breaking.

Or was it detaching?

"That's the *Zephyrus*," said Gildersleeve indifferently.

Finally, Clara understood why Marie Lemot had called the headquarters extraordinary. The building, or at least the upper part of it, was a gargantuan airship. Clara could now plainly see that the cylindrical structures at each corner— which she'd assume were stairwells—were in fact, turbine propellers. The top of the building climbed into the sky, revealing a balloon-like base that puffed out like the belly of a whale wrapped in an elaborate ribbed latticework.

And then Clara realized that WOOBA headquarters—or *Zephyrus*—wasn't the only building taking flight. Behind it rose the shape of the Hive, followed by the other hangars.

"How?"

"Things aren't always as they appear," said Gildersleeve.

Amelia dropped sail and joined the trail of balloons as the world twinkled beneath them. It was easy to see why Paris was called the City of Lights. Everything was aglow, from the grand cathedral of Notre Dame to the pyramid of the Louvre, the glass ceilings of the train stations, to the countless monuments dotting the landscape. In the center of it all, hundreds of light posts glowed along dozens of bridges, turning the Seine into a glimmering golden thread, which they followed like a yellow brick road.

Ahead, the Jollys in *Samsura* let out sail, while to their left, the happy shape of *Primrose* bobbed along with Alberto Furio keeping watch from the crow's nest. On the right, the Newlins passed near the Eiffel Tower. Maybe too near.

"Hit the burner, Niles," yelled Norman. "We need more lift!"

The burner blazed, and Clara saw their anxious faces in the firelight. *Albatross* rose, though not fast enough. The envelope cleared the wrought-iron tower, but the basket rammed into the upper platform. Instantly, the balloon deflated, shrouding the famous monument in darkness as if snuffing out a candle.

"We're okay!" came Norman's muffled voice. "Only a teensy setback!"

Gildersleeve huffed. "That man is either cursed or stupid . . . or both. We haven't even gotten to starting line yet."

"Where's that?"

Gildersleeve pointed and Clara saw two massive spires in the distance held aloft by giant propellers, joined by a sprawling blue banner emblazoned with the WOOBA dove. Close by was the long cigar shape of the Chins-Rattons' balloon.

"*Brigadier Albert*, start time ten thirty-seven and forty-five-seconds," crackled the voice of Guy Gerard over the *Zephyrus*'s loudspeaker. "I'd say good luck, but we're well aware Ophelia has already guaranteed victory."

It was then that Clara realized the balloons would not be racing together. Stage One was a time trial, meaning each team would race independently against the clock. The winner would be the team that finished with the fastest time.

Gildersleeve called the monkeys to their stations. Moments later, *Amelia* sailed underneath the massive banner, which was easily the length of a football field. Fans cheered from spiraling balconies that rotated around the starting towers like gigantic barber poles.

Aboard *Zephyrus*, the word *Amelia* appeared on the observation deck's large scoreboard next to a digital stopwatch.

"*Amelia*, start time ten forty-one and three seconds," announced Guy.

An hour later, the balloons cleared the city limits, and the

CHAPTER THIRTEEN

THE FIRST TEST

CLARA WOKE TO A SCURRY OF FOOTSTEPS above deck.

"Squall!" yelled Gildersleeve. "From the east!"

The monkeys scattered in a blur before Clara had even fumbled to the ladder. The sky swirled gray.

"Bob, Mayhem, take the helm," ordered Gildersleeve as she collapsed the sails. "Houdini, secure the rigging."

As the monkeys took position, Gildersleeve gave a hard blast of the burner, and *Amelia* climbed.

"Are we okay?" asked Clara.

"Not if we don't get above this storm. Our internal skeleton prevents us from buckling in heavy gales, but only to a point."

"What should I do?"

teams sped over the countryside as they caught the southerly wind. Clara was surprised she could hear the barking of dogs and the slamming of screen doors on farms a thousand feet below. To the west, the moon seemed many times bigger than usual, washing the landscape in a bath of silver light.

"Time to get some rest," said Gildersleeve with a yawn.

"But . . . what about the race?"

"We won't reach the coast until morning. That's when the real action will begin."

"Oh. Then . . . where do we sleep?"

"In your room, of course."

Gildersleeve pulled a lever on the side of the basket, and the floor beneath them crackled and shook.

"What did you do?" Clara cried.

"Relax, child."

Clara clutched the railing and peeked over the side to find the bottom expanding, or rather, unfolding. A lower story materialized with bump-outs and a long pulpit, all of it made from wicker.

"It's magic," she muttered.

"Hardly," replied Gildersleeve. "It's origami."

The woman lifted a panel in the basket's floor and descended a ladder to a lower deck that hadn't existed moments before. Clara followed and found herself in a large cabin with a series of bunk rooms on each side. The walls were lined with books, maps, and charts. An astrological mobile made of cardboard hung from the ceiling. At the far end, Clara peered out through a large bay window at a perfectly framed moon.

"How did you . . . ?"

"I told you. Origami. Once you learn to fold things really small, you can accomplish quite a lot."

"But if you had all of this room, why couldn't my father come?"

"Hmm, that," said Gildersleeve, rubbing the back of her neck. "I was trying to find a polite excuse."

"For what?"

"Not *what—who*. The monkeys . . . They don't like him. Especially Bob. I think it's because your father called him smelly, and the others fleabags. I told you that monkey holds a grudge. Besides, I got the feeling he wasn't up for the ride. . . . And that maybe you didn't want him, either."

"I never said that," Clara replied defensively.

"You didn't have to, child. At my age, I know what I see when I see it." Gildersleeve disappeared into one of the bunks, leaving Clara staring out the window.

Something scuffled next to her, and she jumped back to find a rather ratty-looking pigeon cowering in the back of a

birdcage, its bulging eyes darting wildly. (Clara coul[d] but think of Raylee Price.)

"Who are you?" she said gently.

"That's Coo," grumbled Gildersleeve.

"His door is open. Should I close it so he doesn't [ ]

"Don't bother. That good-for-nothing pigeon is[n't] anywhere. Too chicken to leave."

Moments later, Gildersleeve was snoring. Cla[ra] Coo's door anyway and went to find a spot in on[e] other bunks. Inside was a berth with a thin mattre[ss] from bamboo covered by a wool blanket. Clara cha[nged] of her Face of the Race costume into her regula[r] and fell into bed, exhausted. A small window by [ ] let in the outside world, and she counted the clou[ds] changed shape in the moonlight.

Suddenly, she felt a smothering weight as Ho[use] Mayhem flopped their hairy bodies on top of her.

"Get off me," she cried, pushing them away.

But the monkeys were already snoring in stere[o] old woman.

Clara sighed. At least she'd be warm.

"Stay out of the way."

Thunder cracked and pounded the air, and a rush of wind and rain knocked *Amelia* sideways. Clara watched the monkeys' hair stand on end as the atmosphere grew hot with static. She'd felt this before.

Please, no lightning.

The burner blazed again, and Clara's knees turned to jelly as they rocketed higher. She stumbled across the basket, knocking the monkeys from the helm. They tumbled in a heap, sending the balloon spinning.

Above them, a window of electric-pink sky blazed like a trapdoor to heaven. They shot through into silence.

Mayhem climbed back onto Bob's shoulders, and the monkeys captained the helm as Houdini returned to the deck. Below, the world bubbled and churned, dark as a witch's cauldron.

Gildersleeve glared at Clara. "I told you to stay out of the way," she snarled.

"I'm sorry. I stumbled and—"

"Sorry, doesn't cut it up here. Below deck, now!"

Clara sulked away as instructed, down the ladder, settling by the bay window to watch the storm roll off to the west. In her very first test she'd failed, just like that day on the windmill. She pulled her mother's scarf tight around her like a phantom hug.

The day drew on without further incident. Clara watched balloons rise and fall against the changing sky, searching for the strongest winds. Coo, her only companion below deck, did little to keep her company, lifeless in his cage. But there were plenty of books, even if their subjects were as old and dusty as their pages. Clara read the histories of early navigators, from the adventures of the Austronesians, the first to invent ocean-going sailing ships, to the Egyptian spice traders of the Red Sea. Then she got lost in the story of Ching Shih, one of history's most successful pirates (and notably, a woman), who commanded the eighty-thousand-man navy of the Red Flag Fleet. When the moon finally appeared, Gildersleeve descended the ladder and slipped into her room without a word. In no time, the old pilot was snoring again. Clara tried to read over the constant buzz-sawing, but eventually gave up and went above deck.

A warm, steady wind blew in an otherwise calm night. Mayhem and Houdini snoozed in the lookout while Bob manned the helm.

"Can I go up there, too?" she asked, pointing to the hammocks in the rigging.

The big monkey nodded and motioned to a rope ladder

in the corner of the basket. She climbed carefully, one rung at a time, until she reached the lookout and softly rolled into the netting. Mayhem and Houdini stirred, draping long hairy arms over each other, but didn't wake. Puffy clouds shaped like giant buffalo roamed the sky, parting to let the moon cast its beams onto a placid ocean below. Somewhere, singing rose, and Clara listened to the calls and whistles of whale song until their lullaby sent her drifting off to sleep.

CLARA WOKE DRENCHED in sweat, her lips dry and clothes suffocating. Feverishly, she shed layers until she had on only her T-shirt and jeans. Even those clung uncomfortably to her skin. The monkeys were gone, and she was surprised to find they were no longer over water, but groves of olive trees.

"Where are we?"

"Morocco," answered Gildersleeve from the deck.

Clara untied her mother's scarf and used it to shield her head from the burning sun. The groves thinned, and they passed over a massive stone ruin before the land spread out in an array of terraces, sloping down a shallow hillside into the valley below.

"Is that Fes?" she asked.

"No, Volubilis. It was once the southernmost outpost of the Roman Empire before being abandoned and looted to build Morocco's great imperial cities. Many of the wild animals forced to battle in Rome's Great Colosseum came through here. It's only ruins now, but if you look carefully, you can still see the mosaic floors."

Clara squinted, but could only spot families of storks nesting atop the remains of the tall stone columns.

"Are we making good time?" she asked, descending the rigging.

"Hard to say," replied Gildersleeve. "But we passed a few teams who started before us when we came onshore. All right, boys, let's see if we can't find better wind."

She fired the burner and *Amelia* rose into a thick cloud bank. Out of the sun, the temperature dropped quickly. Clara shivered, realizing she'd left her jacket in the hammocks above.

Gildersleeve let out more sail and *Amelia* caught the current.

"How can you see?" asked Clara.

"You don't need to. Just keep your altitude steady and follow your compass."

Clara took her compass from her pocket and watched its

needle spin at random. Evidently, altitude hadn't helped it work any better.

Suddenly, Houdini shrieked from high in the rigging as a dark form broke from the clouds. It careened toward them before rolling to one side, narrowly missing the envelope and the defenseless monkey perched atop it.

"Fools!" growled Godfrey Sway. "I have the right of way!" The black hulk and crimson sails of *Providence* passed overhead and vanished.

They stayed on course for a half hour more, until Gildersleeve opened the deflation port at the top of the envelope, and *Amelia* dropped through the clouds. Ahead, *Providence* passed beneath another set of towers (or possibly the same ones), emblazoned with the words *Stage Finish*.

"*Providence*, thirty-four hours, seventeen minutes, nine seconds," called Guy Gerard over the loudspeaker.

Ussuri emerged from the clouds behind *Amelia*, followed by *Samsara* and *Primrose*, all of which had started long before their team. Clara began to wonder how fast their time was as they neared the finish line.

"*Amelia*, thirty-four hours, nineteen minutes, thirty seconds."

"That's good, right?" she asked excitedly.

"We'll see," replied Gildersleeve. "Okay, Bob, take us in."

The Hive hovered behind the *Zephyrus*, clustered with the other hangars, and linked together by a network of catwalks, which buzzed with dockhands.

"How do we get inside?" Clara asked.

A moment later, they dipped below the Hive and Clara got her answer; the bottom was entirely open except for the central causeway. Bob tapped the burner and *Amelia* rose gently into Bay Thirteen. As it came level with the mooring tower, Houdini sprang onto the metal structure and tied off the balloon.

"Hey, Clara!" called Binder, running down the causeway with Alfie in tow. "Alfie figured out how to detach the sky cabanas on the observation deck from their tethers. We were gonna take one out for a spin and watch the rest of the balloons come in. Wanna join?"

"I don't think that's a good idea," said Ms. Lemot, stepping out from the other side of the mooring tower.

"Oh . . . er, right," Binder said, looking at his feet. "In fact, that's exactly what I told Alfie."

"No, it's not," griped Alfie. "Your exact words were, 'You're brilliant, Alfie!' And—"

Binder smacked him in the head.

"If you'll excuse us," he said, pulling the younger boy away.

Ms. Lemot chuckled, and then smiled at Clara warmly. "I'm here to take you to your Face of the Race interview. It shouldn't take long. I'm sure you'll have plenty of time to meet up with your friends later."

Clara was struck by the use of the word *friends*. She didn't really know Binder or Alfie or any of these kids. Still, she'd probably talked to them more in the past few days more than she'd talked to anyone at Gerald Ford Elementary in years. Certainly, Hatsu had glommed onto her happily. She would've dwelled on it further, but when she reached the broadcast deck, Guy Gerard was standing alongside a stage-hand with the name tag, *Karl,* who was holding a bulky pair of goggles in one hand.

"What're those?" she asked.

"Don't care," Karl replied, placing the contraption over Clara's head.

She stumbled in the sudden brightness. "I can't see."

"Probably because those things are high-powered tele-scoping goggles used for stargazing deep space," came Guy's voice. "Only a moron would wear them in daylight. Just go with it. We're about to begin in three . . . two . . ."

The camera's red recording light cut on, which through Clara's goggles was like staring into the sun.

"Hello, WOOBA fans. Guy Gerard here with our Face of

the Race, Clara Poole, who's wearing Moonies Moon Eyes by Lunar Levard. You'll swoon when you see the moon through Moonies Moon Eyes. So, Clara, you've completed your first leg of the race. What does that feel like?"

"It feels like I can't see a thing."

"No, not the goggles, silly." Guy chuckled. "I meant the race."

"Oh, uh, I don't know. I spent most of it below deck with a pigeon."

"I'm sorry. Did you say a *pigeon*?"

"Yeah. His name is Coo. He's pretty boring, really—hides in his cage all day."

"Surely you did more than that?"

"Uh . . . I also read a lot and fell asleep in a hammock."

"You're flying in the most thrilling race in the world, and all you did was read and fall asleep?"

"And the part with the pigeon."

"Fascinating," mumbled Guy. "Well, before we go, why don't you send us off with one more takeaway?"

"Okay . . . I don't know why anyone would want these Moon Eyes things. They're terrible. I don't think I'll be able to see for a week."

"Clara Poole, everyone," boomed Guy. The recording light switched off, and Clara ripped the goggles from her face. "Listen, kid, try a little harder next time, okay? You're killing me out there."

"Sorry," she said, blinking.

"There you are." Clara spun to see the blurry form of her father hurrying toward her. "I've been searching everywhere. Are you okay?"

"I think so. I mean other than having my eyeballs cooked."

"Well, they're looking for you on the observation deck. Your team won third place."

"We did?"

"I guess you beat the Hoshis by a few seconds. Hatsu was absolutely furious until she realized she'd lost to you. I must say, that child is quite the competitor."

CLARA'S FIRST IMPRESSION of the observation deck was that it looked like a cruise ship. Rows of deck chairs and blue-and-white-striped cabanas surrounded an enormous rectangular swimming pool, its bottom tiled with tiny mirrors, reflecting the sky. Clara wondered whether swimming in it might feel more like flying. At the far end of the deck, hundreds of people sat in a large amphitheater, as Guy Gerard was just beginning to recap the day's events onstage under a screen labeled LEADERBOARD.

"Let's meet our leaders after Stage One," he said. "In a surprise third place, the crew of *Amelia*. Welcome back to the podium, Greta. How nice to see you up here again."

Gildersleeve stepped onstage indifferently and took her place on the lowest podium. The monkeys, however, were nowhere to be seen.

Clara's father prodded her gently. "Go on," he said, and a moment later, she was standing next to the old woman, who dignified her presence with only the slightest of grunts.

"In second place, *Providence*. Congratulations, gentlemen."

The Sways took the podium on the opposite side. Godfrey neither acknowledged Guy, nor waved to the crowd. Instead, he stood like a statue, scowling while Landon hid in his shadow.

"And finally, in first place, *Brigadier Albert*. Bravo, Wallace, Ophelia. The podium is yours."

Ophelia raced to the top tier with an expression of absolute superiority plastered across her face as her father tottered up slowly behind. She bowed and curtsied, soaking up the applause as if the entire audience was there for her alone.

"As the winners, the Chins-Rattons receive ten points, and will have the honor of flying the Dovie in Stage Two.

The Sways receive seven points for second place, and Team Amelia, five points for third. All other pilots tally one point for stage completion. Congratulations, all, even our last-place finishers, the Newlins, who somehow found a way to unstick themselves from the Eiffel Tower. Remember, folks, it's a long race, and anything can happen. Stage Two begins tomorrow!"

"Do you know what they call second and third place?" whispered Ophelia into Clara's ear. "The first losers."

Clara might've reacted to the girl's goading if she hadn't been distracted by Godfrey Sway. His face twitched, making the tattoos under his eyes dance, while his upper lip curled into a sneer. But he wasn't looking at her. His attention was fixed on Gildersleeve.

After a moment, he rushed from the podium toward the elevators, muttering. Clara shot Landon a look, as if to say, *What gives?* He shrugged before following his grandfather.

"Did you hear me?" repeated Ophelia. "I said, *they're called the first losers.*"

"Yeah, first losers," Clara mumbled.

She left the stage, still wondering the reason for Sway's venomous mood, only to find herself consumed by the smell of saffron and cinnamon. A Moroccan feast had been laid out in celebration of the completion of the first leg of the race. Savory stews in clay pots and bowls of couscous covered the tables, along with an array of dishes she'd never seen before. Her stomach growled.

"What is this?" she asked, eating a puffed pastry with a savory filling that exploded in her mouth.

"Pastilla," answered a chef behind the table.

"It's so good," she said, taking another bite. "What's in it?"

"Pigeon," he said proudly.

Clara stopped chewing. Suddenly, she got why Coo had wanted to hide in his cage. She reached for a plate of cinnamon cookies, needing any other taste in her mouth. It disappeared before her eyes, which might have surprised her, if not for the hairy arms and bear ears that accompanied it slipping under the table.

Clara bent down and lifted a corner of the tablecloth to find Hatsu and the monkeys stuffing their faces with treats. From the looks of it, the cookies hadn't been their first plate. They froze, guilty-faced and crumb-covered.

"Bakagari, you did not see this," said Hatsu solemnly.

Clara dropped the tablecloth and walked away, laughing. "I most certainly did not."

CHAPTER FOURTEEN

A SEA OF SAND

LEADERBOARD

AFTER STAGE 1

1ST - Brigadier Albert, 10 PTS

2ND - Providence, 7 PTS

3RD - Amelia, 5 PTS

Often when people think of the desert, they imagine the Sahara. In fact, the name itself, derived from the Arabic word ṣaḥra, literally means desert. Beyond vast, it covers the mind-boggling sum of 3.6 million square miles. However, one would be wrong to call it the world's largest. That distinction goes to the tundra deserts of Antarctica and the Arctic, in that order.

So explained the notebook Clara's father had given her. Accurate or not, it did nothing to help her comprehend the vast emptiness before her—a sea of sand that painted the horizon.

She'd spent the entire morning helping Gildersleeve ready *Amelia* for the two-day trip across the desert. And while it had been backbreaking work resulting in raw, blistered hands, it had also been a distraction, saving her from having to focus on the actual race. Now, the nothingness confronting her was overwhelming.

"Is there anything else besides sand?"

"Just sand and hamada," Gildersleeve replied, checking the rigging.

"Hamada?"

"Barren plateaus where the sand has been blown away, leaving only rock."

The endless dunes looked barren enough already. Clara had trouble imagining the landscape getting any bleaker. She searched the flawless blue sky for a cloud or anything that would provide even the slightest variation to the world around her. Her father's notebook had mentioned the Sahara was located in the horse latitudes where, in this part of the world, clouds seldom formed, making rain incredibly rare.

She licked her lips. "Do we have enough water?"

"Plenty," replied Gildersleeve. "Unless we get lost."

"And what happens if we get lost?"

"Let's just not. Besides, it's the sandstorms you should worry about."

"Why? Are those common?"

"Child, this is the Sahara. Sandstorms are a fact of life."

The balloons had been towed to the starting line and anchored in a row by tethers attached to a fleet of drones. To *Amelia's* left, Satomi Hoshi readied *Ussuri* while Hatsu hurried above, checking the vents. She was as nimble a climber as Houdini.

On *Amelia's* right, the Newlins fumbled about *Albatross*, tripping over supplies strewn across the deck. They appeared to have enough reserves for a month, which made some sense. The likelihood of them going down was virtually a given, so much so that bookmakers had evidently laid odds not on *if* but *when* the Newlins would crash.

Past *Albatross*, yards of wool cascaded across the floor of *Primrose* as Berta sat in her rocking chair, knitting an enormous something. Clara was about to yell to her to ask what she was making when she caught someone else's eye in the distance.

Godfrey Sway glared at her from *Providence's* pulpit, his expression as unblinking as a portrait.

Clara turned away as the loudspeaker crackled from aboard the *Zephyrus*.

"Good afternoon WOOBA fans, and welcome to Stage Two. As always, I'm Guy Gerard, here to bring you every last bit of heart-stopping action. In moments, our aeronauts will begin their harrowing, multiday trip over the Sahara, but before they do, let's check in with our Face of the Race."

In a blink, a drone materialized in front of Clara, its camera's red recording light aglow. A second later, her face appeared on the *Zephyrus*'s giant screen.

"Now, Clara," continued Guy's dismembered voice, "you must know the Sahara is scorching hot. So, I imagine you'll be drinking a lot of water during this next stage, won't you?"

"I guess?" she said into the camera.

"And there's nothing better for you than water, right?"

"Uh . . . right?"

"Wrong! Because now there *is* something even better than water. Diet Water! And it's—"

"I said no cameras on my balloon!" snarled Gildersleeve. As swift as the wind, she lifted a wooden baseball bat high above her head and clobbered the poor machine until it was no more than a pile of smoking transistors. "That means drones, too!"

"It seems we're experiencing some technical difficulties," Guy said quickly. "So I guess it's time to start the race! Best of luck to our pilots. We'll see you at the finish line in Niger."

The drones released the tethers, and the balloons hurtled toward the sea of sand. The Woodrows in *Rumor* shot ahead, immediately taking the lead, followed by *Ussuri*. Off the starboard side, *Providence* banked west and away from the rest of the group.

"Where are they going?" asked Clara.

"Dunno. Maybe Godfrey thinks he can find stronger winds nearer to the coast. Either that, or he's trying to cheat."

"Cheat? Why would he—"

Clara didn't finish because in the next instant, a blur of bear ears appeared, and Hatsu slid onto the deck.

"Bakagari," she cried jubilantly, hopping off her flusterboard. "My mother and I would like you to be our guest for dinner."

"Excuse me?" said Clara, peering over the side to see where the girl had come from.

"Dinner," repeated Hatsu.

"But . . . we're in the middle of a race?"

"Don't you eat?"

"Yes, of course I eat."

"Great. Then we'll see you at six o'clock!"

In a blink, Hatsu and her board disappeared over the edge of the basket. Clara rushed to the side again, and was astonished to find that Hatsu wasn't the only one on a flusterboard. Other kids zipped through the sky, crossing from balloon to balloon.

"What's going on?"

"Kids tend to get a bit stir-crazy on these multiday legs," Gildersleeve explained. "So sometimes the adults let them *get the wiggles out* and visit with one another."

"Is that allowed? I mean, within the new rules?"

"Let's just say, there's an unspoken agreement between parents and WOOBA on this one. You'll understand if you have children someday. Besides, the winds aren't strong enough now for any pilot to gain real advantage. They'll pick up in the morning. That's when the racing will truly begin."

Gildersleeve checked her compass and then adjusted the sails. Clara climbed into Houdini's lookout and spent the rest of the afternoon watching the other kids dart back and forth across the sky. While such sights might be common in the world of WOOBA, Clara reminded herself that they didn't happen anywhere else. She had trouble imagining her life could ever be the same after this—returning to humdrum school and farm chores at home? If Bitter Bend was still home after all this?

"It's almost six," called Gildersleeve. "If you want to see your friend, you better go now. I'll bring us higher so your flusterboard path is easier. When you're finished, have the girl's mother send a flare, and I'll come alongside."

Clara went below to make herself more presentable. She tied her mother's scarf around her neck and tried to smooth her hair, but realized how pointless it would be after falling through the sky. By the time she returned on deck, Gildersleeve had brought *Amelia* well above *Ussuri*. It would be an easy drop to the Hoshis. Clara threw her legs over the side of the basket, slipped on the ancient artifact Gildersleeve claimed was a flusterboard, and prayed her father wasn't watching from somewhere aboard the *Zephyrus*. She'd seen him for only a few moments before the start of the stage, and he'd given her only one instruction: *Don't do anything stupid*.

Clara tried to imagine something more stupid than flusterboarding to dinner. She couldn't, but pushed off the side of *Amelia* anyway. In a matter of seconds, Hatsu was waving excitedly as Clara landed in the Hoshis' basket.

Ussuri, which Hatsu said got its name from the Ussuri brown bear, had three envelopes—one large globe and two smaller balloons attached like ears. The basket, made of cypress, looked like a Japanese lantern with its sleek paper screens, which Hatsu called shōji.

"It's . . . beautiful," said Clara.

"My father designed it. He's an architect," replied Hatsu, and then cupped her hand in a whisper. "But the bear idea was all mine."

"Is he aboard the *Zephyrus*?"

"My father? No, no, he's deathly afraid of heights. But he knows my mother is happiest when she's flying. Building *Ussuri* is like his way of being with her."

Clara thought of her notebook aboard *Amelia*. Maybe *Everything Your Father Would Do That You Should, Too* was her father's way of doing the same thing. There was one difference, though. "At least your dad is okay with you being up here."

Hatsu grinned. "Yes, he knows I'm also happiest when flying. Come. My mother has prepared for you some traditional Japanese dishes. But leave room for my favorite part—dessert!"

It was more a feast than dinner—bowls of rice, miso soup, pickled vegetables, and seaweed. There was also a surprising array of fresh fish—tuna and salmon and halibut—certainly not things one expects to eat while soaring across the Sahara. All of it was amazing, and it wasn't only the food. Clara loved everything about Satomi Hoshi—how she spoke, how she wore her hair, the way she smiled at Hatsu when the little girl didn't know she was looking.

"And where's your mother, Clara?" asked Satomi. "Is she like my husband and chooses to keep her feet on the ground?"

Clara opened her mouth to say something—what, she wasn't sure—but only managed a stuttering exhale.

"Oh," said Satomi with a knowing nod. "I'm sorry."

Clara murmured something like "Thanks" and tried to crack the smallest of smiles.

"I'm sure she'd be proud to see how brave you've become. I heard you were a bit of a hero in PTSD the other day after Hatsu's little escapade with the lollipop. She can be rather impulsive, as you are now obviously aware."

"Deeply," replied Clara, making Hatsu giggle.

The screen to the deck slid open and the silhouette of something large and hairy stood in the doorway.

"Bob, what are you doing here?" Clara asked.

The monkey waddled in, handed her a piece of paper, and sat down in front of the remaining plates, eating whatever was in reach.

"I'm sorry," she said. "He's a bit—"

"Impulsive," said Satomi with a laugh. "Seems we have something in common. It's all right. Bob, here, seems to be quite hungry."

The monkey chuffed in agreement before stuffing a handful of rice balls into his mouth.

"What did he give you?" asked Hatsu.

Clara opened the paper and quickly read the hastily written words.

We're waiting outside. Finish up, and let's get going.

—Greta

"I guess that's your cue," said Satomi.

"Guess so. Thank you. I really don't know what to say."

"How about that you'll come again?"

"Deal."

Clara stepped out onto *Ussuri*'s deck. Houdini and Mayhem sat on *Amelia*'s edge, holding on to the side of the Hoshis' basket. They sniffed the air, possibly lamenting that they hadn't delivered the note themselves.

"Good grief," Clara said, realizing Bob was still inside. "Stop being such a vacuum cleaner, and come on!" He shuffled out slowly, holding his tummy.

"I like this monkey," said Hatsu. "He eats like a bear."

Clara and Bob climbed aboard *Amelia* and the other monkeys released the Hoshis' balloon.

"Good night, Bakagari," said Hatsu. "I'm happy you came."

"Me, too."

"I'll also be happy when I beat you in the race tomorrow."

"Game on, Hoshi." The little girl beamed, and Clara laughed. But as the balloons drifted apart, a hollow, aching feeling rose in her stomach, like the faded memory of a mother's hug. Clara pulled her scarf around her tighter.

THE MOON WASHED the desert in a soft glow as the balloons glided low to the ground where the best winds could be found. Clara counted dunes as if she were counting sheep, folding over the landscape like a giant's blanket in ripples of dark blue and purple.

Gildersleeve had already retired to her cabin, but Clara had no intention of turning in just yet. The world was too stunning to sleep. "Let's go to the lookout," she said to the monkeys. The lookout was quickly becoming a favorite place, a reminder of her rooftop perch at Bitter Bend.

Bob shook his head, motioning that he needed to stay at the helm, but Houdini and Mayhem shot up the rigging without another word, tumbled into the hammocks, and rolled onto each other playfully.

Clara had one hand on the ladder when something hit the edge of the basket, attaching with a loud metal clang. She recoiled as more appeared.

Hooks.

A series of strange cries broke the silence, and moments later Gildersleeve appeared on deck. "Quick," she shouted, pointing at the lines, "cut those or they'll drag us down!"

But it was too late.

Amelia was pulled to the ground in an instant, and a blue face climbed over the railing. However, it was not the blue face of a snub-nosed monkey, but that of a man.

It was also the last thing Clara saw before a sack was slipped over her head, and she was thrust into darkness.

CHAPTER FIFTEEN

THE BLUE PEOPLE

THE SACK WAS HOT, SUFFOCATING, and whatever she was riding on—a camel, she guessed from the horrible smell and bleating—made every part of her body hurt. Clara had no idea how long they'd been traveling, though the sun had risen, because she could see the shapes of people though the coarse weave of the fabric, walking in what looked like a caravan. Beside her, a sack of monkeys barked and kicked furiously.

"Quit it," she whispered. "You'll only make it worse."

At last, the caravan stopped, and Clara was lifted and carried from her camel. The world grew darker, the air cooler. A moment later, she was dropped unceremoniously to the ground like a bag of cement.

Someone next to her groaned.

"Ms. Gildersleeve, is that you? What's happening?"

"Be quiet, child."

Outside, men spoke in a language Clara couldn't understand, talking quickly, urgently. Footsteps approached, and then the sack covering her head was ripped away.

Clara blinked, adjusting to the light, until the inside of a tent came into focus, and with it the blue-veiled face of a mountain-sized man leering over her. Behind him, a group of men in flowing white shirts and similar headdresses hovered outside the doorway. A few carried swords and rifles, while one leaned on a lance.

"You had absolutely no right to bring down our balloon," Gildersleeve spat as the big man bent down and pulled the sack from her head. "Set us free this instant."

He huffed. "You do not give orders," he said in a raspy voice.

"Then who does? I demand we speak to them now."

"In time."

He turned, dropping the tent flap behind him.

"Well, that didn't go as planned," grumbled Gildersleeve fussing with the rope tying her wrists. "But at least we don't have to wear those itchy hoods."

"What's going to happen now?" whispered Clara.

"Well, apparently, we're going to sit here in the dark."

"I know that. I meant—"

"Quiet," snapped Gildersleeve. "Someone's coming."

The clop of camel hooves grew closer, and then Clara heard a man speak loudly, his tone full of authority. There was a raspy response. *The big man?*

"You did *what*?"

"We did as you asked," said the big man. "We climbed the highest dune and waited to take the balloon down."

"You fool. I told you to *wave* the balloon down."

"But you said you wanted to capture the woman."

"I said I wanted to *capture the woman's heart!*"

Cloaked in the darkness, Gildersleeve let out a disgusted sigh. "It can't be . . ." She groaned again.

"Ms. Gildersleeve, do you know these people?" whispered Clara.

The tent flap flew back, and a man paused in the doorway. He was shorter and thinner than the others, though he wore the same blue head wrap. He stepped inside and lowered his veil, revealing a face as old as the desert, and a gleaming white smile.

"Greta Gildersleeve! Do I believe my eyes?"

"Hello, Aflan," she replied gruffly. "I see you're still as ugly as your camel."

The man laughed, which only seemed to increase

Gildersleeve's annoyance. "And who are you, young lady?"

"Clara Poole," she mumbled.

"How lovely to meet you, Clara. My name is Aflan Ag Salla. I do apologize for the scare. When I received news from my people in the north that WOOBA balloons would be passing over, I rushed to send my men to meet you. It seems they misunderstood my intentions, and, well . . . you know the rest."

He picked up one of the sacks from the ground and threw it at the big man standing in the doorway, who caught it with a cringe.

"Where's my balloon, Aflan?" demanded Gildersleeve impatiently.

"Your balloon is fine, Greta. Or it will be. I'm told it needs only a bit of mending."

Gildersleeve gave the man a stern look.

"Well, maybe more than a bit," he added with a Cheshire grin, "but I promise the matter is being resolved as we speak. In the meantime, you must relax. After all, the great Greta Gildersleeve has returned to the desert. This is a day of celebration!"

"Oh no," she said, waving a finger. "No celebrations. All I want is my balloon. If it's not absolutely perfect when I see it, I swear I'll have your—"

"Ah yes, such fire! I can see you are still the same impassioned woman I remember from fifty years ago. Such spirit. Such—"

"Don't pander to me, you desert rat. We're leaving as soon as *Amelia* can fly."

"But of course . . . And not a second longer," he added with a wink. He bowed, then took his leave, snapping as he exited the tent. His men rushed in and untied Clara and Gildersleeve. When the men turned to free the monkeys, they sprang from their sacks, a flurry of barks and bared teeth.

"Relax, boys," commanded Gildersleeve. "They're . . . *friends.*"

The monkeys glared, suspicious of the men and their covered faces, then began primping one another's matted hair.

"It's like a storybook," said Clara as she stepped out into the oasis.

A small lake encircled by palms and lush grasses lay like a mirror, reflecting the cloudless sky. Tents huddled together near the water's edge. Clara watched a group of men tending to a camel train. "Who are they?"

"They're Tuaregs," said Gildersleeve. "A confederation of Berber people, mostly nomadic, or partially so."

"Why are some of their faces blue?"

"Tuaregs color their fabric with indigo. But rather than dyeing it in water, they pound pigment into it, which sometimes bleeds onto their skin, staining their faces. It's why they're sometimes called the *Blue People*."

"How do you know all this?"

"It's a long story—one I'm sure you'll hear if Aflan has his way."

As the morning progressed, Clara sat in the tent's doorway, watching a group of children play a game like tag. Eventually, a boy caught her eye and waved. She gestured back politely before realizing he was signaling her to join.

Me? she mouthed.

He nodded and motioned again.

"I believe the game they're playing is called Abanaban," said Gildersleeve, resting on a pile of pillows. "It's a bit like blindman's bluff, if I remember right. Go on. We're probably going to be here for a while."

Clara got up and hesitantly stepped toward the boy.

"Othman," he said, pointing to himself.

"Hi . . . I'm Clara."

Othman pointed at her white hair.

"Oh, yeah, right . . . different, huh?"

The boy scrunched his face. "How?"

"I . . . uh . . . was struck by lightning."

Othman's eyes went wide.

"Yup," she said. "Ka-boom."

The Abanaban game ended, and the band of kids regrouped for the next one.

"Melghas," exclaimed Othman excitedly, taking her by the hand.

It took some time for Clara to figure out the rules. At first, she couldn't understand why kids kept getting water from the well, until she realized the point of the game was to reach it and drink before being tagged. It was a blast, far more fun than she'd ever had on the playground at Gerald Ford Elementary, even if she couldn't understand a word of what Othman or the other kids said.

They played until the sun cast long shadows across the oasis. When Clara returned to the tent, she found the old pilot missing and a long indigo dress hanging by a makeshift changing area of tapestries. She tried it on—it was light-weight and flowy—and waited for someone to return.

"My, you look like a desert princess," said Aflan, appearing in the doorway. "I thought I might accompany you to the celebration. Your grandmother is already there. Reluctantly, I might add." He winked.

"Oh, Ms. Gildersleeve isn't my grandmother."

"No? How odd. You seem like family to me."

He escorted Clara to the gathering space, where a series of tufted wool rugs were set out in a semicircle. Clara slipped next to Gildersleeve, who had been forced to sit in the middle as the guest of honor.

"Greta, did you not approve of the clothes I left for you?" Aflan asked.

"I'm perfectly fine in my own clothes. In any case, we're not staying, remember?"

Aflan sighed. "At least Miss Poole looks nice in hers."

"I wish I'd had these earlier," said Clara enthusiastically. "They don't stick to me in the heat like my jeans."

"Indeed, blue jeans and the desert are not the best of friends."

Near the camp's edge, a crowd was cheering as men on camelback came galloping across the gravel plain toward a finish line marked by a cluster of colorful flags. Hidden in the throng of onlookers, Clara spied Bob and Houdini wolfing down a platter of dates.

"He's quite a good jockey," said Aflan, taking the seat beside Clara.

"Who?" she asked.

He pointed. "The lead ride, there."

Clara followed his finger and knew instantly who it was.

Though the jockey's face was covered by a blue veil, the rest of him was completely bare.

"That's Mayhem!"

"That monkey is a superior racer," replied Aflan. "In fact, none of my men have come close to beating him. They've even made him switch camels three times, trying to keep things fair."

Mayhem hurtled across the finish line well before the next camel, provoking a chain of groans from the spectators.

"Ah, here we are—the ceremony is beginning," said Aflan, reclining onto a round ottoman. "I think you'll like this, Clara."

A group of women assembled and began to play music on single-string violins, while men circled them on camelback. After, a man with a wooden puppet told stories to the delight of the audience. Even with the language gap, Clara was surprised how much she could understand. Finally, there was a fascinating dance where the performers stayed seated and only moved their heads, hands, and shoulders.

"My grandson, Othman, enjoyed meeting you today," said Aflan, leaning toward Clara's ear as another group of dancers began their presentation.

"I didn't realize he was your grandson."

"Yes, he was excited to tell me all about you."

"He was? What . . . did he say?"

"That you were quite skilled at Melghas once you got the hang of it, and that you laughed a lot." Aflan paused. "He also said you told him how you got your white hair."

Clara jerked her gaze from the dancers.

"My apologies. I didn't mean to surprise you. I only mentioned it because we have something in common."

"We do?"

"Yes. And it happens to be the story of how I came to know Greta."

Clara raised an eyebrow, and Aflan smiled softly.

"Allow me to tell you how I became chief of my people. When I was a much younger man than now, I traveled to the Aïr Mountains at the bottom of the Sahara. I was on my way to a gathering, where a new leader of our confederation was being elected. On the second night, as our caravan traveled, the moon suddenly disappeared. A storm of sand, such as I had never seen, swallowed us like a monster. It roared for what seemed like an eternity, and when it finally ceased, I was alone. Every man and camel except me had been swallowed by the sands. I wandered for days—my lips blistered, my vision swam, babbling to myself in the stifling heat. At last, I gave up."

Someone beside Clara offered her a cup of tea. She took

it with a nod, inhaling its mint aroma, but kept her eyes glued on Aflan's face.

"As you are no doubt aware, water is hard to find in the desert," he continued. "And as I lay there delirious and dying, watching the ravens circle, I wished only for one last drink. So when the first drop of rain hit my face, I was certain I'd imagined it—a cruel trick of my addled mind. But then . . . another drop, and another, and then came the flood. I craned my head back and drank the storm, laughing like a madman, as the rain pounded my face."

Slowly, Aflan loosened the end of his head wrap.

"I may have heard the thunder, though if I did, I can't recall. But I do remember when the world flashed white, and I floated as if in a bubble while the lightning surged through me."

He lifted the side of his head wrap enough for Clara to see the ragged scar that cut from the top of his bald head to his ear.

An ache of emptiness settled in Clara's stomach—hollow and familiar. "But . . . you survived," she whispered.

"Yes, however it was not what I first thought. You see, when I awoke, I was floating in the clouds. 'Am I dead?' I asked myself. And then I saw her: a beautiful young woman standing over me. She had spotted me from her balloon, and in my darkest moment, she had swooped down to save me. She nursed me back to health and delivered me to the Aïr Mountains just in time for my gathering. That day, not only was I elected chief, but I swore my heart to the woman who saved me."

Gildersleeve groaned.

"I even tried to marry her," he admitted with a wink. "But she would have none of it. And that was when I learned Greta Gildersleeve does not stay on the ground for long."

"You make it sound so dramatic," grumbled Gildersleeve. "Honestly, if I'd known better, I would've left you there."

"Ms. Gildersleeve, is that all true?" whispered Clara.

"It doesn't matter. All I care about now is my balloon. Aflan, how much longer until *Amelia* is repaired?"

"Why Greta, your balloon has been ready for hours," he replied slyly, pointing beyond a series of tents.

"And you've kept us here all this time?" Gildersleeve struggled to her feet, accidentally kicking the tea service in front of her.

"But, Greta," Aflan said, rising as well. "I thought you might stay this time, and maybe . . . become my wife?"

Gildersleeve pointed at the spectacle behind her. "Is that what this *celebration* is? Aflan Ag Salla, are you trying to marry me?" She spun away with a growl, hurrying off to find her balloon.

"Can you blame me, my love?" called Aflan. He paused, waiting for her reply, then clapped his hands to his sides and turned to Clara. "Well, Miss Poole, it seems our visit is over. It was my honor to meet you."

Clara stood. "Uh, thank you," she said, not knowing whether to bow or curtsy, "for my dress and . . . well, for everything. And . . . I really liked your story."

Aflan grinned. "You are always welcome here. Perhaps you will even return in your own balloon someday."

As the performance wound to a close, Clara wove her way through the dancers toward where Gildersleeve had stormed off. As she passed the camel station, she noticed a group of men wrestling. Among them were three hairy bodies in blue turbans.

"Come on, dummies, we're leaving."

The monkeys' heads popped up from the melee. They clambered out and followed her to *Amelia*, where Gildersleeve was absorbed in flight checks.

"You weren't going to leave us, were you?"

"Of course not," Gildersleeve replied brusquely. "Just hurry up and get in."

She hit the burner, and the night illuminated in a blast

of orange light. The balloon rose, and *Amelia*'s crew floated away from the oasis. As they passed over the camp, Clara spotted Aflan standing on the crest of a dune. He raised his hand and blew a kiss.

"He really likes you," said Clara.

"That man is as stubborn as his camel. Now, let's hurry. We still have a ways to go to reach the finish line. We will most assuredly take last place for this stage, but we still need to finish."

THE WINDS PROVED unpredictable, and it took most of the night to find a steady current. When morning dawned, they heard the *rat-a-tat* of a helicopter. It drew alongside *Amelia*, and a door opened, revealing a squat man wearing a headset over his gray curls.

"Is everyone all right?" yelled Harold Habberdish.

"We're fine," Clara hollered back. "We, uh . . . got lost."

"Okay. Follow us. We'll guide you back." The door slid shut, and the helicopter took the lead.

"Lost?" said Gildersleeve. "That is an interesting description for what happened."

To be honest, Clara wasn't entirely sure why she'd said

it. But her father knowing she'd been captured by blue-faced men and hauled across the desert in a sack wouldn't help anyone, most importantly, him. And if he thought Gildersleeve was dangerous, he'd demand Habberdish let Clara switch teams. She wasn't sure she wanted that, either. Not now.

Something about the old pilot intrigued her. She just couldn't say what.

CHAPTER SIXTEEN

THE FIVE PERILS

LEADERBOARD
AFTER STAGE 2

1ST - Providence, 17 PTS

2ND - Brigadier Albert, 15 PTS

3RD - Samsara, 8 PTS

THE LEADERBOARD ILLUMINATED FROM the deck of the *Zephyrus*, showing the results of Stage Two. The Sways had won, and not by minutes—by hours.

"How did they finish so fast?" asked Clara.

Gildersleeve gazed briefly at the standings, but only scowled.

Bob hit the burner and *Amelia* rose into Bay Thirteen where Ms. Lemot informed Clara with polite urgency that her father had been "wearing holes in the carpet pacing their room, and that it might be wise to go there right away."

Clara agreed, but only after she helped Gildersleeve make sure everything was shipshape before the next stage. Hopefully, it would earn her a few bonus points with the old pilot (and her blue-faced teammates). Besides, while seeing Sway in first place had been bad enough, seeing *Brigadier Albert* in second was even worse. She'd go down in flames before losing to Ophelia Chins-Ratton.

Clara departed the quiet of the Hive, passing the fleet of balloons bobbing softly on their moorings. She threw back the hangar door and stepped out onto a catwalk where a man stood staring into the distance.

"Oh, good, they found you," said Godfrey Sway. "And here I was thinking you'd become Gildersleeve's latest *unfortunate*."

He smiled with the cheerfulness of a serpent.

"We're fine," Clara said, looking away. "We got a little lost, that's all."

As she pushed past, Sway placed a firm hand on her shoulder. "Odd. What I heard was far more dramatic. Something about being captured by desert marauders."

"They weren't marauders. They were—" She paused. "How did you know that?"

"Bad things happen to those who fly with Greta Gildersleeve." The tattoos under his eyes quivered. "I told you before . . . that woman is a danger."

Clara stiffened. "Ms. Gildersleeve told me something about you, too."

"Did she? And what, pray tell, was that?"

"She said you cheat."

Sway's grip tightened. "Know this, Miss Poole: that woman is a liar. Don't be fooled into thinking she's worth an ounce of your loyalty. She will only bring you suffering . . . or worse."

"You're hurting my shoulder."

"Am I?" He released his grip, then straightened his coat. "Well, I suppose you should run along then. But do be careful. It would be a pity for your poor father to worry more than he already is."

WORRYING MORE MIGHT HAVE been impossible. When Clara finally appeared in the doorway of her room, her father clasped her face and stared at her as if she were a ghost.

"Are you hurt?" he demanded, patting her arms and shoulders.

"No, Dad, I'm fine," she said, pushing him away.

"What happened out there?"

"Honestly, it wouldn't make sense if I told you."

"Well, try me," he urged.

Clara exhaled, thinking how easiest to put it. "I was at a wedding."

"A wedding?"

"Well, an *attempted* wedding. See, I told you it wouldn't make sense. Seriously, I'm here. You can stop worrying I'm—"

"*Stop worrying?* Do you know that I stood on the observation deck watching every balloon return yesterday? Every balloon but yours. I stood there all night, searching the skies."

"Dad, trust me. I'd tell you if I wasn't safe."

"Don't tell me what is or isn't—" He stopped and closed his eyes, composing himself. "Just tell me you read the notebook I gave you?"

Clara nodded.

"Good" he said with a small sigh. "You better start preparing for Stage Three. We're heading to the Tibetan mountains of all places. Someplace called the Five Perils, though I haven't been able to figure out why it's named that. At any rate, it doesn't sound good."

CLARA LEARNED WHY later that day at PTSD class, which began with a Dodge-style safety chat on frostbite. Evidently, this was the same stage that the pilot of *Endurance* had lost enough digits to earn his unfortunate nickname "Five Fingers" Patten. When Raylee asked how they might avoid the same fate, Dodge shrugged and replied, "Bring gloves."

Raylee shuddered and shrank into her down parka like a turtle into its shell.

"Now, the Five Perils is what we call a technical stage," explained Dodge. "It's far scarier than the first two legs you've flown, and one of the only stages WOOBA includes every year. Teams will fly, one by one, in a sort of scavenger hunt through an alpine pass, cresting four peaks. Atop each are a series of flags, one of which you must hook with a pole. You can only approach each peak once, so if you miss the flag on your first try, it's hasta la pasta, baby. The team that returns with the most flags wins."

"That doesn't sound so bad," said Alfie. "Cold, maybe, but not *perilous*. The flag part sounds fun."

"I'm not finished, my young balloon-brah. You see, the pass is shrouded in a soup of clouds, so thick that you'll need to rely completely on your compass to know where you're going. I should warn you, most teams don't even finish this stage."

"But what happens if multiple teams finish with all four flags?" asked Alfie.

"Nobody knows," replied Dodge ominously. "In WOOBA's entire history, no team has ever finished with more than two."

"So there are four peaks and four flags," said Binder. "Then why is it named the Five Perils?"

"Ah, Jedi question, Mr. Jolly. The fifth peril is *you*. How you escape fear and keep from wrecking into the side of the mountain in a giant fiery ball of—well, you get it. By the way, can any of you read a compass?"

A few hands rose, most of them only partway.

"Hmm," mumbled Dodge, pulling at the whiskers on his chin. "Guess I should've reviewed that before. No worries. No time like the present, eh?"

Clara thought she heard Raylee squeak from inside the safety of her jacket. Fortunately, she felt a bit more confident.

She'd read all about plotting points with compasses when she'd been banished to the belly of *Amelia* during Stage One—not that Mr. Bixley's broken one had let her practice.

"Come now," said Dodge cheerfully. "Most of you will be fine. Just remember, the important thing is to have fun and not die."

On that happy (and unsafe) note, Dodge excused them with a big thumbs-up. Clara wished the others luck and headed for the Hive. She wasn't halfway down the causeway to Bay Thirteen when she met an irate Greta Gildersleeve storming toward her.

"I'll make you into hats when I find you!" hollered the old pilot.

"Who are you talking to?" asked Clara.

"The monkeys!"

"What did they do now?"

"They absconded with my supplies . . . the hairy little thieves!"

"What supplies?"

"My potato chips!"

Clara squinted. Of all the strange things she had experienced thus far, potato chip theft might've been the weirdest. She tried to connect the dots in some logical manner, but it made about as much sense as a Dodge safety class having anything to do with safety.

"There they are!" shouted Gildersleeve. "Bring back those chips or I'll knock you back a step on the evolutionary ladder!" She hobbled down the causeway as a gaggle of hairy shapes pushed crates frantically out the Hive's entrance.

As Clara took in the spectacle, she noticed something even more out of place: Godfrey Sway was standing inside the doorway speaking with a WOOBA official.

Why would he be here? Providence *is moored in Regency.*

After a moment, Sway shook the official's hand and left. The man paused a few moments, shuffling through the bundle of envelopes in his arm before walking down the causeway, handing one out to each team.

"Do you have the updated flight chart for this stage?" he said to Clara, holding out a large manila envelope labeled *Five Perils.*

"I'm not sure," she replied.

"Then you better take one."

Inside was a map with four points marked in red, accompanied by compass points, labeled Flag 1 through Flag 4. There were other numbers, too, written within a series of concentric bands. Clara was about to put the map in her pocket for safekeeping when Gildersleeve reappeared, followed by three cowering primates. Each carried a crate overflowing with chip bags, except for Bob, who had apparently eaten all his before being caught.

"A race official came by and gave me this," Clara said, holding out the envelope.

Gildersleeve snatched it, removed the map, and frowned. "Why WOOBA feels the need to change everything at the last moment is beyond me."

"You know, I learned a lot about the Five Perils today."

"You did, did you? Well, don't sound so excited. You're about to freeze your tuchus off. I hope you have a thicker coat than that."

Clara didn't. Moreover, she had no idea where to get one now—or did she?

"Ms. Bortles," she yelled, running across the causeway to *Primrose*.

"Ciao, bella!" Alberto Furio peered over the side with a cheery wave.

"Oh hello, Mr. Furio. Is Ms. Bortles there?"

"Berta? No, non qui."

"Do you know when she's coming back? I was hoping she might have something warm I could borrow. You know . . . because she knits a lot? A sweater, maybe?"

"A sweater?" repeated Alberto.

"Yes, er . . . like a jacket?"

His eyes brightened. "Ah, jacket! Sì, un momento!" The man vanished, and Clara heard bins opening and closing. He reappeared and dropped something over the side to her.

"Jacket!" he said gleefully.

Unfortunately, it was not a jacket. Nor was it a sweater, or even an item of clothing for that matter.

"Uh, thanks," said Clara, holding the tennis racket in her hands. "You know, why don't I come back when Ms. Bortles is here."

"Prego," said Alberto, seemingly pleased with himself.

"Time to go," shouted Gildersleeve.

Clara climbed aboard with only the warmth of her cotton hoodie and Bixley's thin leather coat. Houdini cast off the mooring lines, Mayhem released air from the deflation port, and *Amelia* dipped out of the Hive.

The temperature plummeted instantly as they lowered into the shadow of a giant mountain.

"Oh my . . . Is that M-M-Mount Everest?" asked Clara.

"Of course not. Everest is thousands of feet taller," replied Gildersleeve. Clara couldn't conceive of anything bigger than the black granite monster that loomed in front of her. "That is Mount Kailash. It's sacred to the people of Tibet, thought to be the spiritual center of the universe, and to Hindus, the paradise of the god Shiva."

"And we're going up there? It's—"

"Not a place for people," Gildersleeve finished.

Bob guided *Amelia* to the starting line as *Rumor* emerged from the clouds. One of its twin envelopes sagged heavily as two people in puffy silver coats huddled together at the helm. Alfie was blue, and would've been unrecognizable if not for the few curls of red hair that stuck out from his hood.

The next teams didn't fare much better. *Samsara* ascended only to return minutes later with the Jollys looking more like snowmen than people, followed by the Chins-Rattons, the only team to secure a flag. The surprise of the day was the Newlins, who not only returned in one piece but with two flags. Niles and his father danced a jig on the deck of *Albatross* as they made their way back to the docks, hooting and hollering like they'd won the lottery.

"*Ahm-m-melia* to th-the s-s-start line," announced the quivering voice of Guy Gerard.

If it was any consolation for the cold, Clara doubted there would be any Face of the Race announcement today. At least, she hoped.

"All right, Mayhem, this is all you," said Gildersleeve.

The small monkey took the helm, staring steely-eyed at the granite slope before them. He signaled to Bob to hit the burner, and *Amelia* lifted into the gray.

"Child, take the port side," instructed Gildersleeve. "I'll take the starboard."

"I can't see anything," Clara complained. "How will we see the flags?"

"We won't. Not until we're on top of them. There are four navigation points we'll need to follow. Do you have your compass?"

Clara pulled Barnaby Bixley's broken one from her pocket. As usual, its needle spun aimlessly.

"Put that toy away and use mine," Gildersleeve barked.

When Clara exhaled, her breath instantly froze. Her hands were trembling, though not solely from the cold.

"Now, here's the tricky part," continued Gildersleeve. "We need to measure our rate of climb and descent with a variometer, but we must also stay close to the mountain, or we'll have no hope of seeing the flags."

"So that's what those other numbers on the m-m-map are—elevations."

Clara plotted the first coordinate, while Bob trimmed

the sails and Houdini repositioned the balloon's rotation. The wind rocked the basket, reaching up her shirt cuffs and down her neckline, icy and raw. Gildersleeve kept her gaze fixed on the variometer, calling out the altitude as she alternated firing the burner to add heat and releasing it from the top deflation port.

"If I'm reading this right, we should be nearing the first flag," Clara called.

"Houdini, Bob, you're up," shouted the old pilot.

Bob lifted a long wooden pole over the basket's edge and Houdini scampered to the end. The thick clouds made the little monkey appear as if he were floating in midair.

"I thought we had to use a hook," Clara said.

"We do. We're just adding a monkey."

Houdini barked as the red flag emerged atop a craggy outcropping. Bob adjusted the pole, and the other monkey snatched it before scrambling back to the safety of the basket.

"That's one," said Gildersleeve. "What's the next coordinate, child?"

Clara plotted the next bearing. Mayhem trimmed the sails and Gildersleeve gave another heave on the burner. A momentary wave of heat washed over them. Clara fantasized about climbing inside the warmth of the envelope as she pulled her hands into the cuffs of her sweatshirt, then tugged the strings of her hood to tighten it. Her fingers ached and her nose and ears prickled terribly.

Amelia neared the next navigation point, and Bob lowered Houdini once more over the railing. Moments later, the monkey reappeared holding the second flag.

"Next, child?"

"The map says we continue on the s-same c-c-course," she said, teeth chattering. "It's a s-straight sh-sh-shot across a s-snowfield."

As she pointed out the heading, a rock face emerged from the clouds only feet away. Houdini shrieked in alarm.

"Brace yourselves!" cried Gildersleeve.

Amelia slammed into the mountain, catapulting her passengers across the basket. A searing pain shot through Clara's head as she slammed into the fuel tanks, accompanied a second later by a high-pitched ringing. Gildersleeve scrambled to the helm to help Bob.

"We have to get off this wall," she shouted, "or we'll be torn to shreds."

Bob opened the burner full blast and *Amelia* tore upward with an angry roar, dragging along the rock face with an earsplitting screech like nails on a chalkboard. The starboard boom snapped in a shower of splinters, sending loose lines thrashing across the deck, while debris exploded off the wall, pelting them with ice and pebbles. Finally, *Amelia* blasted through a ridge of snow, dumping a foot of powder into the basket.

Someone cut the burner, and the world fell silent.

Clara peered over the railing at their buried basket and the snowfield beyond, and then collapsed in a corner. Surprisingly, she was still holding the map, although her fingers had grown so numb, she couldn't feel the paper. She stared at it, searching for an answer.

Did I read it wrong? Did I plot the wrong point?

A blast of wind kicked up around the basket, biting into every part of her. She curled into a ball, desperate to make herself as small and warm as possible. Overhead, the sky was growing darker. Even Gildersleeve, with Bob and Mayhem huddled around her, seemed clueless what to do next.

A thought crept into Clara's mind, dark and deathly. She tried to push it aside, but it grew more and more insistent.

Please don't let me become "Five Fingers" Clara.

CHAPTER SEVENTEEN

A PLACE WITH NO PEOPLE

CLARA CLUTCHED HER COAT as she huddled low in the balloon's snow-caked basket. She was sure WOOBA would send help when *Amelia* failed to return. But after what felt like hours of waiting and listening for helicopters, her hope had frozen like the rest of her. Maybe it was too risky now for anyone to fly—if it hadn't been all along. As far as she could tell, the weather had only gotten worse since their crash.

Clara jerked her collar high over her nose and looked at the ice cube shapes across from her, her focus moving from Gildersleeve to Bob to Mayhem, and then—

"W-W-Where's Houdini?"

Gildersleeve's eyes lifted. "He's right over—"

Suddenly, the old pilot was up and stumbling around

the basket, flipping broken panels of wicker and upended crates. She called out for the little monkey over and over—"Houdini! Houdini!"—but only the wind called back. "Bob, Mayhem." Her voice was strained. "We have to find him."

Without another word, the trio clambered from the listing basket and disappeared into the snowfield, hollering and barking for their lost friend. Clara closed her eyes and listened to their voices blend with the wind, until all she could hear was the envelope tugging against the snow-locked *Amelia*.

I should go below deck, she told herself. *It will be warmer there.*

But before she could move, something stirred behind a pile of crates heaped on the far side of the deck. It sounded like crinkling followed by a small *pop*, and then the distinct sound of crunching.

"Bob? Is that you?"

The noise stopped abruptly, then started after a few moments.

"Seriously, Bob? I hope you're n-n-not doing what I th-think you are?"

Suddenly, the top crate shot off the side of the basket, vanishing with a *thunk*. Clara rushed to the edge as fast as her frozen bones would allow, only to see the shape of something hairy disappear into the swirling storm.

"It's your f-f-funeral, Bob! You know what Ms. G-G-Gildersleeve will do to you if she c-c-catches you eating her p-p-potato chips again!"

"Who are you talking to, child?"

Clara spun to see Gildersleeve climbing into the basket behind her, followed a moment later by Mayhem, Bob, and finally Houdini. They slumped slack-jawed, gasping for breath, frosty-white like a family of snowmen.

"He was in the snowfield . . . with this," panted Gildersleeve, holding up a red cloth labeled *#3*.

"He f-found the th-third flag!" cried Clara.

The old woman nodded and coughed. "I'll give him this . . . he's one competitive monkey."

"But w-wait," Clara said, pointing back in the other direction. "If you were all in the s-s-snowfield over there, then wh-who was just h-h-here?"

"What are you talking about, child?"

"Whoever it w-was that took that c-c-crate?"

Gildersleeve stiffened, then staggered to the side of the basket. "Someone took a crate? Where? Are you sure?"

"Yes, I th-thought it was B-Bob. There was all this c-c-crunching and then one of the crates just z-zipped off the—"

"Quick," said the old woman. "Bob, Mayhem, open a few bags of potato chips and scatter them around *Amelia*."

She worked urgently, popping the lids off crates and tossing bags to the monkey.

"Ms. Gildersleeve, w-what's going on?"

"Never mind that now. Houdini, take this girl below deck before she turns blue."

Houdini wrapped his hairy arms around Clara as she got to her feet. Even snow-covered, the little monkey's body heat was rejuvenating. Together, they scaled down the ladder into the belly of *Amelia*, dark except for a sliver of daylight that filtered through the shattered window. Somewhere, Clara heard the shuddering coo of a frozen pigeon.

"There . . . off the port side," said Gildersleeve. "Do you see them?"

"See who?" Clara called up the ladder.

"Hello, friends!" shouted the pilot, her tone unusually jovial. "Please, come . . . we have something for you."

There was a trudging sound, faint at first. It grew louder, fanning out, as if a crowd had arrived, and then the unmistakable sound of crunching chips. Clara craned her head, trying to get a better view, but she could only see shadows passing by the broken window. "Is it rescuers?" she called.

"Can you help us?" Gildersleeve asked, ignoring Clara's

question. "Our basket . . . it's stuck in the snow. If you can free us, all these chips are yours."

Clara tried to imagine why rescuers would want potato chips, but a second later the crunching stopped, and then the trudging sound fanned out around *Amelia*. The basket lurched one way and then the other, rolling back and forth. Whoever it was outside was rocking them free. Clara heard the snow crack, echoing off the granite walls of the mountain, and the world suddenly reappeared through the broken window as the snowfield shot by underneath. They were airborne.

Clara scrambled up the ladder, desperate to catch a glimpse of their rescuers, but the balloon crested the peak before she could reach the railing. "What happened?"

"We were saved from becoming Popsicles, that's what."

"By who?"

"Gorillas," said the old woman matter-of-factly.

"Excuse me?"

Gildersleeve sighed loudly. "Many years ago, I was stranded here when my burner failed. I sat all night freezing in the shadow of the mountain's summit, waiting to be rescued. By sunrise, I'd about given up when a group of mountaineers appeared. I'd gone into shock by then, so I couldn't tell right away that my rescue party was really a troop of mountain gorillas. I was terrified. I threw everything I could at them, hoping to scare them away. The biggest one came at me, gnashing his teeth and spreading his massive arms. I thought he meant to choke me, but instead, he reached into the crate behind me and pulled out a bag of potato chips, then sat down as if we were at a picnic, and ate the whole thing—including the plastic bag. I was lucky to have more; he ate those, too, and everything else he could find. When he finished, he lifted me into his arms and carried me down the mountain, below the snow line, where rescuers could reach me. I still don't know why—maybe payment for the meal. Regardless, I would've died without the great ape's help. Since then, I stock potato chips whenever I fly in Tibet . . . just in case."

Something didn't compute. Clara searched her memory for a book report she'd done on the world's great apes. "But I don't think there *are* gorillas in Tibet."

"No? There aren't? Well, that's what they looked like to me," Gildersleeve said. She released air from the envelope, and the balloon descended beneath the clouds.

Clara tried to reconcile the impossible thoughts swirling in her mind. She'd heard legends of yeti. But they *were* only legends.

"Okay, Bob, take us back to the Hive," commanded the old pilot.

"What about the fourth flag?" Clara asked. "We can't just give up."

"Look at this balloon, child. Do you really want to risk crashing again?"

The old woman was right, of course, but Clara still didn't like it—especially when *Providence* returned from the course an hour later, Godfrey Sway grinning, with all four flags clutched in his fist.

LEADERBOARD
AFTER STAGE 3

1ST - Providence, 27 PTS

2ND - Brigadier Albert, 16 PTS

3RD - Amelia, 13 PTS

Amazingly, *Amelia* finished second, thanks to Houdini's bravery (or stupidity, depending on how you viewed it). *Albatross* was third on the podium until the Hoshis bumped them off in the last run of the day, also claiming two flags, but in less time. Still, from the way the Newlins celebrated, no one would've known.

"Let's meet our Stage Three winners," said a heavily bundled Guy Gerard, crossing to the podium. "Godfrey, impressive performance. Not only are you the first pilot in

WOOBA's history to return with all four flags, you did so with such speed! It's as though you had X-ray vision."

"Try expert piloting," countered Sway smugly. "The first two flags were simple, but the third required a steely conviction few pilots have. However, I knew that I—"

"Yes, what a smashing retelling, old chap," interrupted the announcer. "Now, folks, let's speak to our other big winner: our surprise second-place finisher, Team Amelia. Greta, you're becoming quite the talk of the race these days. People are even referring to you as the *Comeback Kid*. Not a bad title for someone in her eighties. Gutsy performance getting off that mountain, and with three flags, no less. Simply brilliant! I must say, after all these years, it looks as though the great rivalry of Gildersleeve and Sway has been reborn! Isn't that special, folks?"

Sway's nostrils flared. He pushed past Guy, knocking the announcer to the ground, before storming offstage.

"Ah, seems like Godfrey is eager for the next leg," said Guy, scrambling to his feet, "as I imagine all our fantastic aeronauts are. So, I'll see you soon for a hopefully much warmer Stage Four. Until then, I'm Guy Gerard, and don't you wish you were, too!"

The cameras stopped recording, and the audience

crowded the front rows clamoring for Gildersleeve's autograph. The old pilot had quickly become the fan favorite. Clara snuck off the back of the podium with Hatsu before they got caught up in the fanfare.

"Is it weird to you that no one's ever gotten all four flags, and then Sway does it in world-record time?" Clara asked. "It's almost like he knew where to go."

"But how could he?" replied Hatsu.

"I don't know, but I'm going to find out."

"Ooh, a mystery!" squealed the girl with an excited clap. "I love mysteries! Hey, can I be your Watson?"

"My what?"

"You know, Dr. John Watson . . . like Sherlock Holmes."

"I suppose you could help me keep an eye on Sway? I don't trust him, especially after what Ms. Gildersleeve said. If he is cheating, we have to catch him in the act."

"I will become small and sneaky," said Hatsu mysteriously. "Like a shadow he does not see. But I'll need a name . . . a sidekick name . . . something like . . . *The Shadow Bear!*"

"Really? Shadow Bear?"

"Yeah, well, let me work on it." The little girl marched off, mulling the possibilities, stopping briefly to hug a smiling woman in cat-eye glasses.

"No, no, Ms. Lemot, please," pleaded Clara. "I just

nearly froze to death on the side of a mountain. Please tell me I don't have to do a Face of the Race thing right now?"

"I'm sorry, Clara, but I'm afraid you do. However, if it's any consolation, you're about to be plenty warm."

CLARA WAS SURPRISED to find Habberdish waiting at her Face of the Race update. Apparently, some (or all) of the sponsors had complained about her previous performances. Habberdish was, as he put it, "there to mitigate as needed."

Clara had no idea what that meant, other than he didn't trust her, but that concern was overtaken shortly thereafter by the strange, puffy, metallic thing in front of her. "What is this? A sleeping bag?" she asked, slipping her leg into the silver sack.

"Not just any sleeping bag," said Habberdish. "This is a sleeping bag you never have to get out of, because this sleeping bag has legs."

"Who on earth would want that?"

"I'm not sure, really. Lazy people, I suppose."

"If it has legs, why doesn't it have arms?"

"How should I know? I'm only WOOBA's president."

"Oh, she's here," said Guy Gerard, materializing from

behind the camera. "How come no one told me the kid was here? All right, Sara, let's do this."

"It's *Clara*," she gritted out. "And I can barely breathe in this thing."

"All right, *Ca-lair-rah*," Guy mocked, marching her onto the stage. "Don't worry. This update is gonna be *bing-bang-boom*, and we're done. When the recording light goes on, simply read the teleprompter."

"You mean, we're not doing this *live*?"

"Live?" He laughed. "After your recent performances? Goodness, no! The sponsors have demanded that all future promotions be prerecorded. This way, you can't say anything stupid on live television and ruin their businesses. Okay, let's do it. Lights, camera, action!"

Words crawled quickly across the teleprompter.

"'Hello, everyone. It's Clara Poole, your Face of the Race. Have you ever felt like you wished—' Wait, can you go back?"

"Cut!" bellowed Guy. "Try again. And action."

"'Hello, everyone. It's Clara Poole, your Face of the Race. Have you ever wished you could stay in bed all day, but didn't want to miss out on life? Well, you don't have to wish any longer. Meet the Sleepwalker, the first sleeping bag with feet.' Uh, Mr. Gerard? The prompter says I'm supposed to give two thumbs-up, but this thing doesn't have arms."

"Don't worry, kid. Keep going."

"Okay. Where was I? Oh. 'Meet the Sleepwalker, the first sleeping bag with feet. Now, wherever you go, you'll be snug as a bug! So, say goodbye to the snooze button, and hello to the last bed—and pants—you'll ever need. Order your Sleepwalker today. Now for pets, too!'"

Something scuffled behind her.

"Bob?"

The big monkey grimaced unhappily, stuffed like a sausage into a matching silver sleep sack.

"Don't talk to the monkey." Guy groaned. "Just finish your lines!"

"But he doesn't like it."

"Of course he doesn't like it. No one does!" Guy pulled at his hair. "Honestly, they need to pay me more for this. Okay, one more time."

One more time became two, which became five, which became twenty. By the end, the crew looked thoroughly dejected, and Bob was lying on his back moaning from possible heatstroke.

"That's it!" hollered Guy. "I quit!" He threw his headset to the ground and marched off the stage, shouting a string of not-so-nice words.

Everyone around them froze. Clara looked at Habberdish, Habberdish looked at the cameraman, and the cameraman looked at his camera. "Uh-oh," he whispered. "I think I filmed all that *live*."

Not knowing what to do, he pointed the camera at WOOBA's president.

"And . . . cut," said Habberdish with a nervous laugh. "Okay . . . that went well . . . I think. Thank you, Clara. You are free to go."

Clara didn't need to be told twice. She wrestled free from the Sleepwalker, then helped Bob, who poured out sopping with sweat, and sent him back to the Hive before heading to the elevators.

"Destination, please?" requested the elevator's robotic voice.

"Take me to—" Clara stopped. She'd promised her father after returning from the mountain that she'd come right back to the room, but she wasn't ready to see him. He'd only make her start cramming for the next stage. In fact, Clara didn't want to see anyone. After the day she'd had, what she really wanted was time alone.

"Destination, please?" repeated the elevator.

"How about someplace with no people."

"Thank you." The elevator sprang to life. Clara watched

a rainbow of colors shift by the little window as the car went up, sideways, down, and sideways some more.

"Where are we going?"

"Someplace with no people, as requested."

"But I was joking."

The elevator dinged, and the doors slid open. "Arrived."

Clara stepped off the carriage into a dark room with high ceilings. The only light came from a wall of windows, which framed the moonlit peak of Mount Kailash. Balloon-shaped chandeliers hovered above islands of furniture draped in dustcloths. Clara moved among them toward the back wall, where a gallery of old photographs and news clippings told the story of WOOBA's hundred-year history. She recognized a few from orientation, but there were dozens more stretching into the gloom. She ran her hand down the fabric wall until her fingertips brushed a bank of light switches, and she flipped them all on. The chandeliers flickered to life, revealing the full dimensions of what she guessed was a ballroom.

At its center was a cluster of tables, strewn with piles of promotional flyers, felt pennants, and other WOOBA memorabilia. All except one, on which a squadron of origami doves and other animals lay in perfect rows, as if awaiting orders. Clara picked up a tiny monkey made from Wibble

Bibble wrappers to study it, and then caught sight of something even odder.

Beyond the tables, what she had originally thought was furniture was a collection of life-size sculptures.

The first was a heroic but disheveled-looking figure with frizzy hair constructed from wicker and parachute cloth. The second was pudgy-shaped with a thick mustache, posed with a hand on the shoulder of a girl with a long ponytail (and to Clara's delight, a rat tail). Clara didn't need a nameplate—or monogram—to know her identity. Nor did she have any trouble identifying the others: a dapperly dressed, rotund figure with curly hair made from shredded paper; a tall, slender character with a chiseled face and grim expression, punctuated by tattoos under each eye.

As she approached them for a better look, she stepped on something soft—a Dovie pennant like the ones sold at the merchandise counters. This pennant, however, was missing its white WOOBA logo. And it wasn't alone. Other scraps of blue cloth littered the floor, each one with the white dove cut out of its center. Clara picked one up and peered through the hole, and then realized why.

At the far side of the ballroom was the figure of a girl. She stood defiant in a Peter Pan stance, legs wide and hands on hips. Beside her were three smaller, hairier forms (one, twice the size of the others). They were all crafted entirely in blue felt, except the girl's hair, which curled in a bob around her chin in strands of white.

That's me!

The elevator chimed and Clara spun, startled. A second later, a boy stepped off holding a cardboard box. He took two steps, saw her, and stopped dead in his tracks.

"What are you doing here?" demanded Landon Sway.

CHAPTER EIGHTEEN

PIECES OF THE PAST

LANDON MARCHED INTO THE ROOM, anxiously survey-ing the tables of origami. "Seriously," he said, turning to Clara, "why are you here?"

"Landon, did you make these sculptures?"

He dropped a box of fabric on the table and began straightening the rows of paper birds. "What if I did?"

"Well . . . they're incredible."

He shot her a sideways glance. "How did you even know about this place?"

"I didn't. I told the elevator I wanted to go somewhere without people, and it brought me here."

Landon picked up a flyer promoting Ignitus Burners, folded it into a perfect dragon, and placed it in a column with a dozen others. "Then it took you to the right place.

Other than me, no one comes here. It's like nobody knows it exists."

Clara spun in place. "How do you not know about a place this big?"

"Got me. The only thing I've come up with is that maybe WOOBA doesn't need it anymore, now that everything happens on the observation deck. This ship is huge, after all. I only learned about this place after I discovered this."

He walked to a table and ran his hands over a dog-eared map. Clara leaned in to see a diagram of a cross section of the *Zephyrus* with each area labeled: *Bridge*, *Engine Room*, *Passenger Deck*, *Crew Quarters*, and so on.

"So then, we're in the Elysium Ballroom?" she asked, tracing her hand over the ship's stern. "Where did you find this?"

"In a stack of old papers in my grandfather's cabin."

"And no one knows what you're doing here?"

"Absolutely not."

"Not even your grandfather?"

"Especially him," Landon said. "And he can't know, either."

"Why?"

"Because he'd make me stop."

"I don't get it?"

"You don't have to."

"But—"

"Listen. All my grandfather cares about is me becoming a great aeronaut. 'Because that's what Sways do.'"

"But look at all this. . . . You really don't think he'd be—"

"The only thing he'd *be* is furious."

"Still, don't you want people to see your work? Seriously, Landon, these sculptures could be in a museum."

"*Museum?* Yeah, like that will ever happen. Look, just forget it, okay? I'm not like you."

"What's that supposed to mean?"

"I'm not outgoing the way you are."

Clara laughed. "Is that how you see me?"

He mumbled something unintelligible and returned to his origami. In seconds, he was lost, hidden in the safety of his own inner world. Suddenly, Clara saw herself.

"You know, before this race, I wanted to be invisible, too. I just hid in my room all the time, kinda like you coming here and doing all this. It's the same thing, really."

Landon scoffed at her. "Same? You chose to come to Paris to join this race. You chose to be the Face of the Race. If that's your idea of invisible, it's not mine."

"That's different. I . . . had to come."

"Had to?"

"It's complicated."

Landon put down his origami, crossed his arms, and waited. "Well . . . ?"

"Well, what?" grumbled Clara. "I don't know. My dad was making us move, okay? I thought if I joined the race, I could somehow stop it from happening."

Landon squinted one eye. "You know that makes absolutely no sense?"

"I do now. It's hard to explain . . . my father tries to protect me from everything. It's like being kept in a bubble, or something. Then he tells me to be normal—whatever that means—like I can just snap my fingers and be somebody else." Clara paused, looking at the sculpture of the girl and her monkeys. "But what if I don't know who I am? All I know is that all this—this race—it's starting to feel like this is the only place I fit in."

"Well, that makes one of us. Look, just promise to keep this place a secret. My grandfather would freak if he found out about any of it."

"And you say I make no sense," mumbled Clara. "Just tell him this makes you happy."

"You don't get it, do you? No one tells Godfrey Sway anything. Not even me." Landon slumped onto a blue couch and stared out at the snow blowing over the mountain's summit. "He'll do anything to win this race."

"Like . . . cheat?"

"Cheat?" Landon seemed genuinely surprised by the question. Even a bit offended.

"That's what Gildersleeve told me. She thinks your grandfather's cheating."

This time, Landon laughed. "Says a woman whose best friends are apes."

"Monkeys," corrected Clara. "Fine. Then how do you explain crossing the Sahara hours before the next balloon?"

"I don't know. Good piloting?"

"What about the Five Perils? You got all four flags."

"So?"

"So no one's ever done that before."

"You got three. No one's done that, either."

"Yeah, but we weren't cheating."

"Neither were we. Look, is my grandfather like the most competitive person there is? Absolutely. Is he's totally obsessed with winning that dumb trophy? Without a doubt. But does he cheat? I can guarantee you I've never seen anything like that when I've come up on deck."

Clara paused, squinting at Landon. "*Come up* on deck? You mean, you're not on deck during the race?"

"Aren't you listening? I couldn't care less about this stupid race. No . . . my grandfather and I have a kind of unspoken agreement—he gets his copilot and future heir to his aeronaut throne. I stay below deck and do what I want . . . like making origami."

"Then maybe you haven't seen him do anything sketchy. Ms. Gildersleeve said—"

"You're putting a lot of trust in someone you don't really know."

"Come on, I've seen how your grandfather glares at her."

"I think that's different."

"How?"

Landon watched her for a long moment. "Come here," he said. "There's something you should see."

Clara followed him to the wall of photographs, where he removed a pair of black-framed glasses from his pocket, put them on, then squinted at the little brass plaques at the bottom.

"You wear glasses?" she said.

"Yeah, and I *talk*, too."

Clara went red. "I didn't mean it like that the other day. Besides, you were the one standing there like one of your statues."

"Sculptures . . . ," Landon corrected with a smirk. "And

at least *they* have manners." He adjusted his glass and studied the wall. "Okay, this way."

Clara opened her mouth to defend herself, then stopped. Upsetting him more wouldn't help. "What are we looking for, anyway?"

"That," he said, pointing to a series of clippings.

WOOBA CROWNS ITS FIRST WOMAN CHAMPION, GRETA GILDERSLEEVE, IN THE RUNNING OF THE 60TH WOOBA AIR RACE

GRETA GILDERSLEEVE & TILLIMICUS ROCHEMOND: GRAND CHAMPIONS OF 62ND DOVIE CUP

EASY SAILING FOR GRETA GILDERSLEEVE & COPILOT, DECLAN DUNSEY, IN WOOBA'S 67TH AIR RACE

"Okay, so they're just a bunch of old newspaper articles. I'm still not sure what am I looking at."

"Not there. Underneath."

Clara focused her attention on a headline near the bottom that trumpeted, "SHE WINS AGAIN!" The accompanying photo showed a much younger Gildersleeve standing beside a handsome, slender man, maybe in his twenties. Together they were hoisting the Dovie Cup high in the air, smiling triumphantly. In the lower corner was a small inset picture: a boy no older than Clara holding a different trophy sitting in what looked like a one-person balloon. Behind him was a strikingly younger Gildersleeve wearing a flight suit with the letters *A. A.* embroidered on the lapel, her arms raised in celebration.

Everything became clearer as Clara read to the caption below:

> Greta Gildersleeve, winner of the 72nd WOOBA Air Race, with her new copilot, Godfrey Sway. Inset: Gildersleeve and Sway from their earlier days at Air Academy.

"They were teammates," she said, stunned.

"The best ever. They won six races together."

Clara read the caption again. "What's Air Academy?"

"Some kind of school for aeronauts. My grandfather keeps threatening to send me there. Anyhow, it's where they first met. I guess he was one of Gildersleeve's students."

Clara skimmed some of the other articles displayed on the wall, slowly piecing the truth together. "So let me get this straight. Ms. Gildersleeve taught your grandfather at this Air Academy place, and then, after, she won a bunch of races with these other guys, Rochemond and Dunsey . . ."

"Right."

"And later, your grandfather became Ms. Gildersleeve's copilot, and they won six races."

"That's what it says."

"Then . . . why does he hate her so much?"

"That, I don't know. But read this . . ."

A tiny clipping from *The WOOBA Quarterly Journal* had been tucked under a row of headlines recounting Godfrey Sway's victories in the eighty-first and eighty-second races. There was no picture, only a small blurb:

> *In unlikely news, multi-time champion Greta Gildersleeve has decided to end her retirement and return to balloon racing. However, in paperwork filed today with WOOBA officials, Gildersleeve made the unusual request for permission to fly solo in this year's upcoming air race. This action comes years after her high-profile and contentious breakup with longtime racing partner Godfrey Sway. Exact details of the pair's parting remain unknown, though it is rumored to have occurred after a family tragedy. Neither party was available for comment.*

"Family tragedy?"

Landon shrugged as a nearby clock chimed ten.

"Oh, no. Is it really that late? My dad's gonna murder me that I'm not back."

"Then go," Landon said. "But remember, don't tell anyone about this place."

"Yeah, sure," Clara said over her shoulder as she jabbed at the elevator's call button.

"I mean it. You have to promise!"

Clara turned and looked him in the eye. *"I promise!"*

The elevator opened with a *ding*, and she rushed into the carriage.

"Hey, wait," Landon said, stopping the doors before they could close. "Do you ... uh ... really think my art is good?"

"No," she replied flatly. "It's far better than good."

Landon flashed a small smile and let the doors slide shut.

CHAPTER NINETEEN

A COO-RIOUS SITUATION

CLARA HADN'T EVEN PUT HER HAND on the knob when the door flew open.

"Where have you—"

"Dad, I didn't mean it," she blurted. "I lost track of time. I—"

"Do you know how many hours I've been looking for you?"

"I know, I—"

"Four! I have been scouring this ship for four hours. WOOBA security is searching for you as we speak! For all anyone knew, you fell off the *Zephyrus!*"

"Dad, I'm sorry. It won't—"

"Where were you?"

"Oh . . . where?" It was a simple question, but not one

Clara could answer without breaking the promise she'd just made to Landon.

"Don't play games with me, Clara. Where were you?"

"Uh . . . ," she said, squeezing one eye shut. "I was with Hatsu and the other kids. Like I said, I just lost track of time."

"That's odd, because I spoke with Hatsu's mother . . . and Binder's . . . and Alfie's. I even spoke to Sir Wallace. Now, try again. Where were you?"

Clara winced, knowing how bad the next words would sound. "I can't tell you."

"You *what?*"

"I . . . promised I wouldn't say."

"Promised who?"

"A friend."

"Which friend?"

"One of the kids from pilot training. Look, Dad—"

"Clara Abigail Poole, tell me where you were and who you were with this instant!"

She bit her lip—hard. "No."

Anger flashed across her father's face, and she watched his chest rise like a dormant volcano waking. She tensed, waiting for the eruption, but it didn't come.

"You're grounded," he murmured.

"Grounded? How? You can't ground me in the middle of the race."

"I just did."

"But—"

He held up his hand. "You will fulfill your obligations as we've agreed with Mr. Habberdish, but after each stage, you'll return here immediately."

"For how long?"

"Indefinitely."

"Dad, that's not fair!"

Without another word, he walked into his bedroom and turned off the light, leaving Clara broiling with angry thoughts and nowhere to sling them.

"You're the worst father ever!" she yelled, stamping her feet.

"So you've said," came his disappointed voice.

HATSU SAT BEHIND a tower of French toast, covered ear to ear in powdered sugar. Clara hadn't been sure if her prison sentence meant she was supposed to stay in her room and order room service, but her father was gone when she woke, and she was too hungry to care about consequences. Besides, it didn't seem possible she could get into any more trouble than she already had.

"I'm sorry to hear you are on the ground, Bakagari."

"I think you mean *grounded*."

"That's what I said."

"Whatever," Clara grumbled, pushing a slice of watermelon around her plate with her fork. "Just don't tell anyone, okay? I'd rather avoid the humiliation."

Hatsu gave a solemn (and syrupy) nod.

"The worst part is now I can't keep an eye on Sway."

"But you don't need to, remember? You have the Shadow Bear." Clara gave Hatsu a sideways glance. "I know, I'm still working on the name. Just go with it, okay? Anyhow . . . you'll be pleased to know the Shadow Bear has been very sneaky, following Mr. Sway everywhere he goes. And I have news." She lifted her backpack onto her lap and began rummaging through it, placing handfuls of old candy wrappers on the table.

"Hatsu, did you eat all of those?"

"Maybe . . . ?" she mumbled. "Ah, here it is!" Hatsu pulled out a spiral-bound memo pad with the words *Shadow Bear Super-duper Book of Secrets* on it and began flipping through the pages. "Since the end of Stage Three, Mr. Sway's been busy. First, I found him on the shopping and services level having his nails done."

"Sway got a manicure?"

"Yes, his fingers, but not his toes. He didn't choose a color either, even though I noticed a very nice shade of violet that I think would've been perfect for his skin tone."

Sway at a nail salon was the last thing Clara might've expected, but it wasn't relevant, either.

"After, Mr. Sway went to the gym. He walked on the treadmill for thirty minutes, then did twenty-five push-ups, fifty sit-ups, and ten minutes of stretching. Then, he swam twenty lengths in the pool on the observation deck. For a man his age, he's in excellent shape." Hatsu thumbed to the next page. "Then he went to the dining room—the fancy one with white tablecloths. I hid inside a fern for an hour watching him, which was unfortunate because halfway through his meal, a waiter decided to water me. I did note here, however, that I *was* thirsty. Mr. Sway's meal consisted of poached salmon, kale with lemon, and a cup of ginger tea. He did not, however, order dessert. I noted that, too, because I would've ordered the cake—the one I saw Ms. Berta eating. It was three layers of chocolate, with chocolate icing."

"Hatsu, what does any of this have to do with Sway cheating?"

"I'm getting there, Bakagari. Do you want me to skip ahead?"

"Yes."

"So then, you don't want to hear what Mr. Furio had for dessert?"

Clara raised an eyebrow. "No."

"Fine." Hatsu flipped forward in her notebook. "It was panna cotta," she muttered, "and it looked yummy."

"Hatsu, please!"

The little girl frowned and flicked the page. "Okay, here. 'Mr. Sway visits balloons in empty hangars.'"

"Sway went into the hangars when no one was there?"

"I just said that. Really, Bakagari, try to be a better listener. At eight-oh-two p.m., Mr. Sway visited Hangar One, also known as Regency. He walked the entire dock to make sure he was alone, then boarded *Brigadier Albert* for a total of four minutes and twelve seconds."

"What did he do there?"

"I couldn't get close enough without being seen— or heard. After the fern incident, my sneakers were very squeaky."

Clara's mind went into overdrive. "Well, did he move something or take anything?"

"Not that I could tell."

"Did he go on any other balloons?"

"Yes. After, he went to the Hive, which was also empty. And again, he boarded one balloon."

"Whose?"

"Yours, Bakagari, but not for long. Because while the Hive was empty of people, it was not empty of monkeys. I heard a loud bark from somewhere aboard *Amelia*, and then Mr. Sway hollered. A moment later, he rushed out of the hangar holding his hand. When I looked back, I saw Bob flaring his teeth."

Clara had never been so proud of the big monkey.

"But why would Sway only go on *Brigadier Albert* and *Amelia*?"

"I wondered that, too. The only thing I could think of was that you and the Chins-Rattons are second and third on the leaderboard. Maybe Mr. Sway sees you both as the closest threat to win? But don't worry. The Shadow Bear will find the answer . . . at least while you are on the ground."

"Grounded."

"That's what I said. Oh, good morning, Mr. Poole."

Clara turned to see her father in gym clothes, covered in sweat, carrying the most unappetizing plate of food she had ever seen: baked tomatoes, cottage cheese, a bran muffin, and an egg white omelet. He'd started working out, something very unlike him. Clara assumed it was to help relieve the stress of feeling powerless during her races. She'd even encouraged him—especially if it meant him staying off her back.

"I see you've left the room," he said, taking a bite of muffin.

"I have to eat, don't I?"

"I suppose," he said flatly.

"Anyhow, I have to go to the docks to get ready for Stage Four. That is if I have your permission?"

"So long as you return to the room right after the race."

"Hmph!" She shoved her chair back and stormed out of the dining hall.

"Bakagari?" called Hatsu, "If you're done . . . can I finish your French toast?"

IF CLARA WAS HOPING to feel better, it didn't happen at the Hive. Gildersleeve was in a foul mood, for whatever reason she didn't say. Clara gave the woman a wide berth, which on this occasion wasn't a problem. She needed a private word with a big monkey.

"Bob?" she said, climbing the rigging to the hammocks. "I need to talk with you."

"Leave him alone," called Gildersleeve. "He's only sulking up there because I yelled at him for making a mess of the deck."

"Bob, are you okay?" asked Clara quietly.

The big monkey huffed and turned his back to her.

"Something happened here last night, didn't it? Did Sway try to come aboard?"

The monkey growled low.

"That's why the deck's a mess. Because you chased him away, didn't you?"

Bob gave a small whine and motioned to the old pilot below.

"I know. You were only trying to protect us."

He flopped onto her lap with a whimper.

"It's okay," she said, stroking his fur. "You're a good monkey."

"A-hem ... er ... hello! Can all teams please report to the starting line," Harold Habberdish said over the loudspeaker. Apparently, Guy Gerard had not returned after his on-set outburst.

Loud clacks filled the air as balloons detached from their

moorings and dipped out of the safe harbor of the Hive. As they descended into the open air, a wall of humidity struck Clara, and an instant later, every inch of her was soaked with sweat. Forest rolled out in all directions, dense like a jungle, broken by patches of dry grassland—the clouds, little more than thin streamers of vapor.

"Where are we?" she asked.

"Madhya Pradesh," Gildersleeve replied. "It's a central state of India."

"We're in India?"

"Pench National Park, to be precise. You might know it if you've ever read Rudyard Kipling. Some of his most famous stories took place here. Just hope we don't have to put down anywhere—unless you like playing with tigers."

"Wait, we're flying over *The Jungle Book*?"

Stage Four had been designed as a short-distance sprint. Unlike the time trial in Morocco, the balloons would race all at once. In their PTSD class, Dodge had likened it to an aerial roller derby. Raylee, who as always asked for actual safety guidance, had gotten nothing more than the obvious (and unhelpful) advice, "Don't fall out." But after hours of floating in dead air, any thoughts of fast-paced danger, Mowgli, or Shere Khan had transitioned into sheer boredom.

Clara wiped her forehead and groaned. "Where's the wind?"

"Do I look like a weather report?" Gildersleeve grumbled. She sat in a rickety lawn chair huddled with the monkeys under the shadow of an umbrella. Even Coo had left the safety of his cage in the sweltering belly of the basket to come above deck.

"Can't we go back and wait until the wind picks up? It's . . . so . . . hot."

"Toughen up. A bit of grit would do you good. Besides, what's the alternative? Sitting in your room, grounded?"

Clara's mouth fell open. "You know about that?"

"Of course I do. There are no secrets at WOOBA. Everyone here knows everything."

"Maybe not everything," muttered Clara.

"Rubbish."

"Well . . . what about you and Godfrey Sway?"

Gildersleeve tilted the umbrella. "Do you have something to say, child?"

"Oh, I . . . uh . . . no. It's just . . . I heard he was your copilot once."

"And?"

"And . . . that something bad happened."

Gildersleeve sat up in her chair. "I'm not sure where

you're headed with this, but you'd be wise to mind your own business."

"Sorry. I just thought maybe you would—"

"Would what?"

"Tell me why you and Sway stopped flying together."

Gildersleeve glowered. "I will tell you this: stay away from Godfrey Sway. Do not get in his path, or you will most assuredly become one of his unfortunates."

Clara blinked. "That's exactly what he said about you."

If Gildersleeve heard Clara, she didn't say, because the next moment, Coo plunged off the side of *Amelia*.

"Good grief, did it die?" exclaimed Gildersleeve, racing to the edge of the basket.

Coo fell like a rock, plummeting through the air, and then opened his wings and catapulted forward like a rocket.

"Wind!" cried Gildersleeve. "The dumb bird found wind!"

Unfortunately, they weren't the only ones to notice the old pigeon. Other pilots shouted orders, and moments later, the race was on. *Brigadier Albert*, much nimbler than *Amelia*, was the first to reach the air current, and shot ahead of the pack. Gildersleeve pulled hard on the deflation port, and the balloon dipped into second position, just as a jolt shook the deck. *Providence* lifted their basket and broke free, swinging *Amelia* like a pendulum into the passing *Primrose*. Alberto pinwheeled through the air, landing with a *thud* at Gildersleeve's feet.

"Scusi," he said, scampering back over the side to his basket.

"Incoming!"

Clara whirled to see the terrified eyes of the Woodrows, moments before *Rumor* slammed into the stern of the two balloons. They tangled, twisting around each other in a great knot. Wicker cracked and buckled, and the rigging moaned as the lines wrapped over one another with the tension of a slingshot. *Primrose*'s sail jammed into the mouth of *Rumor*'s envelope and over the open burner, before exploding into flames.

"Fire!" cried Gildersleeve. "Cut that sail free, or we're goners."

Alfie's mother, unsheathed a small knife fastened to her shirtsleeve and sliced at the rigging. The sail fell with a fiery *whoosh*, like a diving phoenix, thankfully extinguishing itself before reaching the grasslands below.

Gildersleeve began barking out orders like a general: "Cut your burners! Open your side vent! Free that line from the uprights!"

Slowly, the snarled balloons untangled.

Once free, Clara was amazed to find they were still in contention, not far behind *Ussuri* and *Providence*. Only the Chins-Rattons were too far to catch. Clara's stomach turned, imagining the self-satisfied smile plastered on Ophelia's face. A win would put the aristocrats in range of first place.

The balloons rose and descended together following Coo as the pigeon surfed the shifting thermals. In the distance, *Brigadier Albert* stalled and sank, and a minute later the other balloons caught up and sailed past. Clara watched Sir Wallace racing around the basket, frantically checking the burner tanks.

"How could the blasted thing be empty?" he cried out. "We shouldn't need this much fuel!"

"Father, look! There's a tear," shouted Ophelia, pointing into the mouth of the balloon's envelope.

"A tear?" he exclaimed. "Blast!"

"Do something, Father!" Ophelia whined. "We're going to let them win!" She glowered at Clara as *Amelia* sailed by.

"Sway must've sabotaged *Brigadier Albert*," whispered Clara to Bob. "I know it."

Moments later, *Providence* crossed the floating finish line of Stage Four. Bob howled in protest as *Amelia* took third place behind *Ussuri* and an elated Hatsu.

"I beat you, Bakagari!" cried the little girl, pumping her fists and wiggling her hips in an odd victory dance.

Ahead, floating near the *Zephyrus*, Clara saw Godfrey Sway on the deck of *Providence*, waving to the fans like a hero.

Waving with a hand wrapped in bandages.

CHAPTER TWENTY

THE MAKING OF ENEMIES

LEADERBOARD

AFTER STAGE 4

1ST - Providence, 37 PTS

2ND - Amelia, 18 PTS

3RD - Brigadier Albert, 17 PTS

WALLACE CHINS-RATTON PULLED ON his great wattle of a chin as he examined the tear in one of the nylon gores of *Brigadier Albert*. A crowd had gathered near the balloon, which was held aloft by a fleet of rescue drones alongside the observation deck.

"And you have no idea how it happened?" asked Habberdish, looking equally confused.

"In all my years flying, I've never had a balloon do that. A seam pull, yes, but not an outright tear. No wonder we used so much fuel—hot air was spilling out the side of the envelope as fast as we could fill it."

Music started playing onstage announcing the start of the ceremony for the day's winners, and the spectators peeled off to take their seats. Clara hung back, studying the jagged tear in *Brigadier Albert*'s envelope.

"We better go, Bakagari," said Hatsu, tapping Clara on the shoulder. "Oh, and by the way, I beat you."

Clara rolled her eyes, though she couldn't help smiling.

As they walked toward the podium, Clara noticed Sway was already standing at the top, speaking cordially with Guy Gerard.

"Looks like a solid first place lead for *Providence*," said Guy with his signature plastic exuberance. "I say, Godfrey, it will be tough to beat you now."

Clara took her place next to Gildersleeve.

"Indeed," replied Sway, catching Clara's eye. "You would be a fool to try."

She looked away. The warning was clear.

"I'm afraid that's all we have for today," said Guy. "Next up—Stage Five and the misty spires of the Tianzi

Mountains. Folks, get ready for excitement. And pilots, get ready for danger. I'm Guy Gerard and, as always . . . don't you wish you were, too!"

The on-air light went off, and the announcer's smile vanished in a blink. "You!" he said, pointing at Clara. "Let's get something straight. I wouldn't still be here if I hadn't signed a contract. But nothing in that contract says I need to like you." He grumbled something else Clara couldn't make out before storming off.

"I think you're growing on him, Bakagari," mused Hatsu.

"You think so?"

"Yeah . . . just a hunch."

THE KIDS SAT AT the foot of *Rumor's* mooring tower, gathered around Clara to learn more about the next stage from her father's notebook. *Everything Your Father Would Do That You Should, Too* had become a vital resource, especially for Raylee, who had come to rely on these prerace insights to keep from freaking out—mostly.

"How bad is it?" she asked, wringing her hands.

"Honestly, there's not much info on this one," replied Clara.

"I heard a rumor that Habberdish enlisted Dodge to help beef up safety precautions for the upcoming stages," Alfie said.

Binder huffed. "Then there's at least one thing we know . . . if Dodge is involved, whatever we're facing will be anything *but* safe."

"It'll be even worse if Sway has his way," said Clara.

"Hey, that rhymes," Alfie chimed in with a goofy smile. He turned to the others for agreement but only got a smack in the head from Binder. "What? It did!"

Clara rolled her eyes. "That rip in *Brigadier Albert*'s envelope wasn't an accident. I bet Sway put a slash in it, knowing it would only grow bigger as the race went on."

"And you heard Sir Wallace," added Hatsu. "They had to use all their fuel to keep from crashing."

"What are you talking about?"

Clara spun to see Ophelia Chins-Ratton behind them, arms crossed and scowling.

"Oops," whispered Hatsu.

Binder sighed. "As much as it kills me to say this, OCR does have a point. What exactly *are* you talking about?"

Clara looked at them one by one, then at Hatsu who shrugged. "I think Godfrey Sway is cheating. I think he sabotaged *Brigadier Albert* and tried to do the same to *Amelia*."

"Cheating?" repeated Raylee.

Binder scratched his head. "I wonder if that's why our balloon had issues."

"Yeah. Ours, too," Alfie added.

Clara frowned. "You mean, both of you have had problems?"

"Sure did. . . . Weird ones," said Binder. "*Samsara* ran out of fuel during Stage Two, which seemed impossible, because my mum and I refill our tanks after each race. And I heard Alfie's mother complain that the same thing happened to *Rumor*."

"Twice," confirmed the red-haired boy.

"That's it. I'm telling my father!" OCR spun on her heels and headed for the exit.

"No, Ophelia. Stop," Clara called. "You can't tell him."

"And why, pray tell, would that be?"

"Because he won't believe you. Godfrey Sway is a multi-time champion. In the eyes of WOOBA—and your father—he's a bona fide hero."

"And?"

"And . . . I don't have any proof."

Ophelia glared, but remained silent.

"She right, OCR," Binder added. "Think about it. Without proof, no one will take us seriously. Not even your dad."

The other kids nodded.

"And if I agree to keep this quiet for now?" asked Ophelia. "What happens then?"

"We get proof."

"And where do you expect to find that?"

Clara thought for a moment, then smiled. "From an insider."

"Well, whoever it's from, you have two stages to get it," said Ophelia with a sniff. "After that, I'm going straight to my father."

"Deal." Clara stuck out her hand.

"Ick! I'm not touching you. You probably have fleas from those monkeys."

THE MOON WAS hidden behind clouds when Clara stepped off the elevator into the ballroom. She strained to see the tables of origami and the sculptures, which stood like gatekeepers to another world.

"Landon?" she said in a loud whisper, stepping carefully through the darkness.

Someone stirred on the couch by the windows.

"Landon," she repeated. "We have to talk. Your grandfather could've seriously hurt someone today. You need to tell Mr. Habberdish what's going on."

He didn't move or reply.

"I'm serious, Landon. They'll believe you more than me. Please, before your grandfather does something horrible."

The clouds parted, casting moonbeams across the ballroom, and a figure rose from the couch in the ghostly light. Even in half silhouette, it was remarkable how similar he was to the sculpture beside him—tall, slender. Even the tattoos under his eyes were spot-on.

"I haven't been in this room for years," said Godfrey Sway. "In fact, I'd completely forgotten about it until my grandson started disappearing here ... working on all ... *this*."

Sway circled the sculpture of himself, taking in its uncanny felt-cut likeness. He poked at the face as if it might be alive, and Clara noticed his still-bandaged hand.

"It runs in the family, you know—*art*. The boy's grandmother was an artist. That woman spent all day painting some foolish bridge or bowl of fruit. Self-indulgent, if you ask me."

Clara felt frozen as Sway wove among Landon's work.

"But it's only a phase for the boy. I imagine this *need* for self-expression will cease once he understands that his legacy is to be a great pilot like his grandfather."

"Great pilots don't cheat," Clara said quietly.

"Mmm, still stuck on that wild theory of yours?"

"I know what you did to the Chins-Rattons. Hatsu saw you sneak onto *Brigadier Albert.*"

"Hatsu? *Hatsu?* Is that the little girl with the ridiculous hat? The one with the squeaky sneakers who's been following me everywhere?" He paused at the sculpture of the Chins-Rattons, then turned back to Clara. "I'm sorry, but what was it you say she saw?"

Clara scowled. "What happened to your hand?" she asked, nodding at the bandages.

"Oh, this?" he replied. "I cut it."

"On a monkey's teeth. Bob bit you."

"Good grief, the things have *names*? I've petitioned for years to cage those beasts and send them back to the wild. Really, it's only a matter of time before someone gets rabies. But for some reason, WOOBA continues to let that disgrace of a pilot keep them."

"*You're* the disgrace."

Something like amusement crossed Sway's face. "You view me in such a poor light, Miss Poole. Perhaps, though, you'll indulge me with the telling of a story about *real* disgrace. Of course, you'll need to put aside your allegiances long enough to listen . . . as misguided as they might be."

Sway walked to the wall of pictures and ran his finger over the frames, taking in each image before stopping at the old photo of him and Gildersleeve hoisting the Dovie Cup.

"Greta was my instructor at Air Academy. I was a gifted student—a generational talent, you might say—driven by the goal to become the best aeronaut the world had ever seen. Naturally, we bonded instantly, and after graduation, I became her copilot. It was an obvious choice, even though many were upset I didn't go out on my own—those eager to see the teacher and her star pupil battle it out on the racecourse. Together, we were unstoppable. We won six years in a row—the longest streak in history."

Sway tapped the picture commemorating his and Gildersleeve's sixth victory with a longing look.

"People sometimes talk about living on cloud nine, but our success went higher. Famous, and rich from our winnings, we each married and started families, though we were always more like one big extended family. At least, for a while . . . until . . ."

He paused again, lost in a memory.

"Until . . . ?"

Sway frowned. "Has Greta ever mentioned my son, Thomas?"

Clara shook her head and he smiled sadly.

"When Thomas was small, we'd go flying with Greta's family. He loved ballooning, and each time we went up, he would promise me that when he was old enough, we would race together as father and son. What father wouldn't want that? Yet when that day came, when Thomas was finally of age, he suddenly changed his mind. He said he'd met a girl and she was everything to him. He told me they were moving to the city—for a normal life—not one in the clouds. 'Normal life? You are a pilot—this is what Sways do!' I said. 'Only a fool would choose love over legacy.' But Thomas was unwavering, unable to listen to good reason. I even asked Greta to talk some sense into him when he would no longer speak to me. Thomas left the next morning."

Sway ambled down the wall of photos, stopping at the headlines touting his many victories. Clara watched him silently, trying to figure out where this was leading.

"I've always believed, Miss Poole, that people must be willing to sacrifice for greatness. So I took the pain of my son's abandonment and I turned it into action. I rededicated myself, spending every waking moment in the air, focusing only on being the best. Win another six Dovie Cups,

I promised myself . . . or more. Unfortunately, my wife did not share my resolve, and soon after she was gone, too. And while I might've predicted that end, it was Greta's actions that surprised me most."

Bending low, Sway read the tiny clipping about Gildersleeve's request to fly solo, then shook his head.

"I was confused at first," he continued. "Initially, I thought she'd simply lost her desire to win. But then I realized it was something else. Greta started to become confused, first making simple miscalculations, then critical lapses in judgment. I tried helping her—speaking to her honestly—even though it pained me to see a champion in decline. But whenever I did, she would accuse *me* of making mistakes, refusing to see that she was becoming not just a danger to herself, but others. Eventually, my only recourse was to end our partnership. And that is when the unexpected happened. Thomas came home."

Sway crossed to the table of origami and examined the rows.

"Naturally, I was thrilled by his return, especially when he agreed to be my copilot. I even proposed we begin our training immediately. But Thomas suggested that I might want to focus on something else first. Or . . . *somebody*."

"Landon," murmured Clara.

Sway nodded. "Of course, what my son neglected to tell me was that he'd already arranged to go flying with a family friend—to brush up on his piloting skills as some sort of surprise for me. The next morning, while I was watching my new grandson, Thomas and his wife went up in secret with Gildersleeve. An hour later, they crashed." Sway picked up one of Landon's doves and studied it, spinning it in his fingers, then lifted it high above his head and let it drop to the ground. "An *accident* . . . that's what authorities called it . . . a tragic fluke of an accident. But I knew better."

His eyes met Clara's as if searching for agreement.

"Why are you telling me this?" she asked.

"Because, Miss Poole, you should know how this ends."

"How's that?"

In one powerful sweep of his arm, Sway sent the paper birds swarming into the air. Clara flinched as one connected with her cheek.

"The same way it did for my son." He adjusted his coat, brushing the front, and marched to the elevator, trampling paper doves in his path. "When you see my grandson, tell him I was here looking for him. Tell him we have things to prepare for."

The elevator chimed and Sway boarded the carriage.

"Whatever you're planning, I won't let you do it," Clara

blurted out to his back. "I'll find proof, and then WOOBA will have to listen to me."

Sway faced her with an expression like pity. "Have you ever considered, Miss Poole, that I'm not the enemy—that maybe it is you who is rooting for the wrong side?"

"Where would you like to go?" chimed the elevator.

"To the balloon docks, please."

"The balloon docks are currently closed," responded the digital voice.

"Perfect."

CHAPTER TWENTY-ONE

PAPER BIRDS

AFTER RETURNING THE UNDAMAGED origami birds to the table, Clara sat trying to fix the ones Sway had trampled. She knew she'd never be able to make things perfect, but maybe she could make them better.

Sway's words still rang in her ears. *Was* she on the wrong side?

"Ouch." Clara shoved her finger into her mouth and tasted blood. "Stupid bird." She threw it as hard as she could and watched it bounce pathetically across the floor before stopping at the feet of a black-haired boy.

He bent down and picked it up, his face a mix of anger and confusion.

"Landon, I didn't see you," she said, wiping her eyes with her sleeve. "I tried my best to fix what I could."

"What have you done?"

"*Me?* Nothing."

"Then what's all this?"

"It wasn't me, I swear. Your grandfather crushed them when—"

"My grandfather? He was here?"

"Yes, he—"

"Did you tell him about this place?"

"No, of course not. I haven't told anyone. Don't you know? I'm grounded because I wouldn't tell your secret."

"Then he followed you."

"No. He was here when I came looking for you."

Landon surveyed the flattened birds that still lay scattered across the floor. "You need to go," he said shortly.

"Let me help. I can—"

"Don't."

"But I didn't do anything!"

"Yeah . . . looks that way."

"I'm being honest. Your grandfather was already here. He told me this long story about Gildersleeve—about *you*. Landon, he told me about your parents."

Landon paused for a moment, then continued picking up his origami.

"I didn't know," Clara said in a hushed voice. "I'm . . . sorry."

"Why?" he said, placing a pile on the table. "They died when I was a baby."

"But they're still your parents."

Landon shrugged. "They're just faces in photos."

"But don't you miss them?"

"I never knew them, okay?" He sat at the table and began reorganizing the rows. "You can go now."

"No, not until you tell me what's going on. Your grandfather said to tell you you had 'things to prepare for.' What does that mean?"

"How would I know?"

"Because he's your grandfather. I'm serious, Landon. I think he's planning on doing something really bad."

"Yeah, well, I think you have a big imagination."

"Me?" She picked up handfuls of paper and shook them at him. "I'm not the one folding animals out of old paper and making sculptures out of trash. I'm telling you, your grandfather is sabotaging balloons! What he did to *Brigadier Albert* was wrong. Next time, he might really hurt someone."

"Goodbye, Clara."

"What's your problem?"

Landon leaned back and studied her coolly. He looked

eerily like his grandfather. "Your mother's dead, too." It wasn't a question, but Clara nodded anyway. "But your father's not, even though you treat him like he is."

"I don't treat him that way."

"Oh really? I've watched you two talking. I've seen how you push him away like he's your enemy—or worse—like he's nobody. You know what I think, Clara? Maybe you stop worrying about my family and start focusing on yours."

"Landon, you have to—"

"No," he said, crossing to the elevator. "I don't have to do anything. For anyone." He pressed the call button, gestured for her to get on, then went back to work at the table.

She stood glaring at him as still and silent as one of his felt sculptures until the doors slid closed.

AS CLARA WATCHED the colors cycle through the elevator window, she tried to imagine anything else she could've said to make Landon believe her. Although, he'd said enough for them both—and then some. Now, she was back to square one.

The elevator dinged and the doors opened.

"Bakagari. At last!" exclaimed an out-of-breath Hatsu.

She rushed onto the carriage and threw herself at Clara. "I've been looking for you everywhere. Your father . . . he's on the way to your room."

"I thought you were covering for me?"

"I was. I cornered him on the observation deck, then the hallway, but after a while I ran out of things to say. And trust me, I said *everything*. If you don't beat him back to your room, you're—"

"Dead."

Clara quickly gave the order to the elevator, and it jumped to life. Hatsu slumped against the wall, exhausted.

"Bakagari? What are you holding?"

Clara looked down, realizing she was still clutching the papers she'd rattled at Landon. "I don't know. Old maps, I think."

She handed them to Hatsu, who flipped the pages over in her hands. "That's odd."

"What is?" mumbled Clara, trying not to picture her father's face when she stumbled into the room.

"Why do you have two different maps for Stage Three?"

"What do you mean?"

Hatsu handed them back and Clara flattened the maps on the wall with her palms. Together, they compared the sheets. Each plotted the racecourse for the Five Perils. Each showed the placement of the four flags. They were identical apart from one important detail. The elevations were completely different. Clara recognized the map pinned by her left hand as the same one she'd used during the stage.

"Look, there," said Hatsu, pointing. "The one on the left is missing the WOOBA seal. That must mean this other map is—"

"A fake. Hatsu, you're a genius. You found it!"

"While I do agree I'm a genius, what exactly have I found?"

"Proof! Landon said these maps were in his grandfather's cabin. That must've been why Sway was talking to that WOOBA official inside the Hive the other day—the one who handed out the updated race map. Sway must've swapped them, so the pilots had the wrong elevations. That's why no one could finish but him. That's why we crashed into the mountain when we went for the third flag. Everyone but Sway had bad maps."

Clara clutched the papers in a tight hug.

"So, what do we do now?" Hatsu asked.

"What do you think? We take these to Habberdish."

"Well, I'd get back to your room first, or you'll never see the light of day."

The elevator doors opened, and Clara ran like the wind

down the hallway, reaching her room moments before her father. Panting, she flopped into a chair and opened a copy of *WOOBA Quarterly* as he came through the door. "Oh, Dad. Hi," she said, still trying to catch her breath.

"Hi," he replied suspiciously. "Is something going on here?"

"Where? Here? No, nothing. I was . . . reading."

"Then why are you so flushed?"

"Am I? Hmm, maybe it's hot in here."

"You could try taking off your coat," he said slowly, walking into the room.

"Nah, I'm good. So . . . uh, what have *you* been doing?"

He raised an eyebrow slightly, and then gave a little shake of his head. "I've been talking with some of the pilots about the big stage coming up tomorrow. Have you been reviewing your notebook?"

"Oh yeah, I was just doing that earlier."

"Good," he replied, hanging his red cap on the hat rack. "So you're ready, then?"

Clara patted the maps inside her jacket pocket and grinned. There was nothing Sway could do now to stop her.

"Oh yeah. I'm *so* ready."

CHAPTER TWENTY-TWO

A DODGE-SIZE WRINKLE

THE KNOCK ON THE DOOR came at 5:28 a.m., well before the sun appeared over India or China or wherever in the world they were. Yawning, Clara took the envelope from the apologetic messenger standing in the hall, fell back on her bed, and removed the note inside.

> *Due to unforeseen issues, today's stage has been moved to Hong Kong. Please report to the observation deck at six a.m. for a mandatory briefing.*
>
> *Respectfully,*
> *Harold Habberdish*

"Hong Kong?"

"Long johns?" grumbled her father with a snore. "Check the bottom drawer."

"Dad, this letter says I have to go to a mandatory meeting."

"Yeah, yeah . . . a short story reading . . . You do that, honey."

Clara left him dreaming and hurried to the observation deck, where she found a cluster of bleary-eyed pilots slumped around the swimming pool, their unhappy expressions mirrored in the water's surface.

"Good morning, everyone," said a much-too-chipper Harold Habberdish. "My apologies for the early hour, but we've run into an unforeseen wrinkle—a permitting issue—with the Chinese government. In short, we have had to postpone our planned stage at Tianzi Mountain. But not to worry. I promise the situation will be remedied shortly. In the meantime, we have decided to relocate to Hong Kong to keep on track with our race schedule. As a precaution, I've asked our own PTSD instructor, Dodge Barlow, to oversee today's course and safety planning. Any questions?"

Most pilots, those not asleep in deck chairs, just blinked.

"Excellent," said Habberdish, clapping his hands. "Dodge can explain further. Oh, and speaking of wrinkles, it is my understanding that Dodge has added a few exciting ones himself. I'm sure you'll love them."

Clara heard Raylee gulp beside her, which was a fair reaction. *Wrinkle* in Barlow-speak meant *life-threatening.* But that was the least of her concerns.

"Mr. Habberdish, wait!" she yelled, racing after him.

"Ah, Clara. I'm sorry, but I'm afraid I can't speak now," he said, continuing on toward the helipad. "Off to meet with Chinese officials about this pesky permit issue."

"But I need to show you something."

"Yes, well, it will need to wait until my return. Best of luck in the next stage!" He flashed her a grin, then climbed into a helicopter, and a moment later, it was airborne.

"All right, muchachos. Let's gather round," yelled Dodge, rousing the sleeping pilots. "Now, I'm sure you're going to be as stoked as I am when you hear about the little sky party we have planned today. So hold on to your sombreros and Popsicles sticks, 'cause we're going to have a steeplechase!"

The pilots exchanged confused looks.

"A steeplechase?" echoed Clara.

"Sombreros and Popsicles sticks?" Alfie mumbled, rubbing his eyes.

"Yeah," mumbled Binder with a wide yawn, "I think you're mixing metaphors there."

Clara shook her head. "But what's a steeplechase?"

"It's a race with an obstacle course."

"Bingo, Binder!" said Dodge. "We've set up a floating network of obstacles all over the city. You'll need to fly over, under, through, and around them."

Clara frowned. "But aren't our balloons too big for that?"

"Excellent question, Miss Poole. But who said you'd be in regular balloons? No, ma'am. For this detour, you'll be flying sparrowhawks."

"Are you out of your mind?" barked Sir Wallace, still dressed in a long nightshirt.

"Well, sir, I have been doing quite a bit of introspection lately. Deep meditation to really connect with my inner self."

"I meant are you *mad*."

"Oh, no, sir. You see, I've learned to control any angry and anxious energy I have and put trust in the power of positive thinking. Like I say, 'Always good to have ripe melon, then bad vibes swellin'.' Keep a bit of Pura Vida in the soul."

Sir Wallace opened his mouth to respond when Raylee, who'd been chewing her fingernails to stubs, interrupted. "Excuse me, Mr. Barlow, but what exactly is a sparrow-hawk?"

"Only one of the coolest inventions aeronautics has ever

had to offer. I actually use them quite a bit at my day job."

Clara tried hard not to imagine what other occupational terrors the PTSD instructor could perform on a daily basis.

"Sparrowhawks are one-person training balloons," explained Dodge, "except they're much faster than the airships you've been flying in the race so far."

Raylee raised her hand. "Excuse me, Mr. Barlow, but wouldn't they need to be nimble enough as well to navigate this steeplechase thing you're describing?"

"Primo point, Miss Price, which brings me to that wrinkle we mentioned."

"You mean, you haven't gotten to it yet?" Raylee began gnawing on her other hand.

"I am stoked to announce that Mr. Habberdish has agreed to lift the ban on technology for this one stage. And that means you can all use—"

"Jets!" exclaimed Hatsu, her eyes sparkling.

Raylee gulped so hard that Clara looked to make sure the girl hadn't accidentally swallowed her hand.

"This is insane," Sir Wallace protested. "I haven't flown in a sparrowhawk since I was in school. I doubt I could even fit in one now."

"Maybe *you* can't, sir . . . but Ophelia can. But don't

worry. Those of you who need practice will have all day to work out the kinks. We race tonight!"

The adults exchanged nervous glances and then eyed their children. Those who did not have children appeared even more anxious as they contemplated jamming themselves into the tiny baskets. Only Satomi Hoshi seemed excited as she gave her daughter a high five.

Hatsu tugged on the ears of her hat. "Time to party," she said with a grin.

CHAPTER TWENTY-THREE

ROMAN CANDLE

CLARA STARED AT THE FLEET of one-person balloons lining a series of floating docks, most of which had been claimed already. Dodge walked from berth to berth, checking that pilots were buckled tightly into their tiny baskets like a man who actually knew something about safety.

At the far end of the dock, an empty sparrow hawk bobbed in the breeze. Compared to the others, it was ancient. In fact, it looked as much a relic as *Amelia*.

"Mr. Barlow, is this thing safe?" Clara asked.

"Cheah, absolutely. Like I said before, I use these puppies every day." Dodge slapped the rim of the basket, which snapped off, leaving a chunk of dry wicker in his hand. "Well, maybe, yours is a tad older. No worries, though. I'll, uh, fix that later."

He threw aside the broken piece and gave Clara a not-so-reassuring thumbs-up. Clara climbed into the basket one foot at a time, testing the floor's sturdiness before lowering her full weight onto it.

"These things are so cute!" exclaimed Hatsu from the berth beside her.

Clara examined the large engine strapped to the back, which was nearly as big as the basket itself. The word *cute* did not come to mind. "They look . . . powerful."

"I know!" said Hatsu, almost euphorically. "That's why they've put those nose cones on the fronts of the envelopes and reinforced the uprights. Otherwise, the balloons would collapse from the force, and crash."

"What's going to crash?" Raylee sat trembling on Hatsu's other side, looking very much like a mouse strapped to a rocket ship.

"Don't worry, Raylee," said Hatsu. "You'll figure it out."

"I will? I don't think I will. In fact, I'm pretty positive I won't."

Clara smiled, trying to look reassuring, then disengaged from the berth. As she rose above the docks, the last rays of sun vanished, and the Hong Kong night came alive in a buzz of neon. Skyscrapers shot up like giant matchsticks, disappearing into the clouds.

There was a whir of rotors, and then a fleet of drones appeared. They pushed the sparrowhawks toward the starting line, above which hung an unfortunately unpleasant advertisement: TONIGHT'S STAGE IS SPONSORED BY WIBBLE BIBBLE BUBBLE GUM. TRY OUR NEW SRIRACHA YOGURT FLAVOR!

Something suddenly thumped under Clara's seat—a wild pounding—and then a hairy leg emerged, followed by a second. Clara scowled, stooping to drag out the stowaway.

"Houdini, what are you doing here?"

The monkey shrugged sheepishly.

"What, are you jealous you couldn't pilot this stage?" She paused. "Wait. That's not a bad idea. Have you ever flown one of these things before?"

Houdini nodded eagerly.

"Well, that makes one of us. Can you fly as well as Mayhem?"

He gibbered back, as if the question was not only obvious but insulting.

"Okay, calm down. Just promise me you won't kill us, okay?"

Houdini jumped into action. He pushed a white button on the console, and the sails telescoped out sideways like wings. Then, he pushed another, a red button with a flame symbol on it. The engine coughed to life, rumbling the basket, and making Clara feel more like she was inside a dragster than a hot-air balloon.

A small speaker affixed to the basket by Clara's side crackled to life. "Hello, WOOBA!" yelled a familiar voice. A moment later, Clara watched Guy Gerard materialize on a balcony at the starting line, dressed all in white. Fans cheered, waving pennants from the decks of the *Zephyrus*. "Welcome to the electrifying city of Hong Kong—Asia's World City—which hosts one of the largest collections of skyscrapers found in the world. Before we begin this special nighttime stage, I must first thank all the well-wishers who sent me such rousing get-well cards during my recent sudden illness."

"Try tantrum," scoffed Clara.

"But even more than that, we must all give an enormous thanks to our very own Dodge Barlow, whose creative genius and safety-first thinking made tonight's race possible." Dodge appeared next to the announcer. "So, Dodge, anything to say about the course before we begin?"

"Only that it's going to be totally epic," he exclaimed, raising two thumbs. "Oh, and that you might want to move quickly past the Roman candle. That obstacle is still a bit unpredictable."

"What's a Roman candle?" Clara asked Binder, who hovered nearby.

"I don't think we want to know."

"Okay, here are the rules," Guy called. "On my signal, you'll race in a figure eight around the heart of downtown four times. Along the way, you'll encounter a series of obstacles, some designed by Dodge, and others, landmarks such as the Arch, Hong Kong's famous skyscraper."

"This is completely mental," Binder mumbled.

"It's madness!" groused a familiar voice. A sour-faced Wallace Chins-Ratton sat crammed into his tiny basket, which creaked each time he moved. (Apparently, he liked his chances better than his daughter's.) And he wasn't the only adult in a sparrowhawk.

"Stupida mongolfiera," spat Alberto Furio. He banged on his controls, trying to get his sails to open. "Non capisco! Work!"

"Pilots, are you ready?" Guy called. "Get set! Go!"

Engines growled, blazing with bursts of flames, and the sparrowhawks shot from the starting line into the night. Clara caught a glimpse of bear ears before they disappeared in a blur.

"Eat my dust, Bakagari!" screamed Hatsu as she blazed ahead.

"And Hatsu Hoshi of Team Ussuri flies into the lead," crackled the announcer's voice. "That little girl is quite a competitor, isn't she, Dodge?"

"I'd say! You should see her after she's had sugar!"

Clara's basket tore forward, pressing her into the back of her seat as Houdini clutched the controls.

"Clara Poole of Team Amelia moves into second place behind . . . Wait a moment. What's on her lap? Is that . . . *a monkey?*"

"Or a very small, hairy man," said Dodge with absolute seriousness.

"Er . . . thanks, Dodge. Now, in third place—wow, here's a surprise—Landon Sway of Team Providence!"

Clara craned her neck to see Landon through the blistered air. He was yelling and waving urgently.

"I can't hear you," she shouted.

Houdini slammed his foot on a pedal on the basket floor and followed Hatsu through the gaping hole of a skyscraper.

"That's the Arch," explained Dodge, "which some think is modeled after the Arc de Triomphe in Paris. Unfortunately, the city wouldn't allow us to install too many fireworks on that one."

"Fireworks?" Guy asked. "What fireworks?"

As Clara cleared the Arch, the sky exploded in a trail

of golden comets, and a thousand high-pitched screams pierced the air.

"That's called a palm," said Dodge excitedly, "characterized by the long tendrils that fall like palm trees. We put in extra spoonfuls of whistle mix to make it really festive."

How about safe? thought Clara, patting out a small fire on the edge of the basket.

Hatsu arced around a tall building and headed for a floating tower at the city's edge.

"We've also placed chrysanthemums at the end of each loop," Dodge continued.

"And what do those do?" Guy asked as a sphere of colorful stars erupted next to Clara. Houdini swerved through the rain of sparks, keeping tight on Hatsu's tail.

Landon was still in hot pursuit and still waving at her madly.

"Now, Dodge, I must ask: As a safety instructor, are these large explosions . . . safe?"

"That's a great question, Guy. If I had to answer, I'd say . . . *kinda?*"

KA-BOOM! The heavens flashed red and sizzled in a crisscrossing pattern of hot stars.

"Oh, that's a crosette," said Dodge cheerfully.

KA-BLAM!

Clara flinched as a second set of shells detonated around them.

"And that one's called a ring because of the halo it makes. See the smiley face in the middle?"

You *fly through this and see if you're smiling!*

Landon suddenly appeared on Clara's right, yelling and waving.

"I can't hear you," she shouted back as Houdini piloted the sparrowhawk through a downpour of flickering stars.

Dodge let out an excited whistle. "Isn't it so cool the way that one flitters and falls. It's called a horsetail."

"Indeed." Guy cleared his throat. "But which was the one you were saying was unpredicta—"

KA-BOOOOOOM!

A firehose of stars spewed from the tower ahead of the racers. Houdini banked hard, drafting close to Hatsu's sparrowhawk through the blast as flaming balls the size of elephants shot out like multicolored cannon fire.

"Oh, no," Dodge moaned. "It's doing it again."

"What's doing what?" asked Guy.

"The Roman candle. It's . . . malfunctioning."

Spectators aboard the *Zephyrus* screamed and ran for cover as fireballs arched across the night sky. One of the burning globes extinguished itself in the observation deck's swimming pool, sending a bath of steam hissing into the air. Dodge ducked as another rocketed over the starting line, dumping a trail of ash on Guy Gerard and his white suit.

"Make it stop!" screamed Guy.

"I can't," hollered Dodge. "It . . . needs to do its thing."

"And how long will *that* take?"

"A while?"

Houdini chased Hatsu around the racecourse over the span of three loops, the wreckage of sparrowhawks littering the sky. Some pilots had abandoned ship, while others, like Raylee, had taken shelter underneath the belly of the *Zephyrus*. Alberto Furio, who still hadn't solved his issue with his sails, sat fuming at the starting line. The only other competitor was Landon, and he seemed less concerned about winning than he was about catching up to Clara. Once again, he came alongside her, this time making strange gestures with his hands.

"What are you doing?" she yelled.

He lifted one arm above his head and scratched it, then bent his other arm down and scratched at his side.

He looked like a monkey.

"Monkey?" she shouted. "Is that what you mean?"

He nodded enthusiastically and began making letter-shapes with his hands. *T . . . R . . . A . . .* and an unmistakable *P.*

"*Trap?*" called Clara, confused.

Landon nodded again and then held up his index fingers and brought them together.

"Eleven!" she shouted.

He rolled his eyes and then repeated the gesture.

"Oh . . . I get it. Put the two words together. Monkey . . . trap . . . *Monkey trap?*"

Landon's eyes went wide. He put his finger on his nose and mouthed the word *bingo*, then pointed to himself, before lifting a flattened hand above his head.

"You?" she called with a confused shrug. Playing charades at high speed while being bombarded by pyrotechnics was quickly becoming Clara's least favorite game. "Tall you? Growing you? A *really* tall you?"

Landon knocked his head against the edge of the basket in frustration.

KA-BLAM!

The world went white and hot, and for a split second, Clara saw her mother's shocked face. Slowly, nighttime returned in a frizzle of sparks. Houdini barked angrily as Landon rocketed by into second place, spinning like an out-of-control top.

"Yikes . . . ," said Dodge sheepishly. "Guess we packed a little too much powder into that one."

The Roman candle had finally extinguished itself, its end smoldering like a tired siege gun. Clara watched Hatsu and Landon disappear into its black cloud before being consumed herself. Her eyes burned, and she gasped for air. Houdini chattered loudly, obviously angry with himself for falling into third place.

As they emerged from the smoke, Clara spotted Hatsu rocketing toward the finish line. There was no chance anyone would catch her now. Landon, however, didn't seem interested in following. In fact, if Clara wasn't mistaken, it appeared that he was trying to wave her back.

"Look at that little girl go," Guy Gerard exclaimed. "Say, Dodge, do you know why she wears that funny bear hat?"

"I don't, Guy. Tell me."

"No, I was being serious. I have no clue why. It's weird if you ask me."

"You're weird!" yelled Hatsu as she rocketed beneath them to victory.

A LINE OF DEMOLISHED sparrowhawks clogged the path back to the dock. A few looked repairable. Others, no better than kindling. Covered in soot and ash, the traumatized pilots inside them could have been easily mistaken for coal miners.

Clara and Houdini waited at the back of the line. She was eager to find Landon and demand he explain whatever it was he'd been trying to tell her. But as they approached the dock, she saw Godfrey Sway pulling him by the arm toward the transfer shuttle back to the *Zephyrus*, speaking forcefully into his ear. Sway paused as a group of WOOBA officials disembarked onto the dock. He exchanged a word with the first one, then quickly ushered Landon onto the transfer.

Houdini shrieked.

"I know," grumbled Clara. "I wanted to speak to him, too."

The next moment, the little monkey scampered between her legs, trying to squeeze himself back under the seat.

"Stop it, dummy," she scolded. "You'll get stuck again," She pulled the monkey free, but it was like fighting a bag of cats. "Ouch!"

Houdini pawed her face, and when she let go, he leap-frogged from one sparrowhawk to another, and then onto the farthest dock.

"There it is, over there," yelled one of the WOOBA officials. "Get it before it escapes again."

Monkey trap!

Suddenly, Landon's puzzle made sense. Clara studied the men on the dock. They weren't officials. They were animal control.

"Close off its exit," yelled another man, holding a large cage.

The men gathered at the head of the gangplank as Houdini paced frantically. The one with the cage set it down, opening the door as the others extended long poles with loops on the ends. Slowly, they eased down the dock toward the monkey.

"Go ahead," ordered the cage handler. "It's not going anywhere."

The animal control men rushed the monkey, who flashed his teeth and then leaped off the edge.

"Houdini!" screamed Clara. She clambered out from her basket and ran down the dock, pushing past the men to where Houdini had disappeared.

"It . . . jumped," said one of the men behind her.

"Well, at least we caught the other two," said the cage handler. "They won't be biting anybody else now."

The men left Clara staring over the edge.

"Houdini!" she screamed, tears streaming from her face. "Houdini!"

He didn't answer. No one did, not even the wind. The

lights of Hong Kong merely twinkled back with cruel ambivalence.

She felt a hand on her shoulder. "Clara?"

"He's . . . gone."

"Clara, can you come with me, please?" said Ms. Lemot gently.

"Those men . . . they were trying to trap him. Why?"

"Please, Clara. Mr. Habberdish is waiting for you."

"One of the men said they caught the others. Were they talking about Bob and Mayhem?"

"Mr. Habberdish will explain."

"Explain what? Why can't you tell me?"

"Please," urged Ms. Lemot. "Mr. Habberdish is waiting in your room with your father."

"Ms. Lemot, what's going on?"

CHAPTER TWENTY-FOUR

THE CHEATER REVEALED

C LARA SILENTLY FOLLOWED Ms. Lemot as they snaked down the hallway toward her room, still trying to understand what was happening. When they arrived, Clara found her door open and her father sitting with Harold Habberdish, and, shockingly, the Chins-Rattons.

"Thank you, Ophelia," said Habberdish solemnly. "You can go now."

The girl stood and curtsied, then walked to the door.

"What's going on?" Clara asked as OCR passed her.

"You're a liar, that's what."

"Clara," said Habberdish softly, "join us, please."

"I'd so hate to be you right now," whispered Ophelia. "Then again, I'd always hate to be you." She flung her pony-tail over her shoulder and marched out the door.

Clara turned to the others. "*What is going on?* There were people at the docks with cages and poles. They tried to take Houdini, and then he—"

"Please sit," said Habberdish. He sounded colder than usual, and he kept his gaze fixed on his lap. "Clara, it's come to our attention that someone's been cheating to gain an advantage in the race."

"I know. That's what I was trying to tell you on the helicopter pad before you flew off to—"

"It would be best if you listened. These allegations are quite serious. There have been claims of not only deception, but sabotage, putting other pilots' safety at grave risk."

"I just said—that's what I've been trying to tell—"

"Clara, please empty your pockets."

"What?"

"Your pockets," repeated Habberdish. "Empty them."

She looked from Habberdish to Sir Wallace, who held out a silver tray, and then to her father. "Dad?"

"Just do what he's asking," he said quietly.

Clara frowned, then unbuttoned her jacket and removed Barnaby Bixley's compass, placing it on the tray.

Sir Wallace snatched it. "And whose is this?"

"It's mine," Clara insisted, grabbing it back.

"*Yours?* I highly doubt that. It looks expensive. Where did you get it?"

"From Mr. Bixley at WOOBATech."

"Please, Wallace, let me handle this," said Habberdish. "Clara, is that everything?"

"No. I have two race maps from the Five Perils. But one has—"

"Aha!" exclaimed Sir Wallace, ripping the maps from her hand. "Just as I told you, Habberdish. Godfrey said she'd have these." He waggled a menacing finger an inch from Clara's nose. "Undeniable proof that you're the saboteur!"

"*Me?* I didn't make those! Sway did."

"Yes, yes, Godfrey said you'd say that, too. I'll give the girl this, Habberdish. She's got pluck. I bet you thought you had us all hoodwinked." Sir Wallace poked the tip of her nose with his fat finger.

Clara swatted it aside. "Don't touch me."

"After Ophelia told me about your little scheme to frame Godfrey, I went to see him myself. Known the man for decades. A great pilot, and even greater champion. To level blame on such a decorated man, why it's—"

Habberdish held up his hand. "Clara, Godfrey Sway visited me earlier today. He was visibly distraught, but after some cajoling, he admitted catching you in the act."

"Like distributing false information about the racecourse for example!" barked Sir Wallace.

"What are you talking about? Mr. Habberdish, I promise, Sway came to the Hive right before the—"

"Godfrey said he tried to reason with you, but you refused to listen—that perhaps the Face of the Race business had gone to your head. He claimed you even tricked the Hoshi girl into distracting him while you snuck around the balloon docks after hours."

"Hatsu wasn't distracting him," Clara spat. "She was following him to make sure he didn't do anything dangerous!"

"Clara, you should know that Godfrey wants you to succeed," Habberdish insisted. "Which is why he said he tried to convince you to stop one last time. But when he went to speak with you, you set those monkeys on him."

"I wasn't even there! And Bob was protecting *Amelia* from *him*!"

"How do we know for sure?" grumbled Sir Wallace. "And these maps? How do you explain them, eh? No wonder I couldn't get through the Five Perils."

"Neither could we," Clara snapped. "*Amelia* crashed into

the side of the mountain, and we almost froze, remember?"

"A ploy, no doubt, to make the deception all the more convincing. After all, you did finish second."

Clara turned to her father with a silent plea, but he just stared at his feet. "I'm telling the truth!" she shouted. "Go to the ballroom right now. You'll find Landon there making origami out of these same maps. There are stacks of them, exactly like the ones Sir Wallace is holding. Landon told me he got them from his grandfather's cabin aboard *Providence*. I swear, Sway swapped them out with the official ones. I saw him do it with my own eyes."

"More lies," bellowed Sir Wallace.

"I'm not lying! Ask Landon!"

Habberdish placed his hand on her shoulder. "Clara, we went to the ballroom right after Ophelia informed her father. There was nothing there apart from old furniture covered in dustcloths."

"No . . . that's . . . not right." The room suddenly blurred. Habberdish was still speaking, but she only heard ringing in her head. Closing her eyes, she tried to quiet the noise, searching for some shred that might prove to them she was telling the truth.

"I'm going to ask that you stop all this nonsense," Habberdish said firmly. "Godfrey Sway is an upstanding member of our community. Now, your father mentioned you suffered a great loss, and that maybe the stress of the spotlight has been too much for you. As you are our Face of the Race, I'm willing to look past this incident, but only if you promise to stop making trouble. And that you stay away from Godfrey Sway."

"But I'm telling the truth! I swear, Mr. Habberdish, Sway will do whatever it takes to win. He wants Gildersleeve out of the race. He hates her. He blames her for his son dying. Please, he's trying to tear our team apart. He sent those men after the monkeys."

Habberdish cleared his throat. "No, Clara, Sway didn't send those men. I did."

Anger boiled inside her. "*You?* Then . . . you know about Houdini. You know he jumped off the dock trying to escape those . . . those awful men."

"I'm aware of the accident, yes. I assure you, that wasn't meant to happen."

"It wasn't an accident!"

"The other monkeys have been taken to quarantine. I was wrong to let Gildersleeve fly with them. I see that now."

"No, *this* is wrong. You don't believe me because I'm a kid. But I'm telling you, Godfrey Sway is a liar, and I'll prove it!"

Habberdish rose suddenly, and as he did, any softness in his demeanor evaporated. "I'll say this one more time, Miss Poole: keep away from Godfrey Sway or your time racing here is over."

"Well . . . ," grunted Chins-Ratton, struggling to his feet. "It seems we're finished here. Shall we get on with it, then? I've still got a race to win."

"Yes, Wallace, I suppose we should be on our way," murmured Habberdish. He straightened his blazer and followed the aristocrat out the door, leaving Clara alone with her father.

"This is my fault," he said quietly, his gaze still fixed on the floor. "I should never have let you do this race. This is much too much for you."

"No," Clara said. "It might be too much for you, but it's not for me. I'm not lying and I'm not giving up. Just because you've decided to—just because you want us to live life in a bubble, doesn't mean I have to. So go ahead. Believe what you want. Or you can decide to believe in me. Because that's what fathers are supposed to do."

He looked up, and opened his mouth to speak, but Clara wasn't finished. "And you can't ground me, either. We're thousands of feet in the air."

With that, she stormed out the door.

CHAPTER TWENTY-FIVE

MOUNTAINS OF TRUTH

LEADERBOARD
AFTER STAGE 5
1ST - Providence, 44 PTS

2ND - Ussuri, 24 PTS

3RD - Amelia, 23 PTS

CLARA LEANED AGAINST THE BAY window at the end of the Hive, staring out at a sea of clouds. She'd spent the night there tossing and turning under an old blanket she'd found aboard *Amelia*, using her father's notebook as a pillow. Hatsu had been the first to find her there the next morning, and not long after, the boys and Raylee had joined, too.

"So, Sway really accused you of cheating, huh?" said Binder.

"Brutal," added Alfie. "I mean it's a masterstroke of evil, but still, brutal."

Clara nodded. "I guess news travels fast."

"It does when OCR blabs it all over the docks," Binder replied, grinning.

Raylee rolled her eyes. "I still can't believe she ratted you out like that."

"That's what Chins-*Ratt*ons do," said Alfie. "What I wanna know, though, is what Clara's going to do now?"

Binder shook his head. "Don't you mean, what *we're* going to do. I, for one, am not going to just stand by and let Sway get away with this."

Clara shook her head. "Really, that's nice to say, but Habberdish said if I go anywhere near Sway, I'm out of the race."

"Fine. Then don't." Binder rubbed his hands together. "Leave it to us."

"Yeah," said Alfie, nodding. "It's not like Binder or I have any chance of winning this thing. Let us handle Sway."

"Guys, I don't think that's a good idea. You could get in serious trouble."

Binder raised an eyebrow. "Uh . . . have you met us? Trouble is what we do. Besides, I wanna see Sway's face when you beat him."

"I'm in, too," chirped Raylee. "Especially if getting in trouble means I get to go home."

"That's the spirit, Raylee! You're a rebel now."

"Yeah . . . I'm a rebel. . . ."

Binder clapped the mousy-faced girl on the shoulder. "Then it's settled. Clara will focus on beating Sway, and we'll make sure that he doesn't do anything underhanded."

"What about the monkeys?" Clara asked. "Habberdish said they were taken to quarantine. Wherever that is?"

"I know!" said Alfie, bouncing. "It's next to the cargo hold."

"Sounds like we need to pay a visit," said Binder with a wink.

Hatsu, who had been uncharacteristically quiet, stood and placed her hands on the window. "Whoa . . . is that Tianzi?"

The kids turned and looked at the army of knifelike peaks emerging from a blanket of fog.

"It's like another planet," murmured Binder.

Raylee snatched the notebook off Clara's lap and flipped frantically until she reached the section on China. "It says here that Tianzi is made of dead mountains."

"I'm sorry, but how exactly does a mountain die?"

"Good question," she replied, flipping to the next page.

"Okay, here . . . Over a billion years ago the crust of the earth started rising up, pushing mountains out from the ocean. They wore away over millions more years, turning into the rock towers we see today—those rock towers. Supposedly, the tallest one is three times taller than the Empire State Building! And it's never been . . ."

"Been . . . ?" prodded Binder, waggling a hand in her face. "Earth to Raylee? Been what?"

She closed the book and handed it back to Clara as the silhouette of even taller peaks punctured the mist. "It says it's never been charted for balloons."

"Alrighty then," exclaimed Binder with a single clap. "Have fun dying, everyone!"

No one replied. Not even Alfie had one of his clever retorts. They all just sat in silence, staring into the distance, until the hangar's clock chimed, announcing the start of the stage. One by one they scattered. All except Clara, who turned from the window and watched Gildersleeve across the causeway working alone on deck. Clara wasn't sure whether she could face her. What could she possibly say to the old woman about the monkeys?

"Don't hide in the shadows, child. It's only us today. I hope you're ready to put that ridiculous pilot training of yours to use."

Clara blinked. *Is that it?*

"Are you coming or not?" scolded Gildersleeve.

"Oh, uh, of course."

Clara climbed aboard while Gildersleeve continued through her usual preflight preparations. "Well, don't stand there, child. Check the tanks and then make sure the lines are in order."

Clara gazed high into the rigging and paused, thinking about Houdini.

"Now or never," grumbled Gildersleeve.

Clara jumped to work, topping off the fuel tanks and climbing into the hammocks to inspect the lines. It felt good to be busy, a much-needed distraction from the ugly thoughts swirling in her mind. She looked down at the old pilot standing at the helm and tried to picture her in Sway's story. She was odd, for sure, but not crazy. And she was definitely grouchy, though all the other pilots seemed to like her well enough. But was she dangerous? That was the real question. So far, Clara hadn't seen anything to make her believe that. In fact, she'd only seen the opposite.

Gildersleeve released air from the deflation port, and they dipped into a thick soup of fog. Clara could barely see her hand in front of her face, let alone the balloons around her, but she could sense them from the occasional creak of a rope or disturbance in the mist. "Are we really going to fly through this?" she asked.

"It appears so."

"Why can't we just fly over it?"

"Because Harold Habberdish demands a spectacle. But don't worry, I know where I'm going."

"I heard Tianzi's never been charted for balloons."

"I doubt it has."

"Then . . . how do you know where to go?"

"Because I lived here once."

Before Clara could ask anything more, Guy Gerard's amplified voice rose from nowhere. "Good morning, everyone! As you may have noticed already, it's a touch foggy today. In fact, I have no idea where any of you are, so I am going to make this simple: Go!"

Gildersleeve adjusted the sails, and moments later, the first sandstone tower rose from the fog. Trees clung impossibly to tiny rock ledges, bursting with brilliant pink blooms. They seemed like they were from some alien world. The tower disappeared as quickly as it had appeared, slipping back into the mist like a stone phantom.

"That was only a small one," murmured Gildersleeve.

The crack of wicker signaled other pilots nearby, and

Clara caught a fleeting glimpse of one of *Primrose*'s flower boxes off the starboard side. A second later, there was the crash of boulders tumbling behind them.

"We're okay!" came the all-too-familiar voice of Norman Newlin.

"Child, get to the lookout," ordered Gildersleeve. "Things are about to get tight."

Clara scaled the rope ladder as another rock tower appeared off the starboard side only feet away.

"Use one of the poles to fend us off," Gildersleeve shouted up to her.

Clara chose the longest from those resting in the hammocks and readied herself as the next tower came into view. She pressed it into the sandstone pillar and pushed the balloon away. Suddenly, the memory of Houdini poking away floating lanterns flooded her mind.

"Too much," yelled Gildersleeve.

Another tower emerged on the port side, and the balloon drove into the mountain. It ricocheted off the sandstone pillar, raining pebbles down onto Clara's head.

"Ow," she hollered.

"Quick now—another—starboard side!"

Clara scrambled across the hammocks and pressed her pole into the next rock face with all her might. Again, the balloon hit the rock tower and bounced off. They were coming too quickly.

"Move faster," called Gildersleeve. "If a monkey can do this, then so can you."

"I'm trying."

"Well, try harder."

Clara channeled her inner Houdini, pushing away the thought that he should be the one there doing this. After a few more attempts, she found her rhythm. Her steps became lighter, and she sprang from side to side across the webbing nearly as nimble as her lost friend. She hoped he'd be proud.

After negotiating a dozen more towers, her shoulders burning from her efforts, she heard the sound of rushing water. The fog thinned and the canyon floor emerged, a thread of green water weaving below surrounded by a riot of pink and purple.

"It's like a fairy tale."

"That is the Golden Whip Stream," said Gildersleeve. "We can follow it to the finish line." She trimmed the sails and guided *Amelia* through an opening beneath an enormous land bridge. The air was suddenly a blur of pink and yellow.

Clara watched as shapes fluttered and fell in lazy loops. "What kind of birds are those?"

"They're not birds," answered Gildersleeve. "They're moon moths."

One landed on the railing of the basket. It was easily as big as Clara's hand, with huge orange-sherbet-colored wings and an elegant split tail that corkscrewed at the ends.

"I've never seen a moth with a tail like that."

"It's for protection. They disturb the air, confusing the bats that hunt them using echolocation. Better to lose one's tail than one's head."

"You seem to know a lot about them."

"I told you, I lived here," said Gildersleeve. "This is where the monkeys found me."

Clara blinked. "Don't you mean where *you* found the monkeys?"

"I think I know what I said." Gildersleeve repositioned the sails again, and *Amelia* caught the breeze. "I was living not too far from here, high in the northern mountains. It was a place so remote, it could only be reached by foot or air—not a soul for a hundred miles. That was until the night I woke to an odd disturbance in my kitchen. I grabbed my walking stick and tiptoed down the hallway to find the room in shambles—chairs toppled, cupboards flung open, and dry goods spilled all over the floor. I'd been ransacked, but by what I didn't know. Only that whatever it was had left a trail of floury footprints out the window. The next night, the thief came again, and once more, I crept down the hall, stick in hand, to defend myself. This time I caught a flash of something golden disappearing out the window. My kitchen looked like the dog's breakfast."

"It was a dog?" asked Clara, confused.

"No, no, the dog's breakfast—it means the room was a mess. Anyhow, I refused to have it happen again, so the next night I camped out in the shadows, waiting. It was a dark night, too—not even a sliver of moon—when black hands appeared on the windowsill, followed by three alien faces. They slipped in like assassins, the largest of them keeping watch at my bedroom door while the others looted the cabinets. I sprang at them, brandishing my stick and shouting bloody murder. The beasts shrieked and fled, but the big one, scared out of its wits, ran straight into the doorsill and collapsed in a heap. I jumped on it, pressed my stick into its hairy throat, and yelled, 'You monsters think you can steal from me?' It blinked back, terrified, and I realized it was far from a monster. The poor creature's face was sunken, its body emaciated."

Gildersleeve paused as a light rain began to fall. She checked for other balloons in the vicinity, then gave Clara a poncho from the box by the helm. Gildersleeve pulled hers over her head before continuing.

"I had been to the city a month before—my usual trip for supplies—where I'd heard reports of unusual animal sightings. Colonies of monkeys were being displaced, driven from their homes by farmers burning the forests for land, or killed by poachers. I had never seen any monkeys so far north, but here they were, pillaging my little house on the mountainside."

Clara pulled the hood of her poncho forward as the rain fell harder, but not enough that she couldn't see Gildersleeve. "So, what did you do?" she asked, riveted.

"I fed them, of course. Pancakes. Stacks and stacks of pancakes. It seemed I couldn't make enough. At first, only the big one was bold enough to eat. The thing gorged himself while the others lingered outside the window. But eventually, their fear gave way to hunger, and they joined in the feast. After that, I had three semiconscious monkeys sprawled on my kitchen floor, bellies fat with batter. That morning, I went to the city to restock, thinking they'd move on when they came to, but when I returned, they were seated at my kitchen table as if they were guests at a dinner party. I chased them from the house, but they perched in the branches outside, then slowly crept back in after a while. I tried banging pots and pans, but it didn't seem to scare them. I even sprayed them with water, but they just thought it was a game. Eventually, I gave up."

Clara thought of Bob aboard *Ussuri* and chuckled. "But how did you train them to be pilots?"

"Train them? I didn't. Those beasts are natural aeronauts. But that's another story."

"Please," said Clara. "Don't stop."

Gildersleeve sighed, pulled the witch hairs on her chin, and shut one eye. "Oh dear, it must've been September, because the finches were migrating. I remember sitting on my porch watching the birds' silhouettes dart past the moon and feeling something stir inside me—an urge I thought I'd long since buried. Yet, there it was, rising up as natural as breath. *Fly*, it whispered. *Fly*. The next morning, I left for the city. I had an acquaintance there who was hanging up his piloting hat and taking up the business of trading aeronautical antiquities. He was selling his balloon—this balloon. Strange fellow. . . . Had a passion for alliteration: Barnaby Bixley's Balloon Bazaar and something . . ."

"Other Big Baubles?"

Gildersleeve raised an eyebrow. "I see you've met."

"Are you telling me *Amelia* belonged to Barnaby Bixley?"

"Yes, but she had another name then. *Findley Fiddlesticks* or *Dudley Doolittle* . . . I can't remember. In any case, I loaded my belongings on board and waved farewell to the monkeys. 'Paris is not a place for you,' I told them.

The little monsters were inconsolable—refused to let me go. But in the end, I managed to climb into the basket and release the anchor line. I was miles away before I realized three monkeys were clinging to it. Houdini was the first on deck, and he made his way immediately to the lookout. Mayhem and Bob followed—they were fascinated with the sails and steering apparatus. Mayhem hopped onto the big monkey's shoulders and took the helm as if he'd done so a thousand times before. They pulled this and pushed that, watching the balloon change direction and elevation. I was awestruck—they were complete naturals. The rest, as they say, is history."

As Gildersleeve wrapped up her story, the skies opened, shafts of light piercing the mist. Far in the distance the *Zephyrus* hovered near the finish line.

"Ms. Gildersleeve, you never said why you came to Tianzi in the first place."

"To escape. To heal—maybe both."

The pair was silent for a long time. Eventually, Gildersleeve spoke.

"Go ahead, child. I can tell you have a question burning inside you."

"Oh, um, it's just that Godfrey Sway told me a story. . . ."

The old pilot raised an eyebrow again. "Did he?"

"Yes. About you . . . and . . . an accident."

Gildersleeve frowned. "I doubt he used the word *accident*."

"No, not exactly. He told me he was watching Landon, and you went flying with Landon's parents and . . . and something terrible happened. . . . That his son, Thomas, died."

Gildersleeve remained silent.

"Is it true?"

The old pilot shifted in her seat, then let out a small huff. "I hadn't planned on telling so many stories today. True, you ask? The simple answer is *yes*, but it's far from the whole truth. I'm sure Godfrey failed to tell you about Thomas's wife?"

"No, he didn't really talk about her."

"Well . . . her name was Amelia. And she was my daughter."

Clara's jaw fell open, but no words came out.

"Amelia was a bit older than Thomas, but when they were young, they played together in the hangars, climbing the mooring towers like jungle gyms, playing hide-and-seek among the balloons. She wasn't much like me, apart from her iron will, and ballooning held no interest for her. Her love was art and history and books. Most of the year, she lived in Cambridge with her father, whom I was estranged from, but she'd visit whenever I was nearby. One fall, her university break coincided with the start of the air race. I agreed to meet her at the train station and take her to the opening ceremonies. Godfrey and I were being honored for some achievement—what, I forget—and we planned to celebrate that night. I remember Amelia walking down the platform that day, her arm in Thomas's. No longer were they children playing on the docks. But I knew instantly they were in love."

Gildersleeve fired the burner as the balloon floated under another land bridge, and a blur of moths colored the air once again.

"Naturally, I was delighted about the union, and I expected Godfrey would be, as well, but he cared nothing for Thomas's aspirations—only his own. So, when Thomas announced he was returning to Cambridge with Amelia, Godfrey practically spat fire. 'A betrayal,' he called it, accusing Thomas of choosing—"

"—love over legacy," finished Clara.

"It sounds like you've heard this part before?"

"Yes—I mean, no. Not really. Only that he tried to convince Thomas to stay—and then after that you did, too."

Gildersleeve's brow furrowed. "No, child. I never tried to convince Thomas of anything."

"Then . . . what did you tell him?"

"I told Thomas—and Amelia—to follow their hearts."

"But Sway thinks you—"

"I'm sure he thinks all manner of things, but I never shared with him what I said to his son."

"Why?"

"Because Godfrey only ever considers his own interests. And he never was much of a father the way, for example, yours is."

Clara thought of her father somewhere aboard *Zephyrus*, anxiously counting the minutes until her return.

"After Thomas and Amelia left, Godfrey's bitterness grew. He became obsessed with flying, obsessed with winning, regardless the cost. There was a rash of accidents with other balloons—convenient accidents that allowed us to win races we never should've won—and I started to sense that he wasn't doing things aboveboard. Power can be a terrible thing, child, and those who suffer hubris are weakest to it. Winning had become an entitlement for Godfrey. So, I ended our partnership—the details of which I'll spare you. Leave it to say, it was not a particularly productive conversation. Soon after, Thomas and Amelia reemerged in Paris. Naturally, everyone was surprised—even more so when Thomas announced he would become an aeronaut after all. Godfrey took the decision as a vindication. Not only had his heir returned ready to assume the family mantle, but he'd brought his own heir as well."

"Landon."

"Yet another story, I'm afraid."

Clara drew lines in her head, mapping one connection to another.

"While I was overjoyed to see them, I could tell Amelia was only there for Thomas. I knew she preferred her life in Cambridge to the circus of WOOBA. Godfrey knew, too, and the first chance he had, he drove a wedge between them, warning Thomas that Amelia would keep him from reaching his greatest potential."

"But she was his daughter-in-law!"

"And the biggest threat to the Sway legacy. Thomas, of course, felt trapped in the middle. Eventually, he asked for my advice. Together, we hatched a plan: Godfrey would be tasked with watching his new grandson, and we'd go flying where we could speak privately and figure out the best path forward."

"And that's when—"

"A fuel tank exploded. Flames erupted through the basket. The smoke was so dark, so suffocating, none of us could breathe. That's all I remember, I'm afraid. I woke in a field surrounded by wreckage. Thomas and Amelia were never found." The hood of Gildersleeve's poncho blew off her head, but she didn't reach to adjust it. "Sway accused me of murder, and petitioned WOOBA to investigate me. In the end, it was labeled a tragic accident. Not that it mattered. I was hollow inside, my soul unmoored. So I fled here to the mountains where I could be alone, unable to hurt anyone, and be . . ."

"Invisible?"

"Yes. I suppose that's a good word for it."

"What about—"

"Landon?" said Gildersleeve with a sad smile. "The boy has no idea who I am."

"He doesn't?"

"His grandfather never told him, and most pilots of that era are either dead or long-since retired. Chins-Ratton knew, but he's such a self-absorbed buffoon, I doubt he even remembers. In any case, it's better this way."

"But he's your grandson, too. Landon's as much a Gildersleeve as he is a—"

"Sway."

"Yes, a Sway."

"No," said Gildersleeve urgently. "Off the port side."

Providence broke from the fog and sped past *Amelia*, Sway alone on deck focused on the finish line. But it was the air sock flying from the ship's crown, stiff and fully extended, that drew Clara's gaze. The wind was blowing stronger, but not *that* strong.

"How is he moving so fast?"

"He's using more than the wind."

"Alberto, ready the jumper!"

Off *Amelia*'s starboard side, Berta was hurling large piles of knitting onto *Primrose*'s deck while Alberto Furio fastened one end to the rigging. Together, they heaved, raising what could only be called the world's largest sweater. It unfurled in zigzagging bands of electric color, catching the wind with a great *snap. Primrose* hurtled forward, leaving a stream of flower petals in its wake.

"It's a sail!" cried Clara. "This whole time, she was knitting a sail."

"A spinnaker," Gildersleeve clarified. "Looks like she used a herringbone stitch, too. Makes for a strong, tight weave."

Berta and Alberto screamed, not in fear, but from the thrill of a lifetime. They blistered past *Providence* before Sway had a clue, then rocketed past the finish line, continuing until they were only a speck on the horizon.

"In all my years," said Gildersleeve, "I can honestly say I've never seen anything like that."

CHAPTER TWENTY-SIX

FUR, FEATHERS, AND SCALES

LEADERBOARD

AFTER STAGE 6

1ST - Providence, 51 PTS

2ND - Amelia, 28 PTS

3RD - Ussuri, 25 PTS

"IT'S N-NOT LEGAL!" stammered Sir Wallace.

"Per the rules, it's technically not illegal, either," argued Habberdish.

"It's a clear violation! A travesty! A mockery! It's—"

"—a sweater," said Hatsu. The two men looked down to see the young girl standing between them. "It's a sweater," she repeated. "Get over it."

The podium ceremony was almost an hour behind

schedule. Guy Gerard had been doing his best to fill airtime in front of a restless audience and who knew how many television viewers while the first-place platform remained bare awaiting the return of *Primrose*, which had reportedly reached the East China Sea pulled by Berta's sweater spinnaker (or *sweataker*, as it had quickly been dubbed).

Clara stood alone, the only competitor present from any team. Gildersleeve had mysteriously disappeared right after they'd docked, and Sway, who'd won second place, was also conspicuously missing.

To his credit, Guy was doing a masterful job improvising. He'd conducted a detailed recap of the stages, and then a full update of the leaderboard. He hadn't stopped there, either, listing off every balloon all the way to the finished-challenged *Albatross*, which for the first time in its history had completed six consecutive stages without exploding or catching fire.

Offstage, the cameraman kept motioning in Clara's direction, but Guy was doing everything possible to avoid her. Clara didn't want to be there, either. She only hoped that Binder and Alfie were busy tracking Sway's whereabouts.

Finally, the plastic-faced announcer ran out of things to say. Grimacing, he pivoted toward the podium. "I'll be . . . Clara Poole! Have you been here this whole time?" His grin was so strained it must've hurt. "Tell us, how is our Face of the Race today?"

"Fine," she mumbled.

"Oh, come now. You must be better than fine. You're on the podium after all. Where, I might add, everyone else *should* be," he added bitterly. "Still, quite a performance from Team Amelia. You're giving Godfrey Sway a run for his money."

"Godfrey Sway is a chea—" Clara paused, catching a glimpse of Harold Habberdish lurking in the shadows. His expression said *Think again.* "—champion," she finished with as little enthusiasm as possible. "I'm sure he'll be tough to beat."

"Indeed! Yet, I have no doubt you'll find a way. Because you never know what can happen or when inspiration will strike, right?"

Something sharp jabbed Clara's side. Glancing down, she realized Guy was stabbing her with a Face of the Race promo card.

"Read it," he gritted out, grinning like a ventriloquist.

"Er . . . yes, Guy," she said, scanning the card. "How true that is. You never know what can happen. In fact, inspiration can strike in the most unforeseen ways. Such was the case in 1905, when an interior wall accidentally collapsed between Walter Wibble's hot dog factory and Henry Bibble's waffle house, forging one of the most unlikely sweet-and-savory partnerships ever known. Since that day, Wibble Bibble Confectionary International has been dedicated to making moderately healthy and debatably delicious treats for brave customers everywhere. And now, in their founders' honor, the company is thrilled to reissue its original creation, simply known as the Wibble Bibble Pork Pie Pop."

"Mmm . . . that sounds . . . er . . . unique. Really, it's too bad we don't have some now!"

As if on cue, Karl the stagehand appeared and shoved a box into the announcer's arms.

"Oh, no . . . I mean . . . oh, yay!" Guy declared with a nervous laugh. He cracked the lid ever so slightly, which was far more than enough. A rancid blend of feet and muffins filled the air. Clara's eyes watered as she overheard someone whispering loudly into Guy's earpiece: "Try a piece for the camera."

"You first," she said, smiling innocently up at Guy. "I know how much you love Wibble Bibble."

"Me? Oh . . . boy, I would . . . I absolutely would . . . ," he said, a manic grin glued on his face, "but I . . . uh . . . don't eat sugar."

Clara read the box and smiled. "Then, you're in luck. It says here these are sugar-free."

"You're joking?" muttered Guy. "No, seriously, tell me you're joking?"

"Eat the candy!" shouted the voice in his earpiece.

Guy removed a piece and placed it gingerly between his teeth, attempting to wrap his lips around the candy without actually touching it to his tongue.

Suddenly, Clara had an idea.

"Guy, you know who else loves Wibble Bibble?"

The ashen-faced announcer shook his head. He looked like he might vomit.

"Godfrey Sway. That's right, he told me himself that he can't get enough of Wibble Bibble. I think we should give him some, don't you, folks? That is, unless Guy wants to keep it all for himself?"

The announcer waved his hands, emitted a deep gurgling sound, then ran offstage with a hand pressed to his mouth.

"I'll take that as a no. Well, in that case, let's send a bunch over to *Providence* right now!" Clara continued, playing to the camera. "Really ... Godfrey loves the stuff. I'm sure he'll be delighted to give the good folks at Wibble Bibble his rousing endorsement."

Karl reappeared and handed her a card.

"It says here that Team Primrose will be unable to make today's podium ceremony. However, we congratulate Berta and Alberto on their big victory . . . and their even bigger *sweataker*. I'm your Face of the Race, Clara Poole . . . and don't you wish you were, too!"

The red light cut off, and Karl golf-clapped from offstage.

"Thank you." Clara grinned, sinking into a deep theater bow.

A HALF HOUR LATER the kids watched from the shadows inside Regency as wheelbarrows full of Pork Pie Pops arrived at *Providence*. A confused (and irate) Sway tried his best to shoo away the equally confused workers as they loaded crate after crate onto the deck of his balloon.

"I can't believe you pulled that off, Clara," whispered Alfie.

"Brilliant," added Binder. "Simply brilliant."

Clara smiled from ear to ear. For the first time in a long while, she felt certain she'd sleep well that night.

BY LATE THE following morning, *Zephyrus* had reached its next destination, and the teams had been scrambled to the starting line. Yet instead of the usual lineup, drones had clumped the balloons together in a circle. Around them, a parched landscape of red and orange stretched as far as Clara could see, apart from the spot directly beneath them, where an enormous black scorch mark marred the earth.

Her father's notebook had informed her that "Wolfe Creek Crater, Australia, had been created by a meteorite only a short one hundred and twenty thousand years ago." Though Clara preferred the origin myth of the indigenous Djaru people, who believe it was formed "by a giant rainbow snake passing out of the earth." Either way, that was everything her father had been able to find with any connection to the stage.

"How far do we have to cross today?" she asked Gildersleeve.

"We're not crossing anything."

"Then what are we doing?"

"We're going up."

"Good morning, WOOBA fans, and welcome to the land down under!" crackled Guy Gerard's voice over the loudspeaker. "Wow, you are all in for a treat today, because this morning you are going to witness a brand-new, never-before attempted stage . . . an altitude race! Pilots will speed to a height of twelve thousand feet, just over two miles in the air! Now, you might say, 'Guy, going up and down doesn't sound that hard.' Well, I'm told that lots of bad things can start happening when you ascend that fast: dizziness, nausea, tunnel vision, numbness, fatigue, and mental confusion—to name a few. It will be crucial for pilots to control their rate of climb and descent to avoid vertigo and spatial disorientation. How fun is that?"

Clara glanced from deck to deck at the faces of the pilots assembled around them, each one grim.

"Well then," said Guy nonchalantly, "up, up you GO!"

The air blistered as burners blazed at once, and the balloons lifted. Clara felt bolted to the deck, knees buckling with the force, as she watched *Amelia*'s altimeter beep out numbers.

2000 . . . 2500 . . . 3000 . . .

As they passed four thousand feet, Clara noticed that many of the balloons, including *Brigadier Albert* and *Providence*, were rising at a slower rate, their envelopes evidently not designed for such a quick ascent. However, *Amelia* climbed with ease.

5000 . . . 5500 . . . 6000 . . . Clara sat, feeling queasy.

"Here," said Gildersleeve, handing her a clear mask attached to a tank. "It's oxygen."

Clara inhaled deeply as the world began to spin and the

air temperature dropped quickly, despite the roar of the open burner.

7000 . . . 7500 . . . 8000 . . .

Gildersleeve wrapped a thick blanket around Clara's shoulders as random visions blurred together in her head: the windmill at Bitter Bend; outside WOOBA headquarters; her father dressed in Hatsu's bear hat; a great serpent arching into the heavens in a vibrant rainbow of colors.

9000 . . . 9500 . . . 10,000 . . .

Her arms tingled, heavy and numb. Her breath pooled inside her mask in icy clouds.

11,000 . . . 11,500 . . . 12,000 feet.

The altimeter sang out a sustained beep. Gildersleeve cut the burner, tugged the deflation port open, and the balloon sank quickly.

If going up had been bad, going down was infinitely worse. Clara's ears rang and she doubled over, dry-heaving. As they dropped, she caught warped glimpses of *Rumor*, *Brigadier Albert*, and *Providence* still on their upward path, and then looked up to see the bear-headed shape of *Ussuri* dropping quickly.

Moments later, they passed throngs of fans cheering from the decks of the *Zephyrus*, and Guy Gerard announced Team Amelia the winner of Stage Seven.

It took the rest of the morning to recover and hydrate before Clara and Gildersleeve were able to climb onto the first-place podium, joined by the Hoshis in second, and Berta in third. Evidently, Alberto was still sprawled on the deck of *Primrose*, fighting off the effects of altitude sickness.

Clara was eager for a nap, until an out-of-breath Binder pushed his way through the crowd, Alfie and Raylee on his heels.

"Clara! Hatsu!" he hissed. "We found them!"

"Who?" Clara asked.

"The monkeys," said Alfie, panting. "But we gotta go *now*. We overheard the animal control guys talking. They're moving the monkeys tomorrow . . . to a zoo."

"Fat chance, they are!" said Clara. "No one's moving anyone to any zoo."

TEN MINUTES LATER, the kids huddled together, peering around a corner of the long hallway. A group of men lingered at the other end by a metal-barred door, above which glowed a sign: NO ENTRY—ANIMAL QUARANTINE.

"So how do we get in?" whispered Clara.

"No idea," Binder replied, turning to Alfie. "Woodrow?"

Alfie squinted. "Nah, not a clue," he said.

"Seriously? Don't you think you should've mentioned that before?"

"Easy there, Miss Face of the Race," said Binder. "We found the monkeys, didn't we?"

Clara stared back at the men by the door and frowned. "What we need, then, is a diversion. Something that will distract them long enough that we can free Bob and Mayhem."

"But what?" Raylee wondered aloud.

"I know," said Hatsu, hopping up and down. "The Shadow Bear!"

Binder scrunched up his face. "The shadow *wha*—?"

Without another word, Hatsu slipped around the corner into the hallway and screamed at the top of her lungs. "SNAKE! BIG . . . FAT . . . SNAKE!"

"What? Where?" one of the men called.

"In my room! My mother's trapped in the bathroom. Please, come quick!"

"Take us there," the man insisted.

Hatsu ran down the hallway, giving her friends a huge wink as she passed them. The men, consumed by the emergency at hand, didn't spare Clara or the others so much as a glance.

"That wasn't very shadowy," Alfie remarked, his eyebrow raised.

"Who cares," said Binder. "It worked!"

The rescue party rushed down the hall to the metal door, where Clara yanked on the handle. "Locked!"

"Over there," called Raylee, pointing to an illuminated keypad on the wall.

"It's asking for a three-digit code," said Binder.

"Try one-two-three," Alfie offered.

The keypad buzzed red.

"Three-two-one!"

"Nope."

"Four-five-six?"

Suddenly, everyone was shouting numbers while Binder punched sequence after sequence into the keypad.

"How about one-zero-zero?" suggested Clara. "Like the One-Hundredth WOOBA Air Race."

Binder entered the numbers. The keypad flashed green, and the door clacked. "Blimey, Clara, remind me to invite you to my next escape room party."

A bank of overhead lights glowed to life as the kids rushed through the door, only to take in seemingly endless lines of cages.

"It's like a private zoo," said Raylee, breathless.

Binder moved down the row, reading labels. "Were people trying to keep all these as pets? Cockatoo, steppe cat, Tibetan fox, lynx . . . kinkajou?"

"Just find the monkeys," pleaded Clara.

"Over there!" Alfie pointed across the room. "All the way at the end."

"Hey, what are you kids doing in here? This place is off-limits."

Clara spun to see the animal control officers in the doorway. Apparently, Hatsu's snake strategy hadn't worked for long.

"So, what's plan B?" Alfie asked.

"B?" replied Binder. "I'm not so sure we had a plan A."

Clara scanned the room frantically "The cages. They're our only hope."

She rushed to a bank of pens marked EXOTIC BIRDS and began opening door after door.

"Stop that!" yelled one of the men as a blur of colorful feathers filled the air.

Binder followed Clara's cue, speeding to another group of cages labeled REPTILES. The next moment, a host of scaly creatures slithered and hopped out across the floor. Not to be outdone, Alfie and Raylee freed a family of chinchillas, which scattered in all directions.

The animal control officers floundered about trying to contain the melee, but it was too late—the zoo was loose. In the bedlam, Clara rushed to the end of the room, where two blue-faced monkeys eagerly awaited their turn.

"Go," she said, flinging the pen door open. "Hide somewhere they won't find you."

Mayhem bolted without another word, but Bob lingered long enough to give Clara an enormous hairy hug.

"Go on," she urged again. "Before they catch you!"

Bob followed Mayhem up a tower of cages. They scurried into an open air duct and disappeared. A moment later, a pair of hands reached down to pull the gate closed, and Clara caught sight of a third blue face.

"Houdini?"

A high scream pierced the air. Clara looked up to see the fat form of a massive pelican perched on the tower of cages above her. It fanned its wings and took flight, swooping down over the men and out the door. She cheered at the chaos of fur and feathers and scales before another noise broke the cacophony. The tower of cages teetered precariously, then tumbled.

A split second later, everything went black.

CHAPTER TWENTY-SEVEN

STRIKING TWICE

LEADERBOARD
AFTER STAGE 7
1ST - Providence, 52 PTS

2ND - Amelia, 38 PTS

3RD - Ussuri, 32 PTS

CLARA OPENED HER EYES and groaned. Lying under the crisp sheets of a bed that was not hers, everything around her was too white, too bright.

"Where am I?"

"Bakagari, you're awake! Hold on, I'll go tell the doctor."

The room swam and Clara closed an eye to help focus on the blurry set of bear ears disappearing from her bedside. "Hatsu? Where . . . am I?"

"The infirmary."

Clara rolled the other way and switched eyes. Binder, Alfie, and Raylee were slumped on uncomfortable-looking chairs by a window framing a stormy sky beyond.

"How long have I been here?"

"About four days," answered Raylee with a yawn.

"Four days?" Clara sat up with a start. "The monkeys! What about the monkeys? Did they . . ."

A wave of dizziness washed over her.

"Easy there, animal rescuer," said Binder. "Don't pass out before the doctor gets here."

"But I saw Houdini!"

"Yes, Bakagari," said Hatsu, reappearing. "He didn't jump after all. He must've climbed beneath the dock—the sneaky little monkey."

"Where are they now?"

Alfie shrugged. "Dunno. Could still be in the air ducts."

"Or maybe hiding aboard *Amelia*," Raylee suggested. "It's tough to know. Gildersleeve won't let anyone near Bay Thirteen."

Binder leaned in. "Rumor is when animal control came looking for the monkeys, Gildersleeve threatened to turn the burner on them if they stepped one foot on deck. The last few days have been pretty wild. After you disappeared

under that pile of cages, the fire alarm triggered the sprin-
klers. The entire floor flooded."

"*And* the two below!" tacked on Alfie.

"It was pandemonium, Clara," said Binder, picking up
the thread again. "Like Dodge-level bonkers."

Raylee grimaced. "Which didn't go over well with our
parents."

"*Which*"—Hatsu frowned—"is why we are all now on
the ground."

"*Grounded*," the other kids corrected.

"Whatever."

Clara rubbed her head, then glanced at the sky swirling outside the window. Thinking was hard. "So where are
we now?"

"Venezuela," answered Raylee.

"We're in South America?"

"Yup," said Binder. "Stage Eight was yesterday—Peru. We
raced through the Andes to Machu Picchu. Came right down
to the wire, too—a literal photo finish. Gildersleeve beat the
Chins-Rattons and my mom and me by a nose. Actually,
she held out this long wooden pole, but you get it. Anyhow,
the Chins-Rattons went ballistic! You know . . . formal rules
on what constitutes a balloon, blah-da-dee-blah-blah-blah."

"Even better, *Providence* finished fifth!" Alfie grinned.

"That means Team Amelia is within striking distance of taking first. Sway's absolutely furious about it."

"Speaking of furious," said Binder, peeking at his watch, "Stage Nine starts in less than an hour. Our parents will kill us if we're late."

"We're, uh, only allowed out of our rooms when we're here visiting you," whispered Raylee.

"Because we're all on the ground," Hatsu said with a nod.

The others groaned. *"Grounded!"*

"Why don't *you* all try and speak another language perfectly!"

The kids stretched their tired backs and made their way to the door.

"Wait," called Clara, throwing back the bedsheets. "I'm coming with you."

She swung her feet onto the floor, and the room tilted.

"Bakagari, you need to stay here," said Hatsu, helping her back into bed. "The doctor will be here any moment."

With the others gone, Clara was left to wait and watch impatiently as a line of balloons passed the window. *I don't need a doctor! I need to get to the Hive!*

The room wobbled as she willed herself to her feet, but gradually she found her sea legs. Fortunately, her clothes were neatly folded on a green vinyl chair in the corner, and with some effort, she managed to pull her hoodie over her head. Hopefully, she'd be able to get to the dock before Gildersleeve left.

She hadn't even gotten out the door when she saw a fuzzy figure hurrying toward her.

"I heard you came to, so I rushed here," explained a red-faced Landon. "He's lost it, Clara. It's like he's gone mad."

"Who?"

"My grandfather. Last night, I heard him ranting to himself about Gildersleeve. . . . Calling the other pilots imbeciles for celebrating her comeback. . . . Saying they were fools for not seeing how dangerous she was—that *someone* had to stop her." A bell chimed, announcing the start of the stage. "I have to go. He's expecting me at the dock. But I think he's planning something awful . . . and I don't know if I can stop him."

"I'm on my way to the docks, too, to find Gildersleeve."

"You're too late. They've already left."

"They?"

Landon flinched. "You mean no one told you?"

"Told me what?"

"Clara, after you got hurt, your father took your place as Gildersleeve's copilot."

"What are talking about? My dad's afraid of heights. He can barely handle being aboard the *Zephyrus*."

"Well, turn around, because he's right there. . . ."

Clara whirled and her head swam again, but not from her injury. *Amelia* sailed by the infirmary window. On deck, a man stood next to Gildersleeve—a man wearing an unmistakable red hat.

Clara ran, ignoring the pounding in her head as adrenaline took over.

"Where are you going?" cried Landon.

"To catch them before your grandfather does."

MINUTES LATER, CLARA staggered out of the *Zephyrus* onto the catwalk to the Hive, shielding her face from the pelting rain. Below, a massive wedge of rock rose from the clouds like an island in the sky. Waterfalls cascaded down the side, thousands of feet into nothing.

Where are we? she thought, craning her neck to read the screen high above on the observation deck: STAGE NINE: MOUNT RORAIMA, VENEZUELA.

Brigadier Albert and *Albatross* sailed toward the starting line, only the tops of their envelopes visible in the fog. *Amelia*, however, was nowhere to be seen.

Clara turned her head from the whip of the wind and felt her way along the safety lines, praying that the Hoshis or the Jollys or *anyone* might still be at the Hive. But when she fell through the hangar's door, she saw only a sliver of *Primrose* disappearing from its bay.

"Berta! Alberto!" she cried, running to the berth. "Stop, please!"

She waited, listening to the mooring lines clang against their empty towers as the clouds below rippled like a murky gray marble. There was another sound, too, coming from somewhere at the end of the dock. In the very last bay, the small fleet of sparrowhawks from Dodge's Hong Kong catastrophe thumped and bumped together like bulls in a pen.

Without a second thought, Clara jumped into the first basket and released the dock line. Instantly, the tiny balloon was sucked from its mooring and blown sideways in the gale. Clara fumbled to engage the sails, and then pressed the ignition. The engine kicked to life, and she hurtled forward. Soon, she came alongside *Albatross*, and screamed above the wind to the Newlins, "Where's *Amelia*?"

"Off our port side, I think!" shouted back Norman.

Lightning arced across the sky, followed by a thunder-clap so loud it seemed to lift the clouds. The sparrowhawk shuddered, and then a second streak of electricity splintered the air.

An old memory flashed in her mind.

Where are you, Dad?

Thunder pounded and the sky lit up again. Clara counted until the next set.

Closer, she thought—closer than she liked.

She pressed on, the wind jolting her up and down and side to side, until she drew level with *Ussuri* and *Samsara*.

"What are you doing, Bakagari?" called Hatsu.

Binder was more direct. "Are you completely mental?"

She couldn't stop now. "Come on," she growled. "Where are you?"

And then she saw it: the white balloon hanging inside a break in the clouds.

She pushed the sparrowhawk's throttle to the limit. The engine responded, coughing out a plume of smoke.

"No, no, no!" she yelled, jamming the lever harder. "Don't you stop now!"

The tiny balloon sputtered forward, engine wheezing, until it drew close enough that she could make out her father in his red hat. He moved quickly about the basket, as if he really knew what he was doing, while Gildersleeve barked orders.

It was a strange sight, him there on the deck of a balloon he never wanted her to fly in—let alone, himself—alongside a woman he disliked and her smelly monkeys. Her father had crossed the Atlantic to find her, to bring her back to a new place she refused to call home, and when he couldn't do that, his only choice had been to worry and wait and suffer her mistakes. But here he was taking her place, for her—because of her—and for the first time since her mother's death, Clara felt like he was finally *with* her.

Steering closer, she noticed three hairy shapes climbing the rigging and smiled. Mayhem and Houdini scrambled quickly to the top of the balloon, followed by Bob.

But that wasn't right.

Bob never climbs that high. Not unless something's wrong.

It took a moment to see it—the gleaming metal pole mounted on the crown of the envelope—and then another to piece it all together.

Clara flashed back to the windmill.

That's a lightning rod.

Dark clouds swirled, parting just long enough to glimpse *Providence*'s dark shape above. On the pulpit, as if immune to the raging storm, Godfrey Sway watched and waited.

Thunder pounded the air, then rolled away, replaced by a soft buzz that grew into a crackling hiss.

It was a sound Clara knew too well.

She counted. "One . . . two . . ." But before she reached three, the hair on her arms stood on end, and the sky flashed white.

Electricity shot down, six times hotter than the sun, turning rain to steam. It split in a forking pattern, reuniting at its final destination, surrounding *Amelia* in a cage of heat. The balloon sputtered and flapped as if the hot air had been sucked out all at once, and then *Amelia* plunged out of sight.

Clara screamed, her eyes fixed on the hole in the cloud where the balloon had disappeared. She waited for its return, but the clouds only swirled, closing a moment later.

She had lived this before—everything changing in an instant.

A shadow passed overhead, and moments later, Satomi Hoshi lifted Clara from her basket. She smiled warmly, but her eyes were a story of sadness. Hatsu stood behind her mom, clasping her hat in her hands.

Clara closed her eyes as an old and familiar feeling rose inside her: guilt.

CHAPTER TWENTY-EIGHT

MONKEY LUCK

BALLOONS GATHERED AROUND *Ussuri*, forming a float-ing flotilla of sorts as rescue helicopters returned from the clouds below. The rain had dwindled, and nighttime quickly descended over Mount Roraima. Continuing the search for *Amelia* would have to wait until morning.

The competitors slowly dispersed. Satomi left Clara under Hatsu's watchful eye as she brought *Ussuri* around and back to the hangar.

"This is my fault," Clara murmured. "I shouldn't have come. I should be with him in Chicago."

"Have hope, Bakagari. The rescuers will find them tomorrow."

Ussuri rose into its mooring where a crowd gawked and

waited, including Harold Habberdish. He opened his mouth to speak as Clara stepped onto the causeway, but she walked right past him. There was nothing he, or any of the other pilots, could say. She didn't blame them. After all, they didn't really know her. Only Berta approached, smothering Clara in the great smock of her dress. "You be strong now, lass. Things will be different in the morning."

Clara nodded without looking up, then exited the hangar.

The rain had stopped, but the sky remained moonless and overcast. Clara wasn't sure where she was going— anywhere, somewhere, nowhere when Godfrey Sway stepped out of Regency onto the far catwalk. Their eyes locked for a moment before he continued on with long, heavy strides.

"Monster!" she yelled at his back.

Sway paused but did not respond.

"That thing!" she shouted. "On top of *Amelia* . . . What did you do to them?"

"What did *I do*?" he said, slowly turning to face her, his tone deeply offended. "I believe Mr. Habberdish has warned you about making unfound accusations. You'd do well to remember—"

"No . . . It was you. I saw you."

"You *saw* me?" he repeated coldly. "No, Miss Poole. What you saw was an accident. A terrible . . . tragic . . . accident."

"Liar!"

"Clara?" said a voice behind her.

She turned to see Habberdish and a group of pilots including the Hoshis, Jollys, and Woodrows.

"Habberdish, this girl needs a doctor," called Sway. "She's obviously in shock."

"Yes, yes, right," mumbled Habberdish.

Sway straightened and cleared his throat. "And Harold . . . if there is anything I can do to help, I most certainly will. I assure you if anyone can understand the pain Miss Poole is feeling . . . it is me."

"Yes, uh, thank you, Godfrey."

Sway's mouth pressed into a thin line, then he marched off the catwalk.

"You're a monster!" cried Clara after him. "A coward! A murd—!"

"Clara, please, it's all right," said Habberdish, placing his hands on her shoulders. "Really, it would be best if we got you to—"

"Best?" she spat, ripping herself away. "You don't know the first thing about what's best for me. None of you do!"

"But—"

"Just leave me alone!"

She sprinted across the catwalk onto the *Zephyrus*, careening down hallways and bumping into passengers. Rounding a corner, she crashed into a room-service attendant, upending his cart, sending fruit plates and cheeseburgers flying. The attendant shouted at her to stop, but she managed to duck into an open elevator as the doors were closing.

"Destination, please," chirped the digital voice.

"Just take me far from here," she blurted, holding back tears.

"Far from here," it repeated. "Thank you."

The elevator jumped to life, lurching to the side. Clara collapsed against the wall as colored lights flickered outside the little window. It seemed a lifetime ago, she'd been staring out it for the first time, hunger her only concern, the *Zephyrus* no more than a strange building somewhere in Paris. What she wouldn't give to go back, knowing then what she knew now. Back to Paris. Back to Bitter Bend. Back to her father. He'd only been concerned for her; had she ever once stopped to think of him?

"Arrived at Far from Here," announced the elevator.

Clara stepped off the carriage into the open air. Moonbeams broke through the clouds as the storm rolled away. A pair of helicopters sat idle, awaiting the first light when the rescue party would set out again. She walked to the end of the platform and peered over the edge. A wall of wind blew up at her, and she imagined riding it like a bird, down under the clouds, to her father . . . somewhere.

There was a sound like a frantic trill that rose above the wind. Clara scanned the horizon for a balloon, but saw only a bird winging its way toward the *Zephyrus*. It struggled against the wind, as if strangely unaccustomed to flying. Slowly, it grew bigger, and Clara realized it wasn't flying toward her. It was flying *at* her.

"Coo?"

The fat bird flapped wildly, and before Clara could duck, he struck her smack in the face. She pinwheeled, landing hard on her back, sending the contents of her pockets clattering across the deck.

"Coo!" she cried, spitting out feathers. "You're alive!"

The bird blinked back with bulging eyes, then attempted to claw his way inside the safety of her jacket.

Beside her, Barnaby Bixley's compass glinted up in the moonlight. She picked it up and read its too-familiar inscription: *Always Follow True North.*

To think she'd ever believed it was special, some far-seeing talisman there to guide her. Now she saw it for what it was—nothing more than the rusty trinket of a senile old man.

"Follow this," she shouted, hurling it into the sky.

In a rush of wings, Coo exploded into the air, caught the compass in his beak, and dropped it back in her lap.

"What are you, a retriever all of a sudden? Can't you get it through your bird-brain, I don't want it." She wound up to throw the compass again, but paused. The needle had stopped spinning. It was fixed on a single coordinate—due north.

Clara looked up, following the needle's direction. On the horizon hung a white balloon. She blinked at the ghost, and then blinked again, but each time, it was still there. The basket sagged pathetically to one side, fastened to the envelope by a flimsy rope harness. But none of that mattered.

Beside three hairy shapes stood a man in a red baseball hat.

If Clara had had a flusterboard, she would've jumped into the sky. She waved and hollered, trying to get their attention as they passed by stoically en route to the Hive.

By the time Clara reached the hangar, pilots, a camera crew, and officials were swarming the causeway. She squeezed between the press of bodies until she spotted her father and threw herself into his arms.

"I'm sorry," she sobbed. "I'm sorry for everything. I should've listened. I should've—"

"Just hug me," he replied, burying his face in her hair.

Other arms wrapped around her—long, hairy arms. The monkeys gibbered as they climbed all over her, knocking her on her back.

"You're so brave," she told them. "I saw you. You tried to save them."

Suddenly, they went quiet.

Paramedics rushed from the balloon's deck carrying a stretcher. Gildersleeve lay still, her eyes closed.

"Clear the way!" ordered Habberdish, waving his arms at the crowd.

"Is she okay?" Clara asked.

Nobody responded.

"Dad?"

"She was hurt in the crash," he said softly.

"But she'll be okay, right?"

Once again, there was only silence.

CHAPTER TWENTY-NINE

A SUDDEN CHANGE OF HEART

GILDERSLEEVE LAY PEACEFULLY in the downy white sheets of her infirmary bed. She looked out of place surrounded by beeping monitors and medical equipment.

"Please," whispered Clara pleadingly, "wake up."

She'd spent the night next to the old pilot, talking to her and telling her how she'd be okay and how she'd fly her balloon again soon. And while Clara prayed the first part would be true, she knew the second was near impossible. She'd seen *Amelia* and doubted it would ever race again.

Out the infirmary window, the red rock buttes of New Mexico or Texas or somewhere passed beneath them. The race's finale was in two days, ironically ending in the place she should've been all along: Chicago. Her world had come full circle, yet she was more adrift than ever.

The infirmary door opened a crack, then shut. It repeated the motion again and again every few seconds. Finally, Clara caught sight of fingers covered in golden hair.

"You can come in," she said.

The monkeys threw open the door and rushed in. They sniffed at Gildersleeve, then gazed hopefully at Clara.

"Not yet."

Bob sat vigil at the edge of the bed, while Mayhem and Houdini located a box of rubber gloves and began inflating them with their noses.

"Quit that," Clara chided, taking the box away.

"It smells like monkey in here," said a tired voice.

Bob chuffed, and a moment later, he and the others were sprawled on top of the old woman.

"You're awake," Clara cried. "I was worried you might . . ."

"Die?" said Gildersleeve wryly. "You can't get rid of me that easily." She groaned and pulled back the bedsheets, revealing casts on both legs. "But it seems I won't be flying anytime soon."

Clara opened her mouth, but was speechless.

"Don't worry. *Amelia* and I've seen worse."

Clara glanced away, rubbing her wrists.

"How bad is she?" asked Gildersleeve. "From your reaction, I'd say pretty terrible."

Clara nodded.

The old pilot closed her eyes and sighed. "You saw it happen, didn't you?" she said quietly.

"Landon warned me," Clara blurted. "I tried to get to you, but he was already there—Sway . . . He was watching."

"Yes, I saw him."

"He tried to kill you!"

Gildersleeve shifted uncomfortably. "No, I don't think that's what he meant to do."

"That man's a monster."

Gildersleeve chuckled. "It's more complicated than that."

"How?" Clara said with a frown.

"When you're as old as I am, you start to see the things people do in a different light. I've known Godfrey for a long time, and as appalling as it might sound to you, I still believe in the talented young man I once knew, who had no one teach him right or wrong."

"He had *you*," Clara protested.

"In Godfrey's case, I'm afraid I came too late to matter. I will not recount his childhood, but when you have a start in life like his, you learn to claw and fight for everything you have. As gifted as he was, and as much as I hoped I might've guided him, he was too hardened by the time he met me.

But you're still flexible. . . . You can still forgive. Maybe one day, you'll even learn to forgive yourself."

Clara's face went pale.

"Do you miss her?" she asked eventually.

"Amelia? Every day."

"So, what do you do with . . . *it?*"

"Do you mean the *hurt*? Sometimes the hurt is the only thing that helps us remember how good it all once was."

"I'm starting to forget her," Clara whispered.

"You won't," said Gildersleeve, touching Clara's scarf. "She's still here."

Clara ran her fingers over the fringe, then tucked it safely inside her jacket. It was enough.

"Ms. Gildersleeve, can I ask you one more question?"

"I think you just did."

"What do we do now?"

"That's simple. Beat Sway."

"But how? *Amelia* can barely fly."

"Then fix her."

"Even if I could, I don't have a pilot."

"You're the pilot now."

"I'd need a copilot."

"Funny, I flew the past two stages with a pretty good one."

Clara frowned.

"If you want to get Sway where it hurts, beat him and put your name on that trophy. Go ahead . . . ask him—ask your father to join you."

"There's no way he'll do it. Not after—"

"Ask," said Gildersleeve, squeezing Clara's arm.

Clara took a deep breath. "Okay."

The monkeys jumped to attention and started pawing her.

"Quit it. Of course you're coming. We all know you're the best pilots here."

Mayhem barked in agreement.

"One more race," she said with a nod, then turned to leave.

"Good luck, Clara."

She froze, turning to look back at Gildersleeve.

"What did you say?"

"I said 'good luck.' "

"No, not that. You didn't call me *child.*"

"Because I don't see one."

HOURS LATER, CLARA stood with the other kids scratching their heads in front of *Amelia* as late-morning sun flooded the Hive.

"You really think we can fix her?" Alfie wondered aloud.

"There's only one way to find out," said Clara.

Binder slapped them both on the back. "Well, we sure can't make her any worse."

The balloon hung limp on its mooring, a splintered mess of wood and wicker. Most of the lower cabin was gone, and what remained looked as though it might fall off at any moment. Coo paced back and forth anxiously on the railing. The bay window, already glass-less from crashing on Mount Kailash, dangled by a thread, and the remaining bookshelves lay bare. Surprisingly, the mobile was still fastened from the cabin's ceiling, a pointed reminder of the randomness of survival.

Amelia's envelope hadn't fared much better. Its top had been charred by the lightning. Clara had been particularly interested to examine it, hoping to find proof of sabotage she could link back to Sway. Unfortunately, there'd been nothing to find.

"Bakagari, have you spoken to him yet?"

"My father? Not yet."

"You know the race is tomorrow?"

"I know, but—"

"But nothing," said Hatsu, pointing to the exit. "Go!"

"But—"

"Now!" yelled all the kids at once.

"And to think I call you friends," Clara growled as she stomped away.

SHE WAS ONE thousand percent sure her father's answer would be no. After all, he'd just escaped death. She doubted he was itching to jump back in another balloon, especially without a real pilot. In fact, she doubted whether he'd ever fly so much as a paper airplane after his feet next touched solid ground.

Their room was dark when she entered, his face illuminated by his computer screen.

"There you are," he said. "I heard you and the other kids are fixing *Amelia*. Think she'll be good enough to race tomorrow?"

"I'm sorry? What did you say?"

"*Amelia*—will she be able to race?"

Clara blinked.

"That is what you wanted, isn't it?" he asked.

"Uh . . . well . . . yeah, but—"

"Good. In that case, I have to get to a meeting with Habberdish's attorney. I need to sign a stack of new waivers before we're allowed to race, absolving WOOBA of any responsibility in letting us pilot. I'll meet you after at the Hive."

"The Hive?"

"The balloon dock?" he said. "Are you okay?"

Clara blinked at him again.

"By the way, something came for you. I left it on the desk."

She watched him leave, trying to figure out if she'd accidentally stepped into an alternate dimension. Crossing to the desk, she scanned the top for what she assumed would be a letter from WOOBA. Instead, she found a handcrafted box made from old maps. Inside, resting on a piece of blue felt, was an origami dove. She carefully unfolded it and scanned the message scribbled in black pen.

TOMORROW. A FINAL LESSON.

Clara dropped the paper in her lap.

A lesson for what?

CHAPTER THIRTY

MAYHEM

LEADERBOARD
AFTER STAGE 9
1ST - Providence, 52 PTS
2ND - Amelia, 49 PTS
3RD - Brigadier Albert, 37 PTS

A NY FURTHER THOUGHT about the mysterious origami message vanished the moment Clara entered the Hive. She jumped right in, helping her friends examine each gore of the envelope to ensure there were no hidden tears. It was tedious work climbing up and down the balloon. Clara would have happily traded jobs with the monkeys, who were weaving bamboo through gaping holes in the basket (except Mayhem who, for whatever reason, was making pirate hats instead).

By midday, Clara's father appeared, joined by Satomi, Berta, and Alberto. They helped reinforce the basket's underside, working through dinner and late into the night. All the while, Clara watched the door to the Hive, hoping to see Landon.

When they agreed the balloon was as good as it would get, they retired to bed. Through it all, Clara hadn't had a moment to ask her father about his sudden change of heart, nor did she once they'd returned to their room, where she promptly fell face-first onto her pillow and fast asleep.

SHE WOKE TO HOOTING and hollering outside her door as fans made their way to secure the best viewing spots for the race's final stage. By the end of the day, a new winner would be crowned, and one team would lift the Dovie Cup in victory.

The starting line sparkled outside her window, as if the towers had been dipped in glitter, but Clara focused only on her own reflection. She stared at it, trying to remember the girl in the lawn chair, or the terrified daughter from the windmill. All of that felt like a lifetime ago, yet here she was, back where it all began, looking out over Lake Michigan.

There were still a few more hours until the start, but the party on the observation deck was already in high gear. Women in flowing sundresses and wide-brimmed hats (some so big that mechanical balloons raced around them like carousels) held the arms of men in crisp seersucker suits. Even the children were impeccably dressed, like miniature clones of their parents. Everyone hobnobbed, laughing and sipping fizzy blue beverages that looked like someone had ladled the sky into a drinking glass.

"There's our girl!" Habberdish emerged from the crowd, his arms outstretched. His gray curls exploded from beneath his blue bowler hat, which featured a fleet of miniature balloons floating above on wires. "Look around at all these happy faces, Clara," he said, taking her by the arm. "Not one of them would be here without you—including me. For that, I am eternally grateful. I dare say, if you hadn't had that little adventure in your lawn chair, WOOBA might be retired to the history books. But after the success of this year, well, the sky's the limit. But first things first—are you ready for the final stage?"

"To be honest, I'm still surprised you're letting me fly by myself after everything that's happened."

"Are you kidding me? What more could I ask than to give our WOOBA fans a father-daughter team vying for the Dovie Cup against a multi-time champion?"

"What about Ophelia and Sir Wallace?" replied Clara.

"Yes, except you're someone that people . . . er . . . like. Besides, the Chins-Rattons are far less colorful. I mean, they don't fly with monkeys now, do they?"

"You mean the monkeys you had quarantined?"

"Yes . . . well . . ."

"Habberdish, over here," called Norman Newlin. "Come get a picture with us to commemorate Team Albatross's first-ever WOOBA finish!"

"They do know there's still one stage left, right?" Clara said out of the side of her mouth.

"Let's not ruin their dream just yet," Habberdish replied with a wink. "Be right there, Norman!" The next moment, he was swallowed by the mob of Newlin supporters.

"They do know there's still one stage left, right?" said Hatsu, appearing at Clara's side.

"I said exactly the same thing."

The girls slipped away from the group, then snaked through the crowd onto an empty elevator.

"Balloon docks, please," said Clara.

"This is it, Bakagari. Today's your day!"

"I wish I was as confident as you."

"Why aren't you?"

"Because even though I've flown all these stages, I've never actually piloted on my own."

"You piloted a sparrowhawk."

"Not really. Houdini did most of it. Still, I'm not sure piloting a sparrowhawk is the same thing."

"Sure it is. *Amelia*'s just bigger. And like you said, you have the monkeys to help. Plus, who knows what strange things might happen." Hatsu giggled mysteriously as the elevator doors opened, and she bounded across the catwalk. "See you on the podium, Bakagari."

Clara stepped off the carriage and was immediately met by a blast of wind that almost ripped her scarf from her neck. The day was gray and overcast, and had she not known it was morning, she would've thought it was much later. She felt lost in time, caught between her new life and the old one she would soon return to. It was impossible to imagine waking up without the mayhem of WOOBA.

She paused at the center of the catwalk, taking in the gleaming form of the *Zephyrus*. She couldn't help thinking how much it had come to feel like home.

"So, it's true," came Sway's voice behind her. "You really plan to race today? How ... earnest of you."

"Go away," she said, starting toward the Hive. "I have nothing to say to you."

"It is sad that Gildersleeve won't be joining you," he called. "Although I suppose with two broken legs, and her being so old, one must wonder if she'll ever race again."

Clara turned back, fire in her eyes. "I know the real story. Your son wasn't the only one who died that day. How can you be so cruel? You were family."

Sway's expression soured.

"Accidents are a part of life," she continued. "How long are we supposed to blame ourselves for every bad thing that happens?"

Sway leaned into her, pointing at the infinity symbol under his eye. "Forever," he said coldly.

"Get away from my daughter."

Clara spun to see her father standing behind her.

Sway went stiff, then straightened and casually adjusted his coat. "How precious. Your copilot is here. Even after all your lies and deceptions, he still stands by you. *Family*—thick as blood, isn't it?"

"I *said* get away from my daughter."

Sway motioned toward Regency, then paused. "I shall enjoy myself today, Miss Poole. Tell me, do you know what they call second place?"

"I do," Clara said, taking a step forward. "They call him 'Godfrey Sway.'"

The man sniggered. "You're not a real pilot. You're nothing but a novelty. No one will remember you after today." With that, he strode away to his hangar.

Clara's father huffed. "We're so beating that guy."

"No arguments here," she replied, watching Sway's retreating back.

LESS THAN AN HOUR later, the pilots hugged the starting line, held in place by a fleet of drones, which buzzed against the stiff wind. Clara rushed around the deck, aided by her father and the monkeys, running through final checks. *Amelia*'s sails were iffy at best, and the basket lurched decidedly to one side, but at least she was airborne, and that was a start. Clara peered down at the whitecaps forming over the gray-green water of Lake Michigan and wondered if the storied balloon could survive one last race.

"Dad? Can I ask you a question?"

"Sure," he said, giving a quick pull on the burner.

"Why are you doing this?"

"Aren't we supposed to test the burner?"

"No, I mean, why are you flying with me?"

"Oh," he said quietly. "You know, something happened when I was with Gildersleeve in Peru. I was staring out over that great expanse of mountains, and it came to me, clear as day: I realized everything I've done since your mother died wasn't to protect you from more pain—it was to protect me. I've spent a year waking up and cursing that windmill, wanting every day to tear it down. But you were right, Clara. Chicago was my version of running away—my way of keeping the real world out. I guess I just needed to get high enough to see it." He smiled at her and gave her a nudge. "Besides, a smart young girl told me that this is what families are supposed to do."

Clara leaned into him and exhaled. "Dad?"

"Yeah, kiddo?"

"I miss her."

"I do, too." He knelt and straightened Clara's scarf. "I wish she could see you right now. You really do look like a pilot."

"Me? What about you? You're like a different person."

He chuckled and peered down at the lake. "It's so strange to be back where we started."

"It's different."

"How so?"

"This time, I'm doing it with *you*."

A wave of emotions crossed his face, and he hugged her tightly. Still, for Clara, it wasn't tight enough.

"Welcome, welcome," came Habberdish's voice over the loudspeaker. "We have crisscrossed the globe, spanning six continents, flown over some of the most inhospitable geography known to man, and shown the world the heights of bravery. It is with the utmost sincerity that I thank you all—friends, fans, and dreamers—for making this year's WOOBA Air Race the greatest the world has ever witnessed."

The crowd roared as a sea of white doves flew upon the brilliant blue of a thousand WOOBA pennants.

"Yet we're not done quite yet. We have one stage remaining, one final stage to decide who will lift this year's centennial Dovie Cup. And with that, I say ... GO!"

The drones released the anchors, and the balloons catapulted forward, jostling for position. *Ussuri* jumped to the front of the pack, but only for a moment before *Providence* rammed her, lifting the bear-shaped balloon to one side and sending Satomi sliding across the basket. Clara searched for Hatsu, but couldn't see her anywhere.

"Whoa, a bit of a bully move by *Providence*," came the voice of Dodge Barlow.

"Everyone, once again, please welcome today's guest announcer, Dodge Barlow," boomed Habberdish. "Dodge is stepping in for Guy Gerard, who couldn't . . . or didn't want to . . . or—oh, let's be honest—the man's a complete pain in the butt."

Bob and Houdini struggled at the helm to control *Amelia*'s course. Despite everything they'd done to get the balloon ready, Clara could tell they were in no shape to compete.

"We just have to try," said her father, sensing her worry.

"I wanted to win for Ms. Gildersleeve."

"Hey, it's not over yet," he said, smiling.

But it was. *Providence* sped off into the distance like a hare to their turtle. The race was over before it started. Only an act of God could change that now.

A-HOOORN! A note bellowed from above, followed by replies from the left, right, and behind.

"What is that?" asked Clara's father.

"It sounds like air horns."

A swarm of shapes broke from the clouds, descending on *Providence*. They flew directly at the black balloon, buzzing the deck like mosquitoes.

"Those are sparrowhawks!" exclaimed Clara.

Another shape appeared, heading rapidly toward them. It was smaller than the others, but as it neared, Clara could clearly see bear ears.

"Bakagari!" Hatsu called as she slid onto the deck on her flusterboard. "Like it?" She flipped the ends of her bob. It was then that Clara noticed the girl's hair was not its usual color. It was white, like hers.

"It's a new look I call *Clara-fied*."

"Clara-fied?"

"Yeah, we all have them."

"Who's *we*? Hatsu, what's going on?"

"On behalf of PTSD, I welcome you to your final safety lesson," said the girl with a devilish grin.

Binder materialized alongside in a sparrowhawk, followed by Alfie a moment later, both wearing the same white wigs as Hatsu.

"Get in," yelled Binder.

Before she could think, Hatsu pushed Clara into the basket and climbed in behind her. The monkeys piled into Alfie's balloon, each now wearing one of Mayhem's pirate hats. Binder cast off, leaving Clara's father slack-jawed aboard *Amelia*, and flew at the melee of small balloons, his white bob flapping in the wind.

"Why are you all wearing those wigs?" she asked.

"We're hiding our identities," explained Hatsu, "so our parents don't recognize us."

"And because what's more annoying to Godfrey Sway than one Clara Poole?" Binder asked.

"Dozens of Clara Pooles!" yelled Hatsu.

Binder gave a faux pout. "Besides, don't I look pretty?"

A sparrowhawk took position high above *Providence*. Clara squinted to see its pilot, a girl with long auburn hair.

"Is that . . . Ophelia?"

"She only agreed to help as revenge for what Sway did to *Brigadier Albert*, but she refused to wear the wig," said Hatsu. "What were her words? Something like 'I'd rather die.'"

A second figure emerged behind Ophelia, threw their legs over the edge of the basket, and fell into the sky on a flusterboard. Immediately, their wig flew off, and Clara saw the wild black hair beneath.

"Landon?"

He plummeted toward *Providence*, trying to get his flusterboard under control.

"I asked if he wanted to practice, but he said he didn't want to try it more than once."

"Try what?"

"Landing."

Binder brought them alongside *Providence* as another white-haired person, and three blue faces in pirate hats whizzed by, hurling handfuls of Wibble Bibble at a visibly enraged Sway. The man screamed and cursed at the tiny balloons, unable to stop them, and unaware that his grandson had just landed on the back of his envelope.

"As I said, Bakagari, welcome to your final safety lesson: 'How to Deflate a Balloon Properly.' Your instructor today is Landon Sway."

Landon scrambled to the top of the envelope and rammed his flusterboard into the deflation port, propping it open. A moment later, he jumped back into the air, latching onto a passing sparrowhawk.

Providence lurched to the side as the hot air rushed out, and a startled Sway staggered on deck to keep his balance. The balloon dipped below the clouds and vanished, but not before Clara heard him shout, "*Saboteurs!*"

"But he'll crash," she said, alarmed.

"Nah, he'll be fine," Binder insisted. "The air escapes at a controlled rate . . . but he *will* need to put down somewhere."

Hatsu giggled. "I hope he's a good swimmer."

Clara gaped at her friends.

"I think the words you're looking for are 'Thank you,'" said Binder with a wink.

"I can't believe you did that."

"Did what?" Binder glanced at Hatsu. "Do you know what she's talking about?"

Hatsu shook her head with glee.

"I'm serious, do you all know how much trouble you're going to be in?"

"Technically . . . none," replied Binder, pointing at his white wig, "because we're not *us* . . . We're *you*."

"Right," added Hatsu. "And you couldn't have done it, because everyone already knows you're on the deck of *Amelia* right now."

"It's all incredibly confusing," said Binder.

"Yes, very." Hatsu nodded, grinning from ear to ear.

"Let's get you back to your balloon now," said Binder. "After all, you've got a race to win."

The sparrowhawks had disappeared like phantoms as *Amelia's* sagging basket hovered toward them. Clara's father helped her clamber back onto the deck, but when she turned to wave to Binder and Hatsu, they were gone.

"I'm not sure I understand what just happened," said her father.

"Me, neither. But I don't know that it matters. We're still too far behind to win."

"Maybe not."

The balloons ahead began moving off to the north and south, clearing a path west. One after the other, pilots threw their sails into irons, stalling their balloons in midair.

A window of blue appeared as the pinnacle of the Sears Tower and the surrounding Chicago skyline peeked from the clouds, over which floated the finish line and the gleaming contours of the *Zephyrus*.

"Dad, what are they doing?"

"I think they're giving us passage."

"Why?" asked Clara.

"I'm not entirely sure, except sometimes the things we honor are far more important than the things we win."

Amelia dipped along toward the finish line, listing heavily. As they passed *Primrose*, Berta clasped her hands to her heart like a proud aunt, and Alberto Furio kissed the air madly. Satomi bowed respectfully next to Hatsu, who waved so hard, Clara thought her arm might fall off. Even Sir Wallace gave them a civil nod as they passed *Brigadier Albert*. Ophelia, however, who like Hatsu had magically reappeared on deck, stood beside her father, arms crossed and scowling.

"And here they come," came Dodge's voice over the loudspeaker. "Holy guacamole, it's *Amelia* in first place!"

The crowd erupted from the decks of the *Zephyrus*, and

a brass band began to play. The finish line was less than a hundred yards away.

"You did it," called her father. "For Gildersleeve . . . for you."

Clara held her hands to her cheeks and laughed. She couldn't believe what was about to happen.

The loud rasp of a burner came from below, and the clouds glowed red like a dragon rising. Cheers turned to gasps as the black body and crimson sails of *Providence* surged up and crossed the finish line in front of them.

The world went silent.

Godfrey Sway had won.

CHAPTER THIRTY-ONE

THE DOVIE CUP

LEADERBOARD

FINAL RESULTS

1ST - Providence, 64 PTS

2ND - Amelia, 56 PTS

3RD - Brigadier Albert, 42 PTS

CLARA STOOD ONSTAGE over a piece of blue tape with the words *Second Place* on it. She searched the crowd for her father, who had vanished after returning to the Hive.

On her right, Sir Wallace rocked impatiently on the third-place spot, like a man who didn't enjoy standing still—or losing. Beside him, Ophelia pouted, her expression so sour it could've turned water to lemonade. Falling to third must've felt like the humiliation of the century.

However, Clara found no joy in it.

Godfrey Sway stood defiantly in the center of the stage; his feet firmly positioned over the first-place mark. Still, even with the focus squarely on him, he looked alone. Clara studied the faces of the pilots assembled behind him. Not one wore an expression that hinted at anything celebratory, nor did the audience who watched in awkward disquiet.

"Welcome, welcome to the winners' presentation!" cried Habberdish, taking the stage. He paused for applause, but the only sound came from an empty soda can rolling under the seats. "Goodness, why is everyone so grim? Well, maybe we'd cheer up if we spoke to our winner—the hundredth Dovie Cup Grand Champion—Godfrey Sway."

Sway stepped forward to crickets. After another uncomfortable moment, calls from the audience broke the silence.

"Let's talk to Clara!"

"Yeah . . . I'm with you . . . Talk to Clara."

Other voices called out in agreement.

"*Clah-rah! Clah-rah!*" started Binder and Alfie.

The chant grew louder and more urgent until the entire audience—and most of the pilots—had joined in.

"*CLAH-RAH! CLAH-RAH!*"

"Come now," Habberdish insisted, trying to hush the

crowd. "Even if you were rooting for someone else, let's be gracious. Godfrey won fair and square."

"No, he didn't," shouted Hatsu.

"Hatsu!" whispered Satomi.

"He's a dirty cheater," added Alfie.

"*Alfie Woodrow!*" snapped his mother.

"It's true," said Binder. "He's been cheating this whole time."

"Harbinder Jolly, be quiet!" his mom scolded.

The kids turned to Raylee for confirmation. She scanned the audience, then the pilots onstage, before taking a proud step forward. "I'm a rebel!" she yelled, whirling to face her mother. "And I hate this race! And you're never *ever* EVER going to make me do it again! In fact, you're going to buy me a pony for all this! A white one . . . with an acorn leather saddle!"

"Are you mental?" said Binder, throwing his hands in the air. "What does that have to do with anything?"

"It doesn't," she grumbled stubbornly. "It just . . . seemed like a good opportunity."

Binder rolled his eyes, then motioned to the WOOBA president.

"Okay, fine," Raylee exclaimed, crossing her arms. "Mr. Habberdish, everything they say is true. Mr. Sway's a cheaty-cheater, and everyone knows it."

"Must we go through this nonsense again?" complained Sway.

"It's not nonsense," said Hatsu.

Habberdish frowned. "Children, that's quite a big accusation to make. After all, this man is a seven-time champion."

"Eight time," grumbled Sway. "I just won, remember?"

"Do any of you have proof to back up your claim?"

The kids looked at one another, but no one said a word.

"Well, then," Habberdish said. He picked up the gleaming silver trophy from the table beside him and cleared his throat. "For ninety-nine years, this prize has been awarded to the best aeronaut in the world. And this year is no different. It goes to a team that's demonstrated a long history of excellence. It is my esteemed honor to present this year's Dovie Cup to the winners of the One-Hundredth WOOBA Air Race . . . Team Providence!"

Team Providence, thought Clara. The words couldn't sound any worse.

Or . . . better?

"Wait!" she cried. "Mr. Habberdish, you said '*Team Providence*'?"

"Yes. And?"

"Well, isn't a team more than one person?"

"Uh . . . yes," he replied. "Though I'm not sure why that ma—"

"We're wasting time, Habberdish," snapped Sway. "My trophy."

"Ten-point-four!" hollered Clara.

"Ten-point what?" replied Habberdish.

"Ten-point-four!"

"Is that some kind of code?"

"No, sir. Rule ten-point-four of WOOBA's Race Guidelines, also known as *Rules for Copilots*."

"Really, Clara, I have no idea what you're talking about," Habberdish said.

"But you do," she insisted. Clara scanned the audience. "Is Mr. Longing here?"

"I am," said the lawyer from offstage.

"Mr. Longing, do you have a copy of WOOBA's Race Guidelines?"

"Of course. I'm never without it."

"Can you please open to rule ten-point-four and read it to us?"

"Habberdish," shouted Sway. "Get control here!"

"One moment, Godfrey," said Habberdish, holding a finger in the air. "Go ahead, Mr. Longing. Read it, if you will."

The lawyer produced a volume from his briefcase, laid

it on the podium, and began flipping through the pages. "Ten-point-two . . . ten-point-three . . . Yes, here it is. Ten-point-four. 'For reasons of safety, all balloons must have a full complement of crew members, comprised of at least one pilot and one copilot.' Furthermore, an addendum to this rule, susbset rule ten-point-four-point-one, stipulates 'All pilots and copilots must be human.'"

"Habberdish," Sway growled. "Give me that trophy!"

"Mr. Longing, there's more, isn't there?" said Clara.

"Yes, Miss Poole," confirmed the lawyer. "Language regarding the penalty if teams do not meet the stipulated conditions. It says, and I quote, 'Teams finishing any race without a full crew will be disqualified from that stage.'"

"Enough," barked Sway. "You lost! Accept it!"

"Where's Landon?" Clara asked, scanning the crowd.

"I'm right here," he replied, stepping out cautiously from behind Berta.

"Landon, tell me, were you aboard *Providence* today?"

He glanced at Clara and then nervously at his grandfather's iron glare.

"Yes," he said, looking at his feet. "I was on board."

Clara's heart sank.

"But . . . only for a moment. Only long enough to open *Providence*'s deflation port."

"That was you?" growled Sway.

Clara smiled. "So, then you weren't there when *Providence* crossed the finish line?"

"No," he said with a faint grin. "I was most definitely not."

Gasps sounded from the audience.

"This is preposterous," Sway blustered. "Everyone saw what these children did: they attacked my balloon! What about that, Habberdish?" He drew his finger down the line of kids. "It was them . . . all with white hair!"

Binder scrunched his face and tugged on his black curls. "Funny, last time I checked, I don't think I have white hair. Hatsu, Raylee, do you have white hair?" Both girls raised locks of their dark hair and shrugged. They all looked to Alfie and his fire-red mop. "Yeah . . . ," said Binder apologetically, "must've been someone else."

Sway grunted and turned to Habberdish. "It doesn't matter, my grandson just admitted to opening *Providence*'s deflation port to make me crash. That is clearly sabotage!"

"*His* deflation port," corrected Lester Longing.

"Mine, his, whoever's! I was sabotaged!"

"Technically, sir," said the lawyer, "it is not sabotage if the person who did it is from your own team."

"This is absurd. I WON!"

"May I see those rules?" asked Habberdish, approaching

the podium. The lawyer pointed to the passage, and the WOOBA president studied the text. "I'm afraid it's not absurd, Godfrey. Those are, in fact, the rules."

"Which means?" prompted Clara.

"Which means," interjected the lawyer, "as Mr. Sway was the only person aboard his balloon when it crossed the finish line, Team Providence is therefore in violation."

Clara glared at Sway, who was practically fuming. "And what does *that* mean, Mr. Longing?"

"That Team Providence is disqualified."

A cheer rose from the audience.

Sway grabbed Habberdish by the shoulders, his eyes wild. "My grandson is lying. I assure you, he was with me the whole time. You know how troubled the boy is."

"I'm not troubled," Landon snapped. "And I wasn't with you." He turned to WOOBA's president. "Mr. Habberdish, I can also confirm that my grandfather's been cheating throughout the race."

"Don't listen to him," Sway demanded. "He's upset because he doesn't want to be a pilot . . . because I don't approve of his foolish artwork. The boy can't prove anything."

"And he doesn't have to," said Gildersleeve.

The old aeronaut sat in a wheelchair at the edge of the stage, behind which stood Clara's father.

"Do something, Habberdish," insisted Sway. "This is madness."

Habberdish looked at Mr. Longing and Clara, then finally back to Sway. "I'm sorry, Godfrey, but the rules apply to everyone—even you."

Sway's nostrils flared. "You thankless little man. You're nothing but a weasel—one more circus swindler descended from a family of idiots. Where would you be without me?" He gestured in a wide circle. "These *aeronauts*, as you call them, are no more than a herd of freaks—embarrassments to the profession! *I* made this race—admit it! You . . . owe . . . me . . . *everything!*"

Habberdish stiffened, his chin pressed into his neck. Then, slowly, he stood straighter, removed his bowler hat, and stepped toe to toe with the blustering pilot. "You're right, Godfrey," he said in a cool, measured tone, "I do owe you something. I owe you a hand off my ship."

Security appeared and took Sway by the arms.

"Don't touch me," he snapped, recoiling. He faced the pilots at the back of the stage, glaring at each one until his eyes fell on Clara. "Go ahead, have your foolish race. You all know who I am."

"A loser," sneezed Hatsu.

Laughter filtered through the line of pilots. Even Satomi

Hoshi suppressed a grin and put her arm around her daughter. "Bless you, dear," she said proudly.

Sway snarled. "Come, Landon. We're leaving."

The pilot strode to the edge of the stage, and then stopped. Landon had not moved.

"I said we're leaving. Now, do as I say, boy."

"No," Landon replied.

"Excuse me?"

"I said no. I'm staying here."

"Staying here?" repeated Sway mockingly. "You? A child? Where do you think you'll go after? Do you think WOOBA will let you hide in some forgotten ballroom making silly paper birds all day?"

"That was true?" whispered Habberdish to Clara.

"Now, Landon!" ordered Sway. "I'm your family."

"You're not his only family," replied Gildersleeve sternly. "The boy can stay with me. It's about time he learns a bit more about his *whole* family."

Sway glared at his grandson, who seemed horribly confused, but nevertheless held his ground.

"You were never a real Sway," muttered the man. He pushed his way through the crowd as a boo rose from the audience. It was echoed by another, and another, until a symphony of disapproval filled the air. Godfrey Sway sulked into a waiting elevator with the dignity of a coward, and as the doors slid closed, the jeers turned into applause.

After a minute, the cheering died down and all eyes fell back on Harold Habberdish, who was studying the Dovie Cup still in his hand. "I'm not sure if I have a good segue for that," he murmured, "but it would appear we have a few updates to our leaderboard. So . . . our new third place is awarded to . . . Team Ussuri!"

Hatsu practically levitated onto the podium, buzzing with so much excitement, Clara thought her friend might explode. It was either that or a sugar high, if the thick ring of chocolate around her mouth meant anything. A quick scan of the catering tables revealed three monkeys with similarly chocolatey faces.

"In second place, in a sporting effort, albeit not quite the finish that was promised . . . congratulations to Team Brigadier Albert."

Sir Wallace tottered onto the podium, leaving no room for his daughter, who sulked in front of him.

"We love you, Rat Chin!" screamed Binder.

"And finally, in first place, it is my immense pleasure to present this year's Dovie Cup—and the winner of the One-Hundredth WOOBA Air Race—to a team that personifies grace under pressure. Congratulations, Team Amelia!"

Cheers erupted across the *Zephyrus* as Clara was lifted into the air and deposited atop the winners' podium. Her father wheeled over Gildersleeve to join her.

"Once again, Greta, the cup is yours," boomed Habberdish.

But before the old pilot could take it, Houdini swiped the trophy from the man, stepped onto the podium, and promptly climbed inside. Mayhem had his turn next, and then Bob, who was too big to fit; he opted to place it on his head like a hat, instead.

"Stop that," yelled Habberdish. "That's an antique!"

He chased the monkeys offstage, the trophy clanging on the ground behind them.

"Don't tell him I once used it as a punch bowl," whispered Gildersleeve. She waved Clara to her side. "Congratulations, partner. You did it."

"I'm not sure what I did. It was the other kids, really . . . and the other pilots. They let us win."

"I beg to differ. There are many ways to win a race."

"What do you mean?"

"You captured their hearts and won their respect. That's far better than being the best pilot or having the fastest balloon. And do you know what else?"

Clara shook her head.

"You showed an old woman that she's been a fool to hide from the world all these years. And, most importantly, you reminded her she has a grandson who needs her."

"What will you and Landon do?"

"We'll go to Paris, of course. Where else do aspiring artists study?"

Clara saw Landon standing with the other kids, watching her from across the stage.

"Will you excuse me, Ms. Gildersleeve?" Clara asked.

"Only if you start calling me Greta." She touched Clara's cheek softly, and Clara closed her eyes for a moment. "Now, go on."

Clara raced to join her friends.

"I think this is yours," she said to Landon, removing the origami bird from her pocket. "You know, you didn't have to do that."

"What makes you think I'd do anything for you?"

"Because this time you did. Thanks."

Landon grinned.

"Bakagari, guess what?" chirped Hatsu, holding up a trophy of a figure on a flusterboard, "I won the PTSD Award for Best New Pilot."

"Not only that," said Alfie. "She broke OCR's record as the youngest ever to receive it."

"By *two years*," added Hatsu.

"Hmph!" grumbled Ophelia, who had obviously been eavesdropping. Evidently, the smug girl's day of disappointment was not yet over.

"And guess what else?" said a wide-eyed Raylee.

"You're getting a pony?"

"Two!" she squealed. "Between us, I think my mother is terrified of me right now. But that's not all—Mr. Habberdish asked me to be next year's Face of the Race."

"But . . . you hate this race."

"I know, but here's the catch . . . Habberdish said I don't have to fly in it. I just get to wear pretty dresses. Apparently, the sponsors thought my outburst was hilarious. And, after all of your updates this year, they want someone else with a fiery attitude."

"You *are* a rebel," Alfie reminded her.

"You know it," she said with steely conviction.

"Ahem. Are you Miss Clara Abigail Poole, otherwise known as WOOBA's Grand Champion?"

Clara turned to see a familiar face—or what she thought was a familiar face. The man was dressed in a tweed suit and a yellow bow tie. Freshly shaven, his hair was neatly combed to one side, and he wore bright, red-framed glasses.

"Dodge?"

"For you," he said, holding out a large cream-colored envelope.

"That doesn't look like it's from WOOBA," she said.

"No," replied Dodge. "This is from my day job." He winked, patted her on the back, and moved on.

Clara sat on the podium and opened the letter.

Dear Miss Poole,

It is my honor to inform you that you have been selected for the opportunity to attend Air Academy this autumn at our European campus. As you might imagine, Air Academy is not a traditional school. In addition to regular studies in math, science, and the humanities, you will be immersed in the art of extreme risk-taking. A list of courses has been included.

(Please note that while death is not predicted, there are some electives in which it is a distinct possibility.)

Sincerely,
Bartholomew Douglas Barlow
Dean of Risk

Clara stared at the signature. "Bartholomew Douglas? Dean of Risk?"

"Bakagari! Bakagari! I got one, too!" cried Hatsu, waving her own letter. "We're going to go to school together! Can you believe it?"

Other kids were holding similar envelopes, including Binder, Alfie, and to Clara's dismay, Ophelia Chins-Ratton. Even Raylee had one, though she chose to stomp on hers while hollering, "*I'm a rebel.*"

"Holy cow, we should be roommates," Hatsu screeched. "Oh, I know . . . we can decorate our whole room in bear print!" Hatsu hugged Clara, then skipped back to her mother's side, singing, "We're gonna be roomies."

Clara laughed. How someone that small could be that enormously electric would baffle her forever.

"I told you that you were a pilot," said a gentle voice.

"Mr. Bixley! What are you doing here?"

"Dear me, I haven't missed a final stage in as long as I can remember," he said, waving two ancient, moth-eaten WOOBA pennants. "The Habberdish family is always kind enough to send me a ticket. I flew with Harold's grandfather, Hugo, you know. Anyhow, I didn't want to leave without giving you my congratulations—from one pilot to another."

"Thank you, Mr. Bixley," she said with a deep curtsy. "Oh, I need to give you your coat and compass back. Here, one second."

"No, no, please, keep them," he said, and motioned to her Air Academy letter. "It seems you still have a use for them."

Clara pulled the compass from her pocket. "I still haven't figured it out how to make this thing work, though. Is there some kind of trick to it?"

"Trick? No, not that I'm aware."

He took the compass and pressed his finger on one side. The top flipped open, and he removed something white, which he popped into his mouth.

"Was that . . . ?"

"A breath mint? Yes. Would you care for one?"

"It's a mint container?"

"I've always found it's good to have fresh breath, especially in the tight quarters of a balloon." He snapped the lid shut and handed it back to Clara. "By the way, have you tried those Wibble Bibble candies they are handing out? Simply delicious."

"So I've heard," she said politely.

Bixley turned to leave, then said, "Clara, you do know what 'Always Follow True North' means, don't you?"

"I think true north is me," she replied. "It means whatever direction I decide is the right one. I just have to trust myself and try."

"Then I'd say your compass is working fine." He grinned at Clara and then shuffled slowly into the crowd, passing her father on the way.

"Who was that?" he asked.

"Just someone I met on the long way round."

"This place certainly has its cast of characters. Speaking of which, I just spoke with a rather dapper-looking Dodge. Apparently, you've been given another invitation."

"Yeah, I've been accepted into Air Academy. It's like school, but—"

"—in the air. Yes, I gathered that from the name."

"I know, Dad, it sounds crazy. And I already know what you're gonna say . . . that *it's not our kind of thing*."

"Actually, I was going to say it's not *my* kind of thing."

"Huh?"

Her father kissed the top of her head and then tightened her scarf. "How's this . . . Why don't you and I discuss it more later? But no promises."

"Really? I mean, it does sound cool. Like super cool—and I promise I'll stay super safe, and not—"

"Later," he repeated with a grin.

The winners' celebration was in full swing as the brass band blared tune after tune onstage. Berta spun Alberto Furio in a jitterbug, while Hatsu and Raylee tried to persuade a reluctant Satomi out onto the dance floor. Sir Wallace watched stoically, his foot tapping along to the music in silent mutiny, while Ophelia pouted beside him. She seemed conflicted, caught between the expectations of etiquette and the longing of a girl who desperately wanted to dance. The latter finally won out when Binder and Alfie pulled her onto the parquet, only to be circled by a rowdy entourage of boogeying Newlins. In the middle of the floor, Harold Habberdish shimmied in his blue chicken suit next to a laughing Marie Lemot, as if it were their last day on earth.

The first stars shimmered in the evening sky, the pinks and purples of twilight glowing over the Great Lake. Thousands of feet below on the streets of Chicago, residents went about their busy lives, completely unaware of the party in the clouds high above.

Clara took the tails of her mother's scarf and double-knotted it. She had no idea what would happen next, but she couldn't wait to get there.

ACKNOWLEDGMENTS

DEAR READER,

I did it! I convinced a collection of brilliant and talented people I was worthy of publishing the book you hold in your hands. How I did this, I'm not sure. Nevertheless, they are all exceptional people to whom I owe an enormous debt of gratitude. However, should you have issues with what you've just read, I think it's only fitting to blame them. After all, they are the ones who let me do it.

To my wife and far better half, Liz, whose belief in me goes lightyears beyond good reason: you are the singular best person I know, and it's not even close. Let's admit, choosing to spend your life with me and, thus, my creative demons is not an easy task. I could do nothing in my life without you, nor would I ever want to.

To my agent and literary sherpa, Erin Clyburn, who took a risk on a first-time, dyslexic writer: I could not have found a better advocate to help me navigate this new world of publishing, nor one with such an enormous (albeit creepy clown-loving) heart.

To my editor, Alison Weiss, whose ability to sculpt my manuscript into a book worth reading is nothing short of wizard's work: Collaborating with your kind of talent and mentorship is *pinch-me* kind of stuff. I promise to make you cry in everything I write.

To my parents, James and Patricia, who filled me with the confidence and support to try hard things and pave my own path: You instilled in me a superpower that I pledge to pay forward whenever and wherever I can.

I am also indebted to Rob Raisch, Tom Phillips, Maryrose Wood, Melissa Gaulding, Team Cly-Fi, and the many other writers and early readers who shared their wisdom and time to help shape this story and my fledgling writing career. Furthermore, a deep and humble theater bow to Bethany Buck and the Pixel+Ink team, who so graciously supported all aspects of this book's creation, as well as the team of sensitivity readers whose thoughtful insights helped guide my representation of the many cultures and characters herein.

Also, to Matt Rockefeller, whose imagination exceeds far beyond anything I could have have conceived for this book's cover, your talents floor me.

To the actual, real-life aeronauts who read this book: I know I took a lot of liberties. Please forgive me. It is, after all, fiction.

Finally, and most importantly, to my two beautiful daughters, Harper and Quincy: Whether it be draft reading, in-house editorial, or story development, you share in the success of this book's creation as much as anyone. You are my two muses (whether you like it or not) and the reason I do this at all. I couldn't be more proud of the remarkable and interesting people you are.